ISBN – 13 978-1493505883

ISBN – 10 1493505882

www.sineadhamill.com

D0233916

Sinead Hamill

Scumbags & Handbags

Sometimes you just need balls

Chapter One

Human and rooster locked eyes. 'Keep this up any longer you little shit and I'll fuck a doodle you!' Robbie King was struggling to keep it together as he eyeballed the bird through the bathroom window. He'd woken to the sound of cock crow at 5.30 a.m. and for over an hour the noisy bastard had kept up his constant cock a doodle doo. He grabbed his dark hair in frustration. The rooster seemed to smirk at him again. 'COCK A DOODLE DOO.' 'If I get my fucking hands on ya…' he whispered through gritted teeth.

A slight moan from the bedroom interrupted his murderous thoughts and he swung his head around the door and looked towards the bed. Kim, his fiancée, was entangled in the pristine white sheets. Her thick blonde hair reached the small of her back and her left thigh was exposed. She was flawless. He smiled at her as she lay there breathing deeply, oblivious to the suicidal rooster outside their window. She never had difficulty sleeping, clear conscience. That and not knowing half the crap *he* got up to. The feed of pints the night before had left his tongue as dry as the underside of Ghandi's flip flop. He sipped some water before getting back into bed beside her. Relax, he had to relax. He was supposed to be taking time out from the fast lane. Kim had insisted on it. 'You have to calm down Robbie,' she had said. 'Get a real job and stop knocking around with those guys from Crumlin. Maybe go back to school, college even.' That's what she'd done; dragged herself out of the gutter in the Salmon Leap Estate where they

1

had met. She had studied her books in school when all their mates were out using the skills learned in mechanical drawing to sketch the layout of houses they planned to rob. Salmon Leap? Jaysus, Robbie used to think that must have given the council a laugh when the bloke who built the flats submitted his plans. The only water nearby was the canal and it was so full of shopping trolleys and syringes, a salmon would only leap to get out of the fucking thing. 'COCK A DOODLE DOO.' Even though they had grown up in the same estate, they only started going out together when they were both twenty one. Seven years ago now. They'd been engaged for the last two. She wouldn't marry him till he gave Hawk the two fingers. The only problem was, the last fella who tried that saw the same two digits chopped off and stuck on to Hawk's dart board. He said it helped his aim. Nobody fucked with the Hawk, however much they might like to. Kim didn't know a tenth of what there was to know about the Hawk and that was how Robbie intended to keep it. 'COCK A DOODLE DOO.'

'That's fucking it!' Robbie slipped out of bed. His 9 mm Beretta handgun was concealed under the false bottom of his leather carry-all. The Hawk had them made for all the lads to help transport cash and drugs around town. They would fool the average blue bottle, especially the spud gobblers fresh out of the Garda training college in Templemore, Tipperary. Slowly and quietly he attached the silencer to the gun and went back into the bathroom. 'COCK A DOODLE DOO.' Grabbing the curtains he tore them open and stared out wildly. 'COCK A DOODLE DOO.' The fucker had moved. Robbie's deep brown eyes scanned the farm buildings attached to the old country house that was supposed to be his refuge from violence for a few days. There he was, the noisy bastard. All fluffed up and important looking with his white feathers glistening in the early morning sunshine. Robbie pulled up the old sash window. The noise attracted the rooster's attention. 'Go on. Smirk at me again you feathery fuck!' For a few gloriously silent moments the bird studied him, eyes settling on the gun. Robbie wondered if images of the bird's life from hatchling to noisy bastard were flashing through his pea sized brain. 'COCK A DOODLE DOO.'

Robbie's top lip curled upwards in anticipation. The bird ruffled its wings and plumped up its feathers. Robbie stretched out his left arm straight, careful not to lock the elbow. The bird bent its head slightly and expanded its chest as though drawing in air. Robbie's right hand clasped the underside of his left, stabilising his grip on the gun. The rooster opened its beak and threw back its head to greet the long risen sun with his now familiar call. PHITT! A smile spread across Robbie's face as the rooster's head parted company with its body in a whirlwind of feathers and innards. He admired his handiwork. 'No you cock a doodle fucking don't.' When he finally got up and dressed some four hours later, the sounds of rural family life that Robbie had half heard the day before were different. In place of the quiet hum of conversation there was the repeated sound of a child wailing. Given his surroundings he felt it really wouldn't be the 'done thing' to flip the lid. He was trying, honest to God he was. Maybe the quack therapist at the anger management class he'd been forced to take was doing some good. He had his doubts though. Some of the exercises he had him doing were seriously off the wall. Robbie reckoned he made most of that shit up just to piss him off. Robbie was on his way down the sweeping staircase heading towards the dining room when he paused to listen, realising that his activities earlier that morning had not gone unnoticed. Robbie 1 – Rooster 0. 'Sergeant Major is dead Daddy,' said a child's voice. 'His head is all gone.'

'Calm down sweetheart, I'll sort it all out,' replied a voice of authority. The little girl continued through what sounded like a haze of snot and tears. 'I went out to feed him and the others and he's dead. The fox must have got him.'

'Show me darling, maybe you made a mistake?' asked her father, sounding like he already knew the answer. No mistake, thought Robbie, the headless bastard's on his way to that big chicken coop in the sky. Thankfully he'd had the good sense to leg it out to the yard earlier to retrieve the bullet before anyone else found it and started asking awkward questions. He put on his best disinterested look and pushed his way through the dining room door. Kim had gone down ahead of him, wanting to get a nice spot at the window that overlooked a meandering river. She waved as he entered the room. It would have been hard not to spot her in the vast room. Her wide smile welcomed him as he sat down.

'What was all the commotion?' he asked. 'Something killed the little girl's rooster,' replied Kim, buttering his toast for him. She loved to mother him.

'Why kill one? They're less than a fiver in Tesco.'

'That's hens you're thinking of. You don't eat the cockerel, they're too tough apparently.'

'Not as tough as he thought,' sniggered Robbie.

'What's that?'

'Nothing. Was it a fox or what?'

'That's what the little one thought, but I heard one of the other guests telling the owner that he heard a sound like a slingshot being fired just before the rooster bought it.'

'Which guest was that then?' asked Robbie.

'He's gone now. Some American bloke. He had to rush off to catch a plane.' The door to the kitchen opened and the owner of the country house hotel entered the room. He approached their table. 'Mr King, I wonder if I might have a quiet word.' Kim shot a dirty look in her fiancé's direction. 'What about?' asked Robbie. 'Perhaps it would be better if we chatted in private?' replied the owner, indicating the other couples. 'I'm eating me toast here,' said Robbie, showing off his half chewed bread before receiving a kick to the shin from beneath the table. 'Alright, alright I'm going,' he said, throwing the crust back onto the plate.

A quick glance at Kim told Robbie everything. She was already pink in the cheeks with shame. She knew all about his 'issues'. Hyperacusis the doctors called it. It wasn't his fault. Really loud repetitive noises actually hurt his head. Then his bi-polar like symptoms would flare up, making him completely irritable which generally resulted in his kicking someone's head in. Kim was putting two and two together. He hated loud noise, he had forgotten his medicine, he hadn't slept well and there was a rooster in two pieces instead of one. Her green eyes filled with tears and she shook her head. Robbie followed the man into the grand entrance hallway. Prehistoric elk antlers hung above the open front door through which he could see a squad car pulling up. Thank fuck I found the bullet, he thought. He had managed to evade any serious prosecution from the law over the last few years purely by being one step ahead of them and by getting the more gormless members of the Hawk's fan club to do the dodgy stuff. He would claim he took a slingshot to the bird. They didn't give time in Mountjoy prison for killing big chickens so he wasn't too bothered. He was more afraid of what Kim would do to him than the cops. The worst thing they could do was take away his liberty but she could take away his hole, and God knows a man needs his bit. Without it he might get violent like the Hawk.

Now there was a man who needed to be ridden like a Cheltenham entry. Full of stress and anger he was; a model for a bit of TLC. The only problem was the Hawk only had time for one woman in his life, his mammy. And let's face it; you can't ride your ma. Especially when your ma's claim to fame was ironing her bloke's Man United shirt while he was still wearing it.

The guard walked toward them as the hotel owner spoke. 'Garda, this is the man identified to me by another guest who has signed a statement attesting to the fact that he saw him pointing something at the rooster just before it was killed. His view of Mr King's hand was obscured however, so he can't say with any degree of certainty what the weapon was.' Robbie sighed and looked bored.

'Have you anything to say to this accusation sir? asked the man in the blue uniform. Kim approached just as Robbie was all set to create a plausible excuse.

'Tell the truth Robbie,' she begged, 'you'll never move forward if you continue with lies.'

Fuck, thought Robbie, I could have blagged me way out of this. 'Ok,' he said. 'I hit the little bollix with a slingshot, but he was asking for it. He'd had me awake since half bleeding five in the morning.'

'It didn't bother any of the other guests Mr King.'

'Well maybe he was just targeting me, because he stayed outside my poxy window all morning.'

'What did you expect when you came to the country for a weekend?' asked the guard, clearly amused by the Dublin hard man so obviously out of his comfort zone.

'Well for one thing,' said Robbie, taking out a smoke, 'I thought he'd cock a doodle doo till the sun was fully up and then piss off and start ridin' hens or whatever roosters are supposed to do all day. If it was me like, and I had a choice between ridin' and roaring, I pick ridin' every time.' He flipped open his lighter and lit his cigarette.

'Ahem.' The hotel owner coughed gently.

'Wha?' said Robbie.

'There's no smoking sir, didn't you see the sign?' replied the now clearly uncomfortable owner indicating a large sign which read, NO SMOKING.

'Can't read,' said Robbie, ignoring the owner's stare and looking straight at the cop.

'Ah Robbie, don't start,' pleaded Kim. 'We're supposed to be on holiday.'

It was too late. He was already in 'the zone'. Having grown up with any respect for authority beaten out of him by his father, he'd wasted a very intelligent brain and left school early. He couldn't bear being told what to do. Today would be no exception. 'That's it,' said the guard, realising the scene could turn nasty. 'You're under arrest.'

'What's the charge? Murder most fowl?' laughed Robbie as the man in uniform placed him in handcuffs.

'Let's start with disturbing the peace and wilful destruction and see where we end up.'   'Great Robbie,' hissed Kim. 'Just bloody great.'

Chapter Two

Tommy Boylan hung his greying head, sighed and said 'Shite' as the TV announcer listed the upcoming programme. 'And coming up next, one of our firm favourites, *Reeling in the Years*, takes a look back at 1985.' He continued polishing the contents of his trophy cabinet, a task he relished. The daily routine kept his mind from wallowing in the present and allowed him to reminisce as he buffed the surfaces of countless awards won throughout a glittering career playing senior county football for his beloved Dublin. He knew what was coming. The familiar intro music rang out from the television. He wouldn't mind but he actually quite liked the show normally, especially when they covered 1982 and 1984. He had captained the Gaelic football team that claimed the coveted Sam Maguire cup in both years when they won the hard fought All-Ireland final in Croke Park, the home of the Gaelic Athletics Association in the nation's capital. But the shaggers were showing 1985. The year it all went tits up.

For the two years leading up to that time Dublin had a team the other counties could only look at in awe. Every member of the squad was at the peak of their playing careers. 'Footballing out of their skins' was one of the headlines in the newspapers that summer they won their place in the final. The pundits were speculating on an elusive three in a row. Tommy's muscles tensed as he remembered back to the tortuous training sessions he and the team had endured all through that season.

'Fuck the begrudgers,' he had said to the lads

in the dressing room that September morning over twenty years earlier. The coach had them physically ready and it was his job to prepare them mentally. 'Now there's fellas out there who think we shouldn't be here, that we've no right. They say we only got here because of some soft decisions by the ref. Is that true lads, is it?' 'NO!' came the testosterone fuelled bellow of the twenty strong squad.

'In a few minutes I'm going to lead the fifteen of you that are starting the game out onto that pitch. What are we going to do when we get out there?' he shouted, cheeks crimson with passion. 'WIN!' they roared, not daring to go above a single word when their captain was addressing them. Tommy was easily one of the game's heroes. He liked to lead by example, always the first to arrive at training and the last to leave. In the off season he kept up his crippling fitness regime. He wouldn't touch alcohol or heaven forbid the fags and he had little regard for any of the lads who snuck in a few pints after a match. He was playing football since the age of four when his da lied about his age to get him started in the club. That little white lie was overlooked once they saw his exceptional talent. Nothing got in the way of football. Work was just a means to an end. As for women…? Well that was a whole other story. He'd told himself he hadn't the time for such distractions but in reality it was just awkwardness. He revelled in the male dominated world of football. There was no shyness when he had a ball in his hand, he was in control. It was a mad time but he had loved every second. He would go back to it in a heartbeat if only to ensure he didn't royally fuck it all up. The much repeated programme was showing old footage of the events that shaped that year. The words appeared ticker tape fashion in white at the bottom of the screen.

Live Aid – Bob Geldof organises massive global concert to aid famine victims in Africa.

Woman claims to see statue of the Virgin Mary move.

Garrett Fitzgerald and Margaret Thatcher sign Anglo Irish Agreement.

Tommy had seen it so often he knew what was coming. 'A paddy turning himself into a saint, holy Joe's getting wasted and that stubborn old bitch agreeing to something with the Irish. Wouldn't you think that would be enough?' he said to the empty room. He resigned himself to the inevitable as the narrator continued. '... and in sport, forget the rugby win over the British, the biggest shock in 1985 was...' The screen flashed up images of newspaper headlines. 'BOYLAN BOILS OVER!' 'BAD BOY BOYLAN!'

He shut his eyes, not bearing to watch the footage that he knew was coming. A grainy but fully recognisable CCTV image of the captain of Dublin's greatest ever football team beating the crap out of a man in a black tracksuit. The background showed a parking space marked REFEREE and a Ford Mondeo with all its windows smashed to bits. The body work of the car looked like a crumpled sheet of red tin foil, a mass of dents and scratches. The hurl, used to inflict the damage, could just about be seen in the corner next to the front tyre. Tommy cringed as he remembered one particular reference that was made of that fact. 'Football's Tommy Boylan tries out for the county's hurling team.' Opening his eyes, long devoid of life's sparkle, he sighed as the episode wrapped up with a final newspaper headline. 'IT'S ALL OVER FOR BOYLAN AS FOOTBALL GREAT IS BANNED FOR LIFE.'

Chapter Three

'Right then, you're probably all keen to hear whether the rumours of National Lottery funding are true.' A nervous wave of laughter spread throughout the all-male audience. It was a Saturday night and Ray O'Toole, the top man in Iona Gaels Football Club sat behind a table flanked on either side by the treasurer and the head coach. The meeting had been organised to bring the members up to speed following the annual GAA congress held earlier that day. Already the twitter accounts of some of the younger players had been humming, spreading fact and fiction like Chinese whispers. The game was suffering during the recession as many key players were forced to emigrate in search of work. The days of securing a sales role just because you played for your county were all but over.

'As you all know, the game needs development and that has to start at club level.'

'Here, here,' muttered voices from various points in the room.

'As will be widely reported by many of the country's sports columnists in the Sunday papers, I am glad to announce that the speculation is true. The National Lottery and the EU Sports Council have agreed a joint funding project to promote the game.'

'YES!' 'YAHOO!' Men of all ages in the hall jumped up and clapped each other on the back as if they personally had secured the money.

'Quiet now, there's a bit more to it than that.' Ray urged them with his hands to sit back down. 'There's a catch.' A silence descended on the room as though the air had been sucked out. 'They want more women involved in the game.'

'Ah Jaysus Ray, is that all? Sure there's already a junior, intermediate and senior women's team, so we're sorted,' laughed one of the lads. The chatter started again as everyone began to relax.

'They want mothers,' said Ray, his expression like a slab of concrete. The chatter died down for a few moments as the men looked at each other, unsure.

'For what? Making the sandwiches? Sure they do that anyway,' said one of the coaches. 'I tell my missus she should be grateful. It makes a change from just cooking the dinner and cleaning. Spices things up like.' The group broke into a fit of laughing. Ray banged hard on the table to everyone's shock.

'It's not bloody funny lads. Apparently the Krauts want to tackle ageism and sexism in sport across the EU. Needless to say the shower of pricks in our government are only too happy to bend over and be taken up the arse and are leading the way in this initiative. So the bottom line is—they've offered up our national sport. To get funding, we have to promote a new initiative within the national game. They've even given it a name, "Gaelic for Mothers".'

'Ah fuck off, are ye having us on Ray?' a voice shouted from the front row.

'No. Unfortunately I am deadly serious. We only qualify for funding if we can show we are actively supporting the venture. So, have I any volunteers for a coach?'

'In your bleedin dreams.' 'No chance.' 'Tell them to shove their funding up their arse.' The varied voices all heralded a common theme. This was not something any self- respecting member of the club would want to be involved with. The existing women's teams, while highly skilled, were just about tolerated once they didn't get in the way of the men's training, but a group of mammies? No way.

The meeting descended into chaos, voices sounding more incredulous by the second. This was an affront to their masculinity. The words 'fucking' and 'Germans' became inexorably linked as various conversations gathered momentum and soon their European cousins were being blamed for everything from the shape of bananas to the weather. Tommy sat quietly at the back of the room. He'd renewed his membership with the club again that year hoping that he might be able finally to get involved with the senior team coaching squad. It had been the same for the last ten years, ever since he returned from the UK. He had gone there in self-imposed exile after he'd beaten up the referee in 1985. Fifteen long years he had spent away, living in various shit bins around North London, making a living in the construction game. Finding work hadn't been the problem, he was very fit and a good worker. He tried to keep his past buried but having been such a highly rated player meant that any Irish he came across instantly recognised him. Instead of the almost God-like status he had been used to, he found himself dealing with jumped up little arseholes who wanted to take him on. Even though he desperately wanted to forget his indiscretions, he couldn't bear to pull himself away from everything Irish. In all the years in the UK he still felt drawn to that scene. He had tried to date a few girls from the Kilburn community but their Irish parents knew all about him and gave him a hard time. The only way he had been able to deal with it was to keep himself to himself, which meant not forming anymore relationships with any of the Irish girls he came across. There was less explaining to do that way. That had been fine in theory but he found he had nothing in common with the English girls either. They didn't understand his preoccupation with Gaelic Football and he got tired of trying to explain the game to people who had zero interest. In the end it had been easier to just stay on his own.

Looking across the hall at Ray O'Toole now he felt the familiar knot in his stomach. If he hadn't lost the head that day at the All-Ireland final ... If he had just accepted the referee's decision or even just had a scuffle with the other team on the pitch it would have been okay. But no, he had to write off the bloke's car and put him in hospital. Not exactly the stuff you put on your CV when you want a career in coaching. It didn't matter that he'd subsequently made peace with the injured man or that the judge who heard the case didn't impose a custodial sentence, due mainly to the fact that the episode was deemed so out of character. No, all that mattered was that he'd dirtied his bib. The other club members still spoke to him, but not like he was one of the lads. He was tolerated purely on the basis of his past credentials but if he was honest he knew in his heart that he had tarnished the club. That was the only reason Ray was the man in charge and not him. Throughout their playing career Ray had only trotted after Tommy, often not even making it off the substitute's panel. The lads used to slag him saying, 'Put some Mr Pledge spray on your shorts there Ray, the bench needs a good polish.' And now he was heading Tommy's way. Ray O'Toole, Club Director.

Toole by name and tool by nature.

'How's it going? Are you staying for a drink?' he asked as he ushered Tommy towards the back of the hall where the group were beginning to congregate.

'Just the one, I have the car.'

'Fair enough, you wouldn't want to get arrested and end up in front of a judge again. You mightn't be so lucky a second time huh?'

'Yeah, very witty Ray. That was years ago, can we move on?'

'Sure I'm only slagging. Pint is it?'

'Yeah, thanks.' Ray ordered two pints of Guinness and the two men sat staring at the glasses in quiet admiration as the black liquid settled.

'That was a bit of a curve ball about getting older women into the game, wasn't it?' said Tommy, picking up his glass. 'Pity the poor whore that gets that job.' He took a long gulp of his pint.

'Self-pity is a terrible waste,' said Ray with a sly grin.

'Are you taking the piss?' asked Tommy, having almost choked in shock.

'Look I know it's not how you wanted to get back involved in the game,' replied Ray impatiently, 'but seniors coaching isn't going to happen. The only way you'll get back on the pitch in Croke Park is if someone spreads your ashes there. You fouled up Tommy and people just don't want to forgive you.'

'I was annoyed Ray. I'd spent a year building up to that moment and then that Kerry fucker called a foul where there wasn't one and we conceded a point in the last ten seconds of the match. We lost by one point. Do you know what that feels like?' Tommy paused, a look of resignation on his face. 'I fucked up. It was a mistake, a simple error. I suppose you never made one of those, no?'

'This isn't about me though is it? You're the one who's been hanging around the club since you came back, trying to wheedle your way back in.'

'Football was my life Ray. It's hard to give it all up and they shouldn't ask me to.'

'But that's just it. I'm offering you a way back in here. Spend the year training the Gaelic for Mother's team, put up with the lack of skill and fitness and possibly the whiff of incontinence and maybe the county board will see you're sorry.'

'I'll think about it,' whispered Tommy, quietly devastated.

'Good man,' said Ray patting him on the shoulder before walking away to join the lads, a satisfied smile across his face.

Chapter Four

The Jag's massive tyres crushed the gravel in the driveway as it came to a sharp stop next to the Range Rover. The man in the driver's seat sat perfectly still with his hands on the wheel as the car idled. He took a laboured breath, switched off the engine and got out. Throwing his Barbour coat over the crook of his arm he nudged the car door closed. He stood for another moment looking up at the house and sighed as he turned the key in the front door. Lorcan Sheehy felt it as soon as he entered the hall and walked into the adjoining kitchen. Misery.

'What's wrong this time?' he asked his panda-eyed wife, Ruth.

'This time?' she blubbed, 'God, you make me sound like a total basket case. What happened to the caring … to the nurturing side of marriage?' The last words were almost drowned out by yet more sobs.

'It got swept away with all the bloody tears. Honestly you need to see a doctor.'

'He already said I'm not depressed, I told you that.'

'That's not what I mean. I'd get him to check if you need surgery to separate your voice box from your tear ducts. You can't open your mouth these days without your eyes leaking.'

'Thanks for the support Lorcan,' she sniffed, trying to pull herself together.

'Ruth, I'm serious. You've got to sort this. How do you think I feel coming home from work after a hectic day to be met by this great wall of woe? I only get an hour to eat dinner, which, before you say anything, I appreciate you've prepared. Then I've got to go and train the junior team at the club. I'm trying to stay upbeat and positive but I have to say, you are making it awful hard.'

'See that's just it,' she said, standing up to clear some John Rocha glasses from the counter. 'You've all these things going on to occupy you. My life hasn't changed since the kids moved away. I'm still cooking dinners and clearing up afterwards, just two less plates. I'm like Shirley bloody Valentine without the hot sex in the sun.' 'Thanks a lot,' replied Lorcan, looking every bit as hurt as he felt.

'You know what I mean. This isn't about you. It's all me. I've no interest in anything, no energy.'

'Maybe you should go to the doctor then, seriously. You could be sick.'

'Oh for goodness' sake, I'm not sick. I'm bored ... rigid. Nobody is spending money on gardening so my horticulture degree seems to have been a total waste of time. Ever since the kids moved out I just feel useless.'

'Look love, I've an idea. Why don't you check out the new initiative they have in the club? They're calling it Gaelic for Mothers and they're signing up new players this weekend.'

'Gaelic? As in football? Sure I couldn't kick a ball out of my way. Why would they take me?'

'It's some edict sent down from the GAA headquarters. The club have to be seen to comply to get some extra funding. All the lads are making sure their wives get behind it.'

'I don't know Lorcan. I'm hardly a poster child for fitness am I?' As she spoke she looked at herself in the glass panelled door. The combination of the darkness outside and the bright interior meant it was almost as good as a mirror. Her husband decided not to comment on her weight which had been steadily building over the last year. 'I think you should sign up for it. Do something for yourself for a change. It might be good for you. For us.'

Naomi Walsh stood looking at the A4 poster stuck to the notice board outside the cafe in the clubhouse. 'Ma, come on! The slush puppies will be all gone.'

'One minute Shona, Mammy's just reading this.' Her six year old daughter pulled at her sleeve and continued to whine. They came here every weekend after the football nursery. Most of the time the slush puppy was the only way she could bribe the child to keep turning up to play Gaelic and she was happy to do it. Kids didn't run around enough in her opinion. 'Look, take the two euro and go in and order it. Don't get in anyone's way now.' The little girl raced through the door and straight over to the machine that churned out flavoured crushed ice in a cup with enough e-numbers in it to give a space shuttle lift-off. She was a good kid so her ma didn't mind the odd treat, and it was only the odd one she got because they were always smashed. Her father had stuck around long enough to prove to Naomi that he wouldn't be missed. One too many digs off the bloke when he'd been drinking was all it took for her to throw him out. They hadn't been married and they'd lived in one of the flats in Rosemount Estate so it was no big deal. The young one was better off without him as well. She never ever asked about him which just proved the point. It was only 95% possible that he was the father anyway, not that he knew that of course. Why give him more ammunition? Well maybe it was more like 75%. She'd never been very fond of numbers but one thing she did know was that six years and nine months ago she'd spent a large percentage of her time on her back and it wasn't always with the same bloke. There was one guy, a real hard nut that she'd met at a party she'd gone to with her boyfriend. She had been off her face, got into a fight with her fella and left with the other guy. She remembered shagging him alright but only after he'd punched her boyfriend's lights out. She would've put money on that guy being the father just because of the timings and the fact that she felt nauseous from the next morning, but she hadn't seen him since so there was no way to know for sure. She never could quite remember his name. Anyway, sex was something she enjoyed so she didn't see the problem. The thing was, now that Shona was getting older she couldn't be bringing blokes around the house so much. There would be too many awkward questions in the morning. Like that time a few months back when the little one had gotten up early and found her mother in the kitchen trying to whoosh a fella out the door quietly. 'Hi, my name's Shona. What's yours?' She'd asked the stranger, her big eyes full of innocence. 'Dave,' answered the bloke. 'Jack,' answered her mother at exactly the same time. There hadn't been much time for introductions the previous night. Even so, it wasn't something she wanted her little girl to see. She needed to be shown better examples of how to behave. That was why the poster captured Naomi's attention.

CALLING ALL MOTHERS - Show the kids how Gaelic is a family game. Join the Iona Gaels G4M

(Gaelic for Mothers) team. No experience (at all) necessary and it's free! Sign Up below today. Meet on all-weather pitch at 9.15pm Friday.

This was just what she needed. She'd gone to the gym years ago when she had a bit more disposable income. Since Shona came along any spare money disappeared faster than Superman's red jocks in a phone box. The sign said no experience was needed which was just as well. Apart from the kids games she had only been to one match to watch some bloke she'd fancied the arse off years ago. That was when she learned that when they used one hand to hold the ball and the other to fist it away it was known as a 'hand pass' and not a 'hand job' as she had inadvertently shouted out from the side-line. Still, it got her noticed by yer man ... and he'd been hung like a moose.

Chapter Five

The street lights had been smashed so many times the council gave up repairing them. It wasn't like they needed this laneway lit up for the public's health and safety. Anyone with regard for their longevity on the planet wouldn't be down there at any time of the day. This was the Hawk's domain. The ground floor of his well-protected warehouse held pallets that were shipped in and out as jobs were completed. The one thing he didn't allow though was the storage of drugs. He had other arrangements for that stuff. Despite paying off enough cops to be given a heads up on any planned raids, he still wouldn't risk it. He'd done enough time in The Joy and he would stop at nothing to ensure he never went back inside. The cops that hadn't succumbed to his financial charms knew he was behind most of the crime in the area, they just couldn't pin it on him. On the rare occasions that they caught one of his cronies they would be too terrified to shop their boss. There were detectives out there in need of Valium; such was their frustration in trying to break any of the gang. Robbie dutifully checked over his shoulder before knocking on the metal door. A flap slid back and he saw one of Hawk's protection squad behind the grille. 'Howya Butch, himself wants to see me.' The big man stared at him as if deciding which bit of him to break first, then he grunted and unlocked the door. Once inside, Robbie heard one of the sounds that accompanied his boss wherever he went; a high pitch squeal. Someone was getting a going over. From the occasional squelching thud that accompanied the screams, it was clear to

Robbie that a sledgehammer or baseball bat was likely to be involved. As he made his way to the back of the warehouse he heard the other sound that was synonymous with the man and he took a slow deep breath in an attempt to keep his irritation in check. He had found over the years that he maintained more of his body parts in Hawk's company if he pretended to like the music that was coming from the stereo.

The large light which hung from the roof illuminated the area beneath to show a badly beaten man slumped and whimpering in a pool of blood and bits of teeth. Another man stood over him with a blood splattered baseball bat in hand. He wore a set of workman's overalls which looked strangely at odds with the Stetson hat on his head. 'Turn up the music Macker,' Hawk shouted to another one of his goons. 'I can't hear it with this fucker crying.'

From the corner of his eye he spotted Robbie. 'Howya,' he said while swinging the bat down on his victim who could now only barely moan as he slipped in and out of consciousness.

'How's it going?' Robbie replied. 'Who's yer man?'

'Him? That's young Scooby. The lad who stole a load of gear last week. Thought he'd set himself up a little franchise so he did. I thought you knew him.' Hawk grabbed the young fella's hair and turned his floppy head towards Robbie.

'I didn't recognise him,' Robbie answered, somewhat cautiously, 'what with his not having anything left of his features 'n' all.'

Hawk pulled the lad's head up to waist level and leaned over to look at the soggy mass of tissue and bone gristle that had once been a face. 'Jaysus, you're right. You wouldn't know him at all,' he said before letting go of the hair. There was a dull thud as Scooby's head hit the floor. He raised his ridiculous looking cowboy hat in salute to the bloke. Hawk wasn't a tall man but what there lacked in height was made up for in width. His neck was easily over nineteen inches wide and his arms were as big as some men's thighs. The eyes that looked out from under salt and pepper hair were almost inhuman. They were violet blue but a strange circle of paler blue that was almost white surrounded the pupil. They were the eyes of a shark, cold and predatory. He had a jagged scar that ran all the way down from the inner corner of his left eye to the lobe of his left ear. An altercation with a drug dealer in his youth had been the cause of that. The same bloke was posted back to his oul wan in twenty large jiffy bags a few days later. Hawk thought that was the funniest part, making the mammy go down to the sorting office to sign for the parcels. 'Macker! Butch! Get rid of this waster while me and Robbo here have a mug of scald.' The two men moved as swiftly as their burly frames allowed and lifted the lifeless man into the back of a truck that was parked in the warehouse. Robbie followed Hawk over to the small kitchen area at the base of a flight of stairs. He watched as the heavies then swept up the bits of the bloke that were still on the floor.

'I'm having camomile tea. Me ma recommended it, says it helps to keep me calm. She's a demon for it herself.'

'Yeah? How is your ma?' asked Robbie as the kettle boiled.

'Grand thanks. She's still waiting on her court date for that spot of bother she had with her last fella.'

'Is that the GBH charge or ironing the Man City shirt charge?'

'The GBH and it was a Man U shirt.'

'Fair enough. So the camomile tea works she reckons?' asked Robbie with a look of utter confusion on his face. 'Bloody right, if she hadn't the tea to calm her down she'd have chopped the bollix off him with a hatchet.' Hawk poured the gurgling water into the tea cups while singing along to the Johnny Cash song blasting out of the stereo. 'I hear a train a comin'. Robbie smiled as best he could while clenching his teeth together. There were only two types of music he detested—Country and Western. Unfortunately that caused him huge grief because this cold blooded, psychotic, baseball bat wielding maniac really liked it. He insisted on it being played endlessly wherever he went. Robbie and he had once driven from London to Holyhead and across on the ferry to Dun Laoire with a consignment of pigeons. The Hawk had gassed a whole racing loft of the birds belonging to a Brit who had crossed him. Then he had the enlightened idea to get a taxidermist to stuff a load of stolen diamonds into the bellies of the dead birds and then sew them up to look like they were sleeping. He threw in a fair few live ones to make the consignment look authentic, robbed the Brit's pigeon transporter and hit the road. During the entire journey he insisted on playing country music and by the end of it, if Robbie had heard 'a train a comin' he'd have gladly thrown himself under the fucking thing.

The tea was made and they sat on some garden furniture. 'No point in putting it in the garden,' said Hawk petting the soft cushioned seat. 'It never stops bleedin raining. So …,' he grinned, winking over, 'I hear you got into a spot of bother on your dirty weekend away.'

'Yeah, Kim's fucking raging at me so she is.'

'Hey, you got away with it. You're some jammy bastard.'

'I was up in the district court just yesterday. They upped the anger management classes they have me doing and I have to do some job sharing bollocks. Not only that, I have to do a load of community service as well.'

'Sure that's ridiculous. When are you supposed to go on the rob?' asked Hawk, appalled.

'I know, it's criminal,' agreed Robbie as he took a slurp of his tea and immediately fought the urge to puke. 'Lovely isn't it, the old camomile?'

'Yeah,' gagged Robbie, 'fuckin' deadly.'

'When do you have to start the community service? Better not be too soon cos I've something that needs sorting.'

'I've to meet some probation officer bloke and he's going to sort it out. I'll probably have to scrape graffiti off some poxy north side wall.'

'Well so long as you spray "yis are all wankers" on it when you're finished it'll be alright,' laughed the Hawk. He never hid his intolerance of his neighbours on the other side of the city.

'So what's the job you mentioned?' asked Robbie, getting down to business.

'Remember Carcass Mulligan?' said Hawk lighting a smoke.

'The fat bloke?'

'Yeah, anyway he got lifted a few weeks back and he's doing time in the Joy. He had a mobile smuggled in and he gave me a shout. Wanted to cut me in on one of his deals so he did.'

'Cut you in?' laughed Robbie.

'I know. I laughed too, only not so he could hear me. I wanted him to think I was well interested. Cheeky fucker, thinking I'd be happy with a piece of his turf when I can take the whole lot anytime I please.'

'So what's the story?'

Hawk stretched back in the seat and scratched his balls. 'Seems like our friend Carcass has a bit of a problem and as you know, one man's problem is another man's opportunity. There's a shipment of his cocaine coming from the US that the cops are on to it. According to my sources on the job, they are expecting it into Cork next week. Only it's coming in Friday, to Dun Laoire. It's mine for the taking.'

'There's a bleedin ferry terminal out there for fucks sake. It's crawling with coast guards and coppers waiting for some dumb shit to sneak in smack or whatever in his rucksack. How are you going to manage that?' asked Robbie.

'That's where you come in. There's a lad in the Coast Guard who's a bit fond of the old white powder. He likes to keep me sweet if you know what I mean. If you want to know about anything nautical, he's your man. Anyway, he tells me there's a big yacht race scheduled for Friday out in Howth. Get yourself out there today and figure out a way to make a few of them sink. I need a big enough distraction off the east coast to get the gear in.'

'Great,' sighed Robbie, 'so all I need to do is lasso an iceberg and pull it down from the arctic. No bother.'

Hawk stared in silence for a moment. Shite, thought Robbie, he'd gone too far. His boss knew he'd understood. 'It's only a few fancy boats, not the

fucking Titanic. Just blow them up.'
'I'll need some Semtex and timing devices then.'
'Well we both know who has shit loads of them.'
The two men laughed.

Chapter Six

Tommy stood on the all-weather pitch illuminated by floodlights and held his blue plastic whistle in one hand. In his other hand was a sheet of paper with a list of names. There were twelve on it. Not even enough for a full squad never mind any substitutes. He had mulled over Ray's offer for a few days and eventually gave in, just like the jumped up little prick knew he would. He wasn't sure which was worse, being viewed as a pariah for bringing the club into past disrepute, or as a pathetic fool for taking a job coaching middle-aged mothers. Either way, he was here now so he had to get on with things, if they ever turned up. He checked his watch, 9.00 p.m. There was an east wind blowing harsh cold air into his face and he zipped up the front of his track suit. The astro pitch was slightly elevated and from this level he had a clear view of the car park and the back entrance to the clubhouse where the main function room was located. Several cars were dotted around so assuming the women were using the changing rooms, he began to lay out the little orange cones for some of the training drills he had prepared. That was about the only part of this whole thing that was within his comfort zone. Training lads would have been no problem but for the love of God, he thought, what do I know about talking to women? The most meaningful conversations he'd had in his life were about construction or some match or other. One too many women's eyes had glazed over on dates throughout the years. After a while he lacked the confidence to even try. Over the last few nights, since he had agreed to take on the task, he had given the training schedule a lot of thought. The more drills they did, the less time there would be for banter. If they stuck at it and he got more comfortable he might relax a bit more with them. He took a deep breath,

'Fake it till you make it Tommy,' he muttered. Much and all as the lads in the club had joked, he doubted that the women would all be big pot wallopers. They couldn't be, by the law of averages. There was bound to be at least a few of them who had played county football on a girls' team in their youth. That was another thing; there hadn't been any mention of age restriction on the poster so he was expecting them to be older than the girls who played junior football. It would be grand, sure nobody would sign up to play a game they knew nothing about, regardless of what it said about 'no experience necessary'.

The four separate exercises were all laid out and Tommy suddenly realised he'd forgotten to take the extra footballs out of the large equipment container in the car park. Of all the things to forget. Definitely out of practice, he thought. With only a few minutes to go before the 9.15 start time he hurried over and used the key he'd been entrusted with to open the padlock. Flicking on the light he quickly spotted the bag marked G4M. That was a pleasant surprise, having footballs supplied especially for his fledgling team. Maybe it was actually being taken seriously after all.

'Ahem.' The gentle sound of someone clearing their throat made him turn. A large woman with more spare tyres than a Ferrari Formula 1 team stood at the entrance to the container. Tommy was grateful for the little energy saving bulb that struggled to illuminate the interior because they wasn't a chance that the shine from the pitch lights was going to get past this woman. She smiled broadly and stepped back to let him out. 'Eh, I don't know if I'm even in the right place. I'm here for the Gaelic for Mothers training but I don't see anyone else.' Tommy tried to look her up and down without seeming offensive. Maybe she'd eaten the rest of the recruits, he thought. 'You're in the right place alright,' he said, leaving down the football bag to extend his hand. 'I'm Tommy Boylan, the coach.'

'I thought you looked familiar,' she said reaching for his hand. 'If you can teach us a tenth of what you were able to do on the pitch we'll be brilliant. I'm Alison,' she beamed. For a few moments Tommy was shocked into silence and he just smiled back at the exuberant woman. It had been so long since anyone acknowledged his career without commenting on its demise, it was a pleasant surprise. He nodded toward the smattering of cars and a group of women walking down the backstairs of the clubhouse. 'I expect this is the rest of them now. First night nerves and all, maybe they feel safer travelling in packs.'

'Oh no, that's the local Weight Watchers group. They meet there every week.'

'Right,' he acknowledged, glancing at his watch—9.17pm.

'I tried it before but it's not for me. All those points and calories,' laughed Alison. 'I think they try to wreck your head so much with the counting that you're too shagging tired to eat!'

A car pulled up and two nervous looking women emerged. 'It's alright I don't bite,' smiled Tommy. 'Is this the mother's soccer training?' asked the smallest woman he had ever seen, a pretty redhead.

'No luv, this is Gaelic for Mothers. Soccer is for poofs.'

'Sorry, I'm useless at sports. I'm Mary and this is Brid.' She indicated her friend who had turned bright red and seemed to shrink within herself. Tommy felt sorry for her. The four of them walked up onto the astro pitch and the girls took in the sight before them. 'It looks bigger than when the kids are on it,' said one of the women nervously.

'Your kids play in the club do they?' asked Tommy encouragingly, facing the women with his back to the pitch entrance. 'Yes my son plays under-14's with her lad,' replied the woman, indicating her friend.

'There's a few more after arriving,' said Alison excitedly, nodding to the gate at the top of the pitch. Sure enough, seven more women came through the gate. A wave of relief engulfed Tommy, three would have been disastrous but he could work with ten. Greetings were exchanged. Many of the women knew each other vaguely because their kids either attended school or sports together. 'So let's get started,' said Tommy, clapping his hands together.

'Sorry, are we too late?' called a girl as she walked onto the pitch followed by another lady.

'No,' said Tommy recognising the second woman. She was married to one of the men in the club. She was about fifty pounds heavier than when he'd last seen her. 'Sorry I'm late,' said the younger looking of the two, 'I had to wait for my ma to take the young one. I didn't want to miss this, I'd say we'll have great crack. Howya everyone, I'm Naomi.'

'Hi Naomi,' replied eleven people. 'Are you sure it's

not Alcoholics Anonymous for mothers!' she laughed as she joined the group.

The lady Tommy recognised stood awkwardly to one side looking at the ground, her cheeks tinged slightly pink. 'It's Ruth isn't it, Lorcan's wife?' he asked quietly. 'It's everyone's first night so it will take a while to get to know each other.'
'Lorcan thought it would be a good idea,' she said quietly, barely lifting her gaze off the floor. 'I'm not so sure.' 'It will be just fine,' he said gently. 'What's more, I bet you'll be a better player than the husband ever was!' Turning to the motley crew standing on the pitch he asked, 'So have any of you played football before?' He was fairly confident of the answer. Twelve heads shook a negative response. 'Ok, not to worry. We'll have you up to speed in no time. Let's start with a light warm up. I don't want you pulling any muscles and getting injured your first night. Get yourselves into pairs and follow me.'

Taking off into a light jog he felt strangely positive and uplifted. Maybe it was the fact that, no matter how minor, he had a purpose once again. God knows, there had been more than one occasion over the last few years when he had found himself in some very dark places. They said suicide was a plague on young men but he knew better. As he ran, he remembered how good he felt at the height of his fitness. How, spurred on by natural endorphins, he felt he could have conquered the world or at least the county. He felt the good hormones flooding through his blood. He was more alive than he had been in years. Turning around he ran backwards to check out how his new team were doing. It was like a scene from The Walking Dead. The two larger women,

Alison and Brid were bent over looking like they were about to puke. The small red haired one was still running but looked to be powered by determination rather than energy. Ruth and three others were walking but looked very red in the face. Naomi was the only one keeping up with him and although panting heavily, she seemed to be enjoying herself. 'I still prefer the horizontal jogging but this will do for now,' she winked at him as she ran past. For a few moments he wasn't sure he had heard her correctly then he chuckled to himself.

The other four women were making their way slowly around the perimeter of the pitch, cutting sizeable chunks off the corners as they went. 'Good Jaysus,' said Tommy quietly. 'Ok ladies,' he continued, 'tell you what. As it's our first night I won't go too hard on you. If you're not up to running, just walk as fast as you can. Maybe try to run a little, and then walk a little. Those of you who can jog or run, carry on as you are. We need to complete two laps and then we'll do a little bit of stretching.' The group started out again and when Tommy reached the end of the second lap he stood waiting for them all to catch up. Some of the very big women were walking so slow he wondered whether they would be finished by the time the session ended. Finally, all twelve women stood before him panting like dogs stuck in a car on a hot day. 'Let's do a bit of stretching while you catch your breath. We'll work on the inner thigh first. Just copy me.' Spreading his legs apart he leaned onto the left leg bending at the knee and pushing all his weight to that side. 'Ok then, switch to the same position on the other side. Nice and gentle now. Right, let's stretch out the hamstring, that's the one you've got to watch. Most prone to injury is the hammer.' He crossed one leg in front of the other and bent forward. 'Try to touch the ground with our hands. Just go as far as you can.' The women all followed his instructions.

FART!

Nobody moved. The noise of the bum trumpet hung in the air like an arching high jumper, waiting to land in front of the person with the guiltiest face. Dutifully ignoring the issue, Tommy continued with his routine. When he trained with the lads years ago there was ferocious farting. It was no coincidence that the ozone layer started to deplete around the same time. He continued with his instructions. 'Because we use our hips a lot in football it's important to warm up the hip flexors. So lift up your knee like this,' he demonstrated, 'and turn it out to the side. Repeat that five times on each side.' The ladies complied and a volley of farts rang out like bells in a cathedral. Tommy pursed his lips together and carried on. Naomi he noticed was also trying to stifle a laugh. 'Oh Jesus!' called out one of the heavier women and Naomi looked towards her fearfully, hoping to Christ she hadn't lost complete control of her arse and dropped a loaf onto the floor.

'Are you alright there?' Tommy asked.

'Yeah, sorry about that. My hip cracked but it's grand. It's stiff from lack of use is all.' One of the oldest looking of the group piped up 'Well girls, I'd say most of us are the wrong side of forty so give the hip hell, it won't be too long before we'll be going for replacements. Maybe we could get a group discount.'

'If there are any bodily enhancements going, I think I'll start by lifting my arse back to where it used to be,' said Alison. Tommy laughed along with the rest of them and was grateful it wasn't Gaelic for Grannies he was coaching. At least this lot still had their original joints.

'Ok, one last stretch before we start working on some drills. Place your legs a little wider than hip width apart and bend slowly from the waist. Try to place a hand around each ankle.' Another flurry of farts rang out as each woman hit maximum stretch. Tommy thought fuck it and let one off himself. They were supposed to be a team after all. Naomi was the first to break. The rim around her lips turned white as she struggled to press them together. Her face threatening to explode in laughter as her shoulders shuddered. She had to decide which to release first, the laughter or the pee that threatened to leak out. The giggles won and she burst out laughing, 'I'm sorry, I couldn't hold it in any longer.' Alison came next, her entire body wobbling like a fresh jelly as she shook with laughter.

'This is mad,' she said. 'It was two years before I was on farting terms with my husband!'

Tommy smiled. The group were bonding, even if flatulence was all that was holding them together.

The scene on the floodlit pitch was being watched by two men from the overlooking clubhouse bar window. Ray O'Toole and Mick Murphy, the head coach, stood drinking pints. 'That was a stroke of genius getting Boylan to train the mammies,' said Mick.

'Did you honestly think I'd ask anyone else?' laughed Ray. 'Yer man is willing to do just about anything to get back involved in the game. He thinks it's a stepping stone to getting on the seniors coaching panel.'

'It is like fuck,' laughed Mick. 'There's more chance of a horse trotting out of my arsehole than him coming onto my squad. I've my hands full keeping a lid on things as it is. The last thing I need is some hot head coming in and blowing a fuse.'

'I know that and you know that but he doesn't, and that's just the way to keep it,' winked Ray. 'Let him mess about trying to teach the yummy mummies football while we get to use the extra funding for the lads teams. It wouldn't be the first time I pulled the wool over his eyes.'

'Sounds good, except for one thing.'

'What's that?' asked Ray.

'There's not much on that pitch I'd call yummy!' The two lads laughed, clinked glasses and returned to the bar.

Lorcan Sheehy looked at them from his seat where he had overheard their conversation. Ray's comments made him wonder about something his son had mentioned years before.

Chapter Seven

Dublin's Parliament Street stretched away from the river Liffey up towards City Hall. It was 1 a.m. and Robbie was looking for a coffee shop. This was not your normal coffee shop. It didn't even have a name over the door which was why he was wandering up and down alleys full of johnnies and fags, and he didn't mean the ones with tobacco. Unusually for him he decided to go into a pub to ask for directions. It was like stepping into an alternate universe. Fully grown men walked around dressed in a variety of costumes. Two blondes, obviously bodybuilders, walked by arm in arm. One was dressed as a ballet dancer, complete with tights and the other in a white naval officer's uniform. A few more were standing at the bar discussing the IMF's bailout of Ireland. Fair enough, thought Robbie, except they were wearing nothing but leather thongs and studded dog collars.

'Fucking sausage jockeys,' said Robbie subconsciously clenching his arse tight. He shivered as men of all varieties squeezed by him, some leaning a little closer than was really necessary. The things he did for the poxy Hawk. With his temper close to simmering point he eventually bulldozed his way to the front of the queue at the bar. He tried to get a barman's attention, all the while doing his best to ignore the hard lump he felt against his jeans exactly at arse crack level. He had to get the information he'd come in for. The body attached to the erection could be dealt with once that had been achieved. 'Scuse me' he shouted. The bar man was busy pouring tequila from a bottle with a penis attachment down the throat of a young lad who wore a nipple ring attached to something in his Superman Y-fronts. 'Hello?' he shouted again, waving his hand at the barman. 'Oh he won't leave Simon till he's ready,' said a voice behind him. Pinned to the counter by the voice's chest and erection, Robbie found it difficult to turn around. The blonde giant was undeterred.

'You do know I'm standing in front of you buddy?' Robbie asked, refocusing his attention behind the counter. 'Oi! Come on man, I just want directions,' he shouted to the barman as he minced past preparing another cocktail for nipple pierced Simon.

'If you're looking for heaven I can show you where it is,' the owner of the pressing appendage whispered in Robbie's ear. Feeling his gun in the inside of his jacket Robbie turned. 'Trust me pal, I could get you there even quicker.' The gay man chose to misinterpret the response and smiled at the dark haired, solidly built younger man in front of him.

'Such dark eyes you have, like melted chocolate. Was your daddy a chocolate bar sweet cheeks?'

'I'm pretty sure he wasn't,' replied Robbie, inwardly cursing the Hawk for sending him in search of a coffee shop with no bleedin name.

'I know everywhere around here. What's the name of the place you're looking for?' said the man, deciding to be helpful.

'I don't fucking know. It's some coffee shop on Parliament Street. Opens late apparently.'

'Oh that's Cafe Woo Woo, that's a wild place. It has two entrances, one out the front, down the lane on the left or there's another out the rear,' he leered. 'If you like I can show you the back way.'

'No thanks,' said Robbie as he tried to push past the man mountain and wondering what these fuckers ate.

'So can I at least get your number?'

'Don't think so pal' replied Robbie, walking away.

'Even tell me where you work?'

'The Disney Store on Grafton Street and FYI, I get all the Mickey I want in there.'

If the Hawk wasn't a psychopath and the job hadn't been so important, Robbie would have been tempted to head-butt the poof in the bar. At least he had the information and was out of the place at last. Lighting up a smoke, he took a long drag and looked around. The lane the bloke mentioned was right beside him so he walked down looking for anything that resembled a coffee shop. Nothing. There were some shops for fellas who liked clothes Rupert the Bear would have worn, but no place with people sitting drinking coffee. Just as he was about to turn back and try another lane, a heavy metal door opened. A tall blonde woman dressed in a canary yellow evening dress and towering heels backed her way out of the entrance blowing kisses to someone inside. That's weird, thought Robbie. It didn't look like a hotel and yer one was all dressed up like she'd been at a ball or something. Then she turned around and the first thing Robbie saw was heavy black stubble. The rest of the face was plastered with vibrant make-up. 'You're fucking kidding me,' he erupted, almost choking on the cigarette smoke he had just inhaled.

'What's your problem shithead?' boomed the baritone voice of the six foot man as he tottered over holding up the end of his flouncy ball gown.

'No problem at all. You look ... eh ... very well,' he managed to answer; almost breaking his bollix to stifle more laughter. 'When I said "are you kidding me" I meant nobody told me I had to dress well to get into Cafe Woo Woo.'

He was back tracking faster than an extended bungee cord but decided it was the only way he was going to find out if it actually was the place he'd been looking for. Unsure but deciding to give him the benefit of the doubt, the man backed down a little. 'It's not required but most people like to.'

'Grand so. Here I don't suppose you know Martin Brick? That's who I'm looking for,' Robbie asked. 'Only I'm not sure I'm at the right place at all.'

'Martin? Yeah he's always here,' replied the man as he scurried toward a waiting taxi. 'He owns the place.'

The car moved off leaving Robbie staring after it with his gob wide open. 'This is like Alice in fucking Wonderland. Jaysus only knows what I'm going to see in here,' said Robbie as he approached the metal door. Two heavy thumps resulted in a flap dropping at head height, revealing a normal looking, make-up free man. He looked Robbie up and down.

'You a member?' the bouncer asked.

'No. Hawk sent me to see Martin'

'Ok, come in.'

The door opened. Robbie stepped through and went down a couple of steps. The foyer was draped in red velvet curtains and the lighting was seductively dim, probably to hide the facial hair of the 'women' that frequented the place. He didn't know where to go so he turned to question the bouncer and found himself at a loss for words, again. The man was standing with his back to him looking through the door flap. From the neck up he had been totally normal looking. Now Robbie found himself looking at a sixteen stone bloke in a mini skirt, boob tube and fishnet stockings wearing shiny red leather thigh-high boots. 'Excuse me?' ventured a bewildered Robbie.

'Oh sorry. Martin is in the workshop at the back. I'll radio one of the lads to bring you through.'

'Great,' smiled Robbie. At this stage he wondered if someone had slipped him LSD earlier in this exceptionally weird evening. 'Eh, do you mind answering me one question? And I swear I'm not taking the piss.'

'What?'

'I was just wondering like … how the fuck do you get home without having the shite kicked out of you?'

'Martin owns a taxi firm as well as this place. None of the drivers have a problem with us. Can't say the feeling is mutual though.'

'Oh? Why's that then?'

'Cos they're all a shower of queers,' he replied as he adjusted his boob tube and turned to answer a rap at the door. 'I can't stand poofs, me.'

Robbie was led to a set of black double doors marked 'Do Not Enter'. He knocked and a gruff northern voice shouted, 'Come on ahead.' As Robbie entered the well-lit room he looked around for the man he'd come to meet. The last time they'd met, Martin was taking possession of a shipment of guns. Hawk's gang had nicked them from an aircraft hangar in the military aerodrome at Baldonnel. Martin had been a senior member of the IRA and had to diversify after the ceasefire. His area of expertise had been bomb making, specifically the timing devices. He and a lot of the top brass in his old network had squirreled away money over the years from various big bank jobs so he'd been able to set up a few businesses. He once told Robbie and his boss that while he was passionate about the Provo cause, in his heart he was really an entrepreneur.

'Martin, where are ya man?'
'Ah Robbie, what about you?' called a voice from behind a large plastic sheet in the back of the room. 'Come on over, I'm just testing out a new product line I've been developing.' He followed the voice and stuck his head around the plastic drapes. The ex-senior officer of one of the most dangerous terrorist organisations in the western world turned to shake hands. He was dressed in fuchsia hot pants and a diamante encrusted bikini top. His lips were smeared with bright pink lipstick and his eyes were barely visible under the false lashes. There were tears on his cheeks. 'Good to see you man,' he sniffed. 'Have a seat.' Robbie just nodded vaguely. Assured at this stage that this was indeed a dream, he viewed the rest of the scene in front of him. There were bloody bits of what looked like some sort of medium sized black animal all over plastic sheeting on the floor. 'Eh, what happened?' he asked.
'Ach I've been trying to come up with a new product so I have.' he said. 'I've all these bastard components for making bombs left over since the bloody ceasefire. I'm trying to find a use for them, shame to waste them y'know. So anyway, I thought of a fantastic idea.'
'Yeah?' asked Robbie, his voice unsure as he viewed the bits of fur and limbs.
'People hate when their dogs won't stop barking on the lead, right? So I said why not make a collar that

gives the animal a wee jolt whenever it starts barking.'

'There's a market for that stuff is there?' Robbie said, incredulous.

'Oh aye, there is surely. Don't you watch The Dog Whisperer?'

'Can't say I do, no.'

'Anyway, I came up with a way to use the detonators to make an anti-bark collar. They didn't work on the toy barking dogs I practised on though. The batteries interfered with the timing device, so I thought I'd practise on wee Fred here, my cocker spaniel. I don't know what I did wrong. I never thought he'd get hurt,' he said as he swept up bits of the family pet. 'I've to go back to the drawing board.'

'Sorry about that,' said Robbie. 'Hard one to explain to the kids I'd say.'

Martin nodded, 'Ach they'll be devastated right enough.'

'Hawk is in the market for some of your expertise,' said Robbie, keen to move the conversation on to the purpose at hand.

'So he said. Something to blow a few boats up. Semtex is your only man. When do you want them for?'

'The job's Friday night so I need to set them Thursday.'

'They'll be ready.'

'That's deadly man, thanks. Listen by the way. If I ever slagged off queers in front of you, I'm sorry.'

'Why?' asked Martin, confused.

'Well,' Robbie looked the other man's outfit up and down. 'I didn't realise you were, you know, that way.'

'Would you piss off? My arse is for one way traffic only. This, I'll have you know,' he said indicating his clothing, 'is Couture.'

Chapter Eight

Ruth stared into the drinks cabinet. The truth was she didn't really fancy anything. It was just boredom bringing her there. It was Saturday night and Lorcan was at yet another function at the club. For several months now, he had been spending more time there than at home. She'd mentioned it of course, and it had led to a humdinger of a row with him saying he only wanted to spend time around positive people for a change. That had hurt. Lately everything did. She poured a large Vodka and tonic. It was just so difficult to buck herself up. She needed to lose weight and buy some new clothes, maybe even change her look totally. But she couldn't be bothered. Her marriage was beginning to slip through her fingers and that really wasn't what she wanted. Lorcan had always been a good man, he still was really. It was her fault he was backing away. She rarely went with him to the club but that was because it was such a male dominated place. Even when she did go for a drink she ended up sitting with another one of the wives while their husbands huddled around the bar yapping about some game or other. What was the point of that? Not exactly a romantic night out.

She was forty nine years old, nearly half a flipping century for God's sake. She wasn't a bad looking woman she supposed. The thick black hair that fell to her shoulders was all natural. She had her late mother to thank for that. Her cheeks always had a little pink tinge which contrasted with her fair skin. Lorcan used to call her Snow White when they met first. Twenty five years and two children later she'd have been happy if he called her the Wicked Witch so long as they were communicating. That was partly the reason she decided to do the Gaelic for Mothers thing. She needed him to see that she was prepared to give it a go, to get involved. When she drove down to the club for the first session the other night she had purposely parked a little further back from the all-weather pitch so she could see if anyone bothered to turn up. There had been one or two familiar faces that she'd seen around Stillorgan. Even though they'd moved to Sandycove when Lorcan sold one of his many businesses, she still spent a lot of time in her old neighbourhood. It had been a surprise to see Tommy Boylan was the coach though. He'd been such a big star in his day. Ruth could never quite understand why everyone continued to treat him so badly. What happened was years ago and you only had to be in his company a few minutes before you realised that he was a kind soul really. She wondered if he was like her, a little shy. In fact, she found him to be a gentleman which was more than you could say for a lot of the guys in Iona Gaels. Sexist pigs would be a more appropriate label.

Take the other night for example. He'd been really good not to make a big deal about the flatulence. Ruth giggled just thinking about it again. It had been like something out of comedy. She dreaded to think what some of Lorcan's friends would have said had they been there. The other women all seemed nice and most of them were close enough to her age so she didn't feel like a total pensioner. Sitting in the Range Rover after training she tried to remember who was who. There wasn't a hope she could remember all of them but some of them had stood out. Alison looked like she might have been the same age as Ruth. God, was she a big lady, but very nice. Ruth had seen her around the area once or twice. The small woman seemed a fiery kind of character. Maybe it was the red hair. Ruth hadn't heard her talking about kids but then she looked as though she could be in her early fifties so they might have been grown up. If she and Brid hadn't come to training together Ruth would never have put them as friends. She was the total opposite of the red head. Tommy only had to look at her and she went puce. Tracey was another big lady. When they were chatting earlier she mentioned that she was a teacher. Then there was Naomi. She was fascinating. It was hard to put an age on her but if she had to guess, she'd say mid to late thirties. They had walked into the enclosed pitch at the same time, both late. Everyone assumed they had come together. Ruth thought she was familiar but hadn't been able to place her until she found out where she worked. She was a beautician in a salon in Stillorgan. Ruth had her monthly facial there and although she didn't remember Naomi actually treating her, they would've passed each other in the reception area on occasion. She appeared to be a very energetic girl. Just watching her wore Ruth out. She seemed to have a very unique way of telling a story, all actions and mimicking. There was hardly a pick on her, well, not when compared to the rest of them anyway. Everything seemed to elicit a giggle from her and boy was she open! They had only been in each other's company for half an hour before the talk turned smutty. Alison had been talking about the new Chinese restaurant that opened beside the pub on the hill. It was called Lee Hung and Naomi had piped up that she knew his brother 'Well'. Of course Ruth didn't get the joke and had to have it explained to her by one of the others. Typical, she thought, the others probably saw her as a right square. When Ruth first met Lorcan she was a little racy too. She used to dress up in fancy lingerie every Saturday night but it got tired. A bit like herself. Then the weight started to pile on, well not pile so much as sneak. It had been a gradual increase. A pound here and there was all very well except when it only went one way—up. There was the usual half a stone gain over the school holidays and at Christmas. Before she knew it, when she looked in the mirror a size eighteen was looking back. Who could blame her for not wanting to flounce around the bedroom in sexy lingerie? Besides, it was hard to show off lacy knickers when the flab from your belly hung down over them like an apron. From what Ruth had gathered in her fact finding mission with the other women, most of them were doing the football to try and lose a little weight. Alison had told the group that she loved swimming but that it was a bit solitary. Naomi sounded like she was doing it more for the social side of things. It mustn't be easy to find time for herself when there was no father around to pick up the slack. Anyway, it didn't matter what reasons any of them had. It was more enjoyable than Ruth had anticipated and although her muscles felt like she had been struck by a train the following morning, she knew it was a good feeling. The best part was she wanted more of it. That was definitely a start.

Naomi studied her little girl's football nursery training session more intently than ever before. Any of the other times she'd been there she had just gossiped with the other parents at the side-line, barely registering what was going on with the kids. Being Irish she assumed playing Gaelic would be some sort of natural instinct. The first indication that it wasn't as simple as it looked was when she nearly went arse over tit while trying to solo the ball. That was partly due to the intense mortification brought about by being the first one asked to do it. She was scarlet thinking back to it. All the women were lined up behind each other. There were four little orange cones. The idea, Tommy said, was to solo the ball in and out of each of the cones.

'You mean go on my own?' Naomi had asked innocently.

'Go where on your own?'

'In and out of the cones, you said "solo" so do you mean just me?' As she spoke she looked to the other women to see if maybe they knew something more. It didn't look promising.

'You don't know how to solo?' asked Tommy with a neutral expression.

'I might, if I knew what it was,' she giggled. He was taking it so seriously that she couldn't help it. Turning to the group, half of whom were indulging in idle chit chat, he asked, 'Do any of you know what it means to solo the ball?' Several of the girls who had been chatting nodded.

'Could you demonstrate for the group Alison?'

'Tommy, I said I knew what it meant to solo not that I could actually do it. I only know from watching the older kids.'

'Anyone?' The coach looked around the sea of blank faces. 'Ok, we better start at the beginning so.'

The majority of the training that first night had

been spent trying to teach them how to do it. The practise was simple enough, in theory. You were supposed to drop the ball from one hand onto the foot and kick it back up into your hand. Easy. If you weren't blessed with the co-ordination of a pissed llama on ice-skates. After at least twenty attempts Tommy thought it might be necessary to pinpoint the exact part of the foot that was supposed to make contact with the ball. He blew the whistle to get their attention.

'Ladies, you want to aim for the part of your foot just behind the base of the toes. Imagine you were double jointed ...'

'Now you're talking!' Naomi had quipped with a wink much to Tommy's mortification, although she'd been sure she saw a bit of a smirk.

'As I was saying ... if you were able to bend your toes backwards it would form a little u shape. Imagine when you let the ball drop onto the foot, it is being cupped in this u shape. What you want to do is give it a quick flick of the foot, like this.' He demonstrated the technique effortlessly. 'Now go off and find a spot. The first one of you that gets to fifty of them without dropping the ball over the next few weeks gets a pint from me, or whatever your poison is.'

The women joked about how the offer of a free drink was a wonderful incentive as Tommy shouted encouragement. 'Go out tomorrow and buy yourself a football. That's the one we use for ladies. Try to practise for just ten minutes a day. You could be doing it in the house while the dinner's cooking or whenever you can. The more you do it, the better you get.'

Naomi, determined by nature, set her sights

firmly on winning the little incentive and had taken possession of her daughter's football that night when she got home. Tommy interested her. When she put his name into Google she found out all about his playing history and the incident that ended it. More importantly, he was only ten years older than her and didn't appear to be married. There weren't many blokes of fifty that looked as good as him. He kept himself fitter than most his age. His thick hair that was probably auburn in his youth was flecked with grey, making it the colour of harvested hay. He wasn't conventionally good looking, far from it actually, but there was an aura about him. She had sensed it the first time she looked at him. His hazel eyes were kind yet sad as though harbouring a lot of hurt and regret. It was hard to put a finger on it. He was totally different to the men that normally caught her eye. Most of the ones she had been with were the type you wouldn't throw out of bed for eating cornflakes. It helped matters that she was cute. Picking up blokes wasn't a problem, though getting them to piss off when she'd had enough sometimes was.

Her black hair was cut short and she kept it styled with gel in a flick that partly covered one eye. This made her face appear even more impish than it was. She was blessed with high cheekbones that almost looked like a chalice holding up her piercing green eyes. One guy she dated told her she had eyes like a cat. To this day she wasn't sure whether it was a compliment or not. None of her friends were members of Iona Gaels so there was no real way to find out any personal information about Tommy. Anyway, it wasn't that she wanted to jump his bones or anything, at least she didn't think so. Fancying the arse off him would have been easier; she knew how to handle that. This was odd. She wasn't able to pinpoint what way she felt about him apart from the fact that it was different from normal. One thing she had picked up from the other girls at training was that he worked as a caretaker in the local girl's school and that he had lived abroad for a long time. Naomi knew for sure that there was more to Tommy Boylan than met the eye. She couldn't wait for the next training session to start finding out.

Chapter Nine

'Fuck,' said Robbie, rubbing his hands together as quickly as possible. The quayside in Howth was the last place anyone with designs on keeping their nuts attached to their body should have been on that miserable night. The rain kept coming in waves across the open harbour, blown by a sharp wind that Robbie felt sure was rattling his bones. He had never been so cold or so pissed off. He had driven out on a borrowed Honda Fire blade motorbike so he had nowhere to shelter. Martin was supposed to meet him here at nine o'clock with the explosives. It was almost 10 p.m. and there was no sign of the prick. Robbie had tried his mobile countless times and it just rang out. At first he gave him the benefit of the doubt, assuming he got held up in the club. Now that he was freezing and wet all he wanted to do was go home and jump into Kim's warm bed. He cursed the Provo again.

One by one the curtains were drawn in windows of the St. Laurence apartment buildings which overlooked the marina. The streets were deserted thanks to the elements and the crews for the yacht race were all attending a pre-race safety briefing in the yacht club. He had managed to check the floor plans of the building online and saw that the conference room was at the back of the club. That had been a real stroke of luck because Robbie knew there was no manned security in the area after 6 p.m. The last thing he needed was a couple of hundred people eyeballing him from an overlooking window. There was the CCTV to think about but Robbie was well used to sneaking around those yokes. The sound of car tyres splashing through pockets of water interrupted his thoughts. He chanced a quick look around the industrial-size rubbish container behind which he had been failing miserably to shelter. A dark Mercedes was approaching with its lights turned off, a brave move on an unlit harbour road without a fence. Robbie pulled the collar of his leather jacket up further to shield his face as it came to a stop a yard or two away from him. Its door opened. The smell of lavender and cigar smoke that reached his nose was a very welcome distraction from the reek of fish guts that, up to now, had threatened to make him hurl. Then again it was his own fault for picking a hiding spot right next to a fishmonger's bin. He held his breath, he couldn't risk being spotted now. A known scumbag hiding in the pissing rain, down the bottom of a dark road leading to a marina full of expensive boats? The cops would just love that. The unmistakeable tip tap of high heels on concrete surprised Robbie. He edged his face forward in an effort to sneak a peek, fully expecting to see some tart with her knickers around her ankles being pummelled up against the wall by a fat man in a suit. To his relief it wasn't two people but one.

'Martin?'

The man turned and walked toward him, his brilliant red stilettos causing him to stumble on one of the cobbles. 'Nice shoes,' grinned Robbie, 'but I'm not sure they match the outfit.'

'Shut your mouth you. The fucking club got raided. I'm after spending all night down the cop shop so I have. They got a great laugh out of it all, the fuckers. That's why I'm late.'

'Don't tell me they got the gear?' asked Robbie anxiously.

'Catch yourself on! D'you think I'd be here if they had? No, I'd the stuff in the boot of the car and thank fuck I hadn't parked it at the club.' He shivered as a huge gust of wind blew up under his ra ra skirt. 'Come on. Get into the car so I can show you how to set these wee bombs.' Robbie was grateful for the reprieve from the pounding rain and listened attentively to his instructions. 'Ok, so the explosives are set to detonate from a radio signal. To activate that, you have to send a text. Here's the phone you need to send it.' Martin handed him a dated looking mobile phone. 'There's only one number programmed in so any eejit can do it.' Robbie nodded.

'And you're sure this shit is waterproof because I have to plant them beneath the water line to maximise the damage to the hull.' The Provo looked at Robbie with a deadpan expression. 'I've used a wee bit of Semtex in my time. Don't you worry your head.' He looked out towards the various boats moored along the fishing harbour. 'Which ones are you blowing up anyway?'

'None of those yokes,' laughed Robbie, eyeing up the lobster pots adorning the decks of the fishing boats closest to them. 'Hawk's contact said there's a load of big Cruiser yachts up in the Marina. I have a list of the mooring numbers.'

'So why don't you stick the explosive on the propane tanks? That would create some spectacle!'

'Yeah,' agreed Robbie. 'That's what I thought but yer man said these racing yachts don't normally carry propane tanks. The fuckers chuck anything that weighs too much. They'd only have the bare minimum of diesel to get them in and out of the harbour. Apparently they don't even have a jacks on board. They shite in a bucket.'

'Dirty bastards,' replied Martin, shaking his head. 'C'mere anyway, the suction pads on the surface of the bomb will hold them in place no matter what the sea conditions are. Then send the message whenever you're ready and sit back and watch the fireworks.'

Robbie watched in envy as the Mercedes world he had briefly inhabited pulled away, taking with it the cosy cream leather interior and leaving him on this exposed, fish gut festooned slipway. Kim and he had come out here the previous afternoon for a nice walk along the harbour. She was off for a few days because she was playing the dutiful aunt, minding one of her nieces while her sister shot yet another baby out like a cannonball. Now there was a baffling thing. His future sister in law, who had as little regard for him as her mother, had a face like a trout—big gaping eyes and a gob that seemed to hang permanently open giving her a gormless expression. Even looking like that she was never short of a ride. Bizarrely, at the age of thirty she seemed to be blissfully unaware of the advances in modern contraception. She had four kids already and not a sign of any of the fathers. Robbie reckoned a fella would feel more sensation sticking his knob in the port tunnel. No wonder they never stuck around.

Kim had readily agreed to the walk out in Howth, totally unaware of her fiancé's ulterior motive. She oohed and aahed at the pristine yachts in the marina as they were lovingly attended to by their respective crews. As luck would have it she had even got chatting to some frog off a French boat who explained all about the yacht's layout. Robbie had feigned disinterest as he kept an eye on the toddler but actually he was taking it all in. There weren't many million euro yachts moored on the balconies of the flats in The Salmon Leap Estate when he was growing up so he needed whatever details he could get. Like the fact that entry to the marina from the road would require knowing the PIN number for the gate. There was no barrier to approach by sea though. He had watched while people approached on water. They seemed to radio ahead. Robbie supposed it was to find out where they could stick their posh boats. Hawk's contact had said that since they put the cameras in, there was no-one manning the airwaves at night. It was Kim who told him later about the crews all having to attend a safety briefing on the Thursday night.

So here he was with rainwater dripping from his jocks onto his bollix. He had a knapsack full of explosives and the patience of a two year old outside a locked sweetshop. He slipped off his jacket and hid it behind the dumpster. However cold he was, it was about to get much worse. He squeezed his hands into a pair of latex gloves and pulled down his balaclava. He eased himself into a small dingy that was tied up conveniently at the bottom of the slipway. Even though there was a motor on it, he didn't want to risk drawing attention so he unhooked the paddles on either side and began rowing out towards the mouth of the fishing harbour. It was tougher than he had anticipated because of the wind which hit with full force once he rounded the harbour wall and headed into the marina where all the cruisers and puppeteers were moored. Robbie put the rucksack on his chest and tied the dingy up. He threw his legs over the side and slid down into the dark water. 'FUCK that's cold.' His teeth chattered uncontrollably and he regretted not kitting himself out in a wetsuit. He swam breast stroke until he reached the first of the cruisers. There wasn't time to scope the boats out for any fancy gear he could nick and flog later. This was to be a quick in and out job and if he wanted his kneecaps to remain a feature of his legs he'd better not fuck it up. The Hawk was relying on this little distraction. It had to go like clockwork. The yachts would only be off the coast between Howth and Dun Laoire for a short while and if the bombs didn't blow at the right time it would be rescue crews from the Howth side that would be first responders which was fuck all use to Hawk who'd be left with a boat full of drugs loitering suspiciously just outside Dun Laoire.

Opening the rucksack he took out the first unit. He peeled off the strip of paper covering the suction cup base and held it next to the hull about two feet below the water line. The pull was fierce and he grinned, knowing there was no way it would be dislodged. He moved on to the next boat. He knew he couldn't be identified even if there were cameras recording his movements. The four boats he had lined up were British as it happened, which was funny because once they sank and were subsequently salvaged, any forensics examination of the bomb's components would point at the disbanded IRA. That would keep the coppers running around in circles for ages. The media and politicians would be in uproar claiming the terrorist's ceasefire was over and all the while Hawk's shipment would be making its way throughout the city. It took less than thirty minutes to plant all the explosives. At least a third of that time was wasted trying to keep his shivering hands steady. Once he got back to the motorbike he stripped off his sodden sweatshirt and pulled his leather jacket back on. It wasn't much defence against the cold but it was better than nothing.

By the time Robbie eventually got home it was close to midnight and he was pleasantly surprised that he hadn't frozen to death. He had arranged with Hawk that he would return to Howth the following day to verify the yacht's locations before detonating. The race was scheduled to get under way at about 2.30 pm. There were a few spots on Howth Hill that he could use as vantage points, then, all he had to do was send the text and boom! Job done. The flat he shared with Kim was in Harold's Cross, just down the road from where they'd grown up. She wanted to stay near her mother. Robbie often thought how he would have loved to get close to her oul wan too. Near enough to put a bleedin pillow over her face! It was because of that pox bottle's interference that Kim wouldn't marry him yet. If she had her way they wouldn't even be living together. Apparently her fella, Kim's da, had been a bit like Robbie. Always on the rob and up to all sorts. The only difference was, he was a thick bastard and kept getting caught. He got sent down when Kim was still in nappies and pissed off the wrong bloke in the Joy. He was only 36 when he was stabbed to death with a scissors in the prison library. As a result of her experience with Kim's da, her ma had it in for anyone in the 'local business' as she called it. She didn't even bother to hide her dislike of Robbie and reminded her precious daughter on a daily basis that she shouldn't marry him till he'd a proper job and could prove he'd gone straight.

Creeping into the second floor flat he eased the door shut behind him and tiptoed into the bedroom. Kim was tangled up in the duvet sleeping peacefully. She was probably worn out looking after her niece all day. Thankfully her sister's other rug rats had been farmed out to the rest of her family. If he'd had any sense, Robbie would've just taken his medication, dragged his half frozen body into the bed beside her and gone to sleep. But he couldn't. He had things to figure out. He got out of his wet clothes, pulled a tracksuit out of the ironing pile and slipped it on. The parole officer assigned to him had left a message on his phone earlier. He left the bedroom and dialled his voicemail to listen to it again as he wandered into the kitchen.

'Mr King, this is Peter Gaughran. I've been assigned to your case. Your community service has been arranged. You are to present yourself at Iona Gaels Gaelic football club at 9 p.m. Friday night. In addition I have agreed terms for a trial employment. I will go through the details with you in person tomorrow night'.

'Bleedin typical,' said Robbie, cracking open a can of Budweiser from the fridge and necking half of it in one go. He was going to be spending his Friday night pulling up weeds or whatever off some tosser's football pitch. He had been into GAA himself for a while when he was younger, even got picked for the first team. His particular forte was lashing out the digs without the referee or even his coach noticing. Then things changed once Hawk started clicking his fingers. Robbie stopped showing up for training and it all just petered out.

The other message on the phone was from his anger management therapist. Honestly, the shite he had to do to stay out of jail. He had almost finished the last set when that poxy rooster made him see red on his weekend away. Now he was back to square one. Having to meet that Edward Flynn man twice a week was about as enjoyable as a dose of crabs. He wasn't even totally convinced this bloke was the genuine article because some of the shite he came out with was warped. He didn't care if yer man's qualifications came out of a Christmas cracker once he wrote a report for the probation officer confirming Robbie had attended the requisite sessions. He grabbed a second can and thought about the session he had endured earlier that day. This Flynn character had an office which overlooked the canal at Portobello Bridge. Robbie had declined the invitation to sit on the couch. Instead he'd stood looking out at all the young ones having their lunch along the water's edge. Fashion, it seemed, was more important than warmth to the girls.

'Isn't false tan a great invention all the same?' he had ventured to the bespectacled man who barely filled his suit on the large leather chair.

'Why's that Robert?' the bore asked.

'Well it means the young ones can wear the greyhound skirts all bleedin year, not just in the summer time.' 'Greyhound skirts?' Mr Flynn seemed totally baffled.

'Yeah, an inch from the hare like. D'ya know what I mean?' Robbie grinned mischievously. The poor man turned purple, realising the connotation.

'Has this derogatory view of women stemmed from a specific incident Robert?'

He hated it when anyone called him that. His father was the reason. He had always thought the name too posh for a son of his and said the boy's mother had ideas above her station. Typical of some court appointed prat to insist on using his full name. 'What derogatory view?'

'No need to become defensive. I'll come back to the issue in a moment. Now, how have you been getting on with your exercises?' smiled the man gently as though he was talking to a lobotomised budgie.

'Can't do them cos they piss me off, make me angry like,' replied Robbie, deliberately trying to wind the bloke up.

'Ok, well let's review them shall we? When we get angry we ...' began the counsellor.

'What's this "we" shit? Are you telling me they've appointed a fucking head case just like me bleedin self to try and sort me out?' he laughed in response. The counsellor continued unperturbed.

'When we get angry we follow our five steps. Number one – find a safe spot to relieve the anger building in us.' Robbie thought yer man's bollix looked like a good place to start kicking off some steam. 'Then two, we take a deep breath. Three, we count to ten, slowly,' the counsellor closed his eyes as he spoke while his patient picked his nose, rolled it into a ball and flicked it across at the man who was seriously doing his head in. 'Four. Take a break. If necessary we take ourselves away from the situation making us angry.'

'I would,' Robbie said, 'but I'd be arrested for violating a court order.'

'And finally step five,' the counsellor said sighing like a yoga instructor, 'we find the sweet spot.'

'So we're back to talking about the tarts out there are we?' laughed Robbie, a mocking tone to his voice. He indicated the window and the girls beside the canal. 'Aren't you the dark horse?'

'Step five,' admonished the man, 'as you well know, is where you learn to act rather than react. If life gives you lemons you make lemonade.'

'Them young ones look like posh sorts though. I'd say if life gave me lemons I'd have more chance of me hole if I cut them into slices and put them into gin and tonics.' Robbie got such a kick out of watching the counsellor struggle to keep it together.

'I feel you are displaying some anti-female behaviour Robert. I have been devising some alternative therapies to help men deal with such issues. I am going to give you an exercise to do for your next visit.' The counsellor got up and crossed to a tall cabinet on the other side of the room. He removed a medium sized box from one of the shelves. With his back to Robbie it wasn't possible to see what was in the box but as soon as he turned it was perfectly plain. A Barbie doll.

'I'm dying to hear what you want me to do with that' said Robbie.

'I want you to treat this Barbie as you would your partner,' the counsellor outlined.

'You want me to ride it?' replied Robbie, incredulous.

'No Mr King, I do not. The purpose of this exercise is to see if you can take care of this doll. Your relationship with the Barbie is representative of your relationships in general.'

'Are you for real? said Robbie. 'That's the craziest

idea you've come up with yet and you've come up with some fucked up stuff over the months. Jaysus!'

'I believe that the act of selecting clothes for the doll and arranging her hair will have a calming influence on you Robert,' replied the counsellor confidently. Robbie's forehead creased as he raised his eyebrows and bent his head slightly to the side. 'Are you trying to suggest I'm some sort of poof?'

'I assure you I am not suggesting any such thing. Sometimes in life we need to try the unusual to achieve the usual. On your next visit we can review your progress. My secretary has to finish early today so I will call you later with our next appointment.'

That was what the other message had been about. Another meeting had been arranged. Terrific. He drained the can of Bud and wandered back into the kitchen to pull some more out of the fridge. Kim didn't really like him to drink too much. She thought it interfered with his medication but he hadn't had an episode in ages. Well, not if you didn't count blowing the head off the rooster. His doctor said he was borderline bipolar but it seemed to him that it was just the fashionable thing to be these days. You were no-one in the celebrity world if you didn't suffer from it. It seemed to be used as an excuse for all sorts of mad behaviour. Britney Spears playing golf with a Jeep's windscreen, Mel Gibson shouting at Jewish people. If it was good enough for that lot, it was good enough for him. Besides, since he was diagnosed he'd been getting away with all sorts of shit he should have been locked up for.

Chapter Ten

Naomi spread the warm wax all over her client's calf, applied the strip of material and pulled.

'Ouch!'

'Sorry, it's nearly over. Next time think about taking a Nurofen before your appointment, it helps a lot.'

It was the end of a long week. She had been distracted most of the afternoon, trying to think where she knew that woman Ruth from. She had said she was a housewife but had a degree in Horticulture. Naomi was a little surprised at that revelation. It was a degree in digging, not brain surgery. The very fact that the woman felt the need to tell people she had a degree at all said a lot. Smearing on more wax she suddenly got it. Ruth had been a client in the salon. She wasn't one of Naomi's clients but she did remember one time when Ruth's regular beautician was double booked and she'd come in for a leg wax. In the beauty business she was used to seeing people in all conditions but she had been particularly surprised to see this well-to-do woman's legs in such a state. She didn't know whether to wax or braid. It was strange because she knew for a fact that this lady had a facial at least once a month which included an eyebrow wax so she wasn't a total stranger to the idea.

She remembered thinking that it was unusual for a woman who took such obvious pride in her outward appearance to be so unkempt beneath her fine clothes. Her husband must have thought he had crawled into the dog's basket at night when he got into bed. Naomi would rather die than let herself go like that. In fact she was the total opposite. She waxed her legs so often that hardly any hair grew anymore and the bit that did was so fine you wouldn't see it unless you were up close ... very close. And then you were more likely to be occupied doing something else. Brazilian waxes were practically her own invention ever since she accidentally spilt hot wax all over herself when attempting to do her bikini line while watching TV. She had no choice but to whip the lot off. The result was very satisfying, except for the initial few times when the hair started to grow back and she scratched like a hooker with crabs. Up to that point she had just tended to the garden down below by trimming the hedges. Ever since she went for the whole deforestation it had opened up a new world. Her latest craze was the vajazzle. It was all the rage since it featured on that reality programme with the UK's only living brain donors. The vajazzle was a jewelled makeover for a woman's newly bare pubic area. It was fantastic! She had introduced it to some of the more adventurous women who frequented the salon. She told them that if they wanted sparkle in their love life they had to sparkle downstairs. A little body glue and a multitude of coloured Swarovski crystals later, they were on their way home to some very surprised partners. Thinking about the other women on the football team she wondered what they were really like. She'd had a chat with a few of them but not enough to really gauge anything. Alison seemed nice. Naomi wondered if she had always been a big woman, it seemed hard to imagine how she'd ever been slim. Then there was little Mary the feisty one. She had told Naomi that she was officially four foot eleven inches which meant she wasn't a midget, not that she seemed to give a flying fuck. During the course of their brief conversation she had mentioned a couple of names which Naomi assumed were kids but Tommy had blown the whistle before she had a chance to find out.

They were due back in the club that evening for the next training session. It would be interesting to see if everyone turned up. She really hoped they did. It felt good to be part of something. Her mother was minding Shona for the night. That meant Naomi was able to go on a date after training. She rubbed soothing cream onto her client's newly waxed legs and left her to get dressed. Naomi had one more lady to do and then she could refresh her vajazzle, just in case it got an airing later. 'You never know the day nor the hour,' her mother used to say, although probably not with the same thing in mind.

Tommy sat in the kitchen of his house and looked around. Why had he never noticed before just how dull the place was? The only pictures on the wall were two team photos from the All-Ireland winning finals he had played in and a couple of shots of sea birds that his father had taken years ago. The walls were painted a pale green colour. The rest of the place wasn't exactly bursting with modernity either. It hadn't changed in years. There was no reason for it to. No woman to change it for, he thought sadly. There were even dado rails in the hall and floral print wallpaper in the sitting room. Maybe he was just used to it now. He had inherited the house from his mother when she died. She had been the reason he returned from England. There wasn't much point paying rent over there when there was a free gaff in Dublin and besides, she needed taking care of. There was nothing else keeping him in the UK. His father had been diagnosed with throat cancer just two months before he died. He had asked Tommy to take care of his mum. It never crossed his mind to say no, given that they were two of the very few people who had understood his moment of madness all those years before. They had seen first-hand the rigorous training he endured, the strictness of his diet and most of all his lack of socialising. His mother had been well aware that he used his strict training regime as an excuse not to go out on dates. As an only child he had been painfully shy and it hadn't eased as he got to the awkward teenage years and beyond. It still felt like it was his parent's house. What was the point of doing it up when he was the only one looking at it? Maybe he would get around to it sometime but for now he wasn't too bothered. The wardrobes full of his parent's clothes had long been emptied and given to the Oxfam shop. There had probably been enough Dublin football jerseys to tog out half the county. He smiled at the thought as he flicked through various training booklets he had compiled over his years as a player. He had a folder where he kept all the up to date theories on new ways to get the most out of an athlete. When he was at his peak they used to start the sessions off with a little light stretching and then move on from there. Nowadays the feeling was that static stretching was damaging to the muscles, so a little light warm up was deemed appropriate beforehand. The problem Tommy faced was that half his bloody team were in need of life support after just one lap of a warm up. God alone knew what would happen if they had to play on a full pitch like Croke Park. 'Sure the game would be over by the time some of them made it out to the pitch,' said Tommy to an empty room.

It was funny but even after just one session he had warmed to the women. Fair enough they were not exactly the type of team he had envisaged getting involved with. Most of them had never even held a football, let alone played a match. But there was something about them, he felt comfortable around them, which was strange. He wasn't sure if he was right but he sensed that, a bit like him, they needed to do this to prove something to themselves or others. He knew Lorcan, Ruth's husband, would have pushed her into doing it simply because Ray O'Toole had suggested it. Ever since his son got selected for the senior squad back in the eighties, if Ray had asked the bloke to wipe his arse he probably would have offered to do it barehanded.   Tommy had seen a few of the lads looking down from the bar that first night of training. In a way he had been a little annoyed that Ray didn't come down to the pitch, given that he was supposed to be supporting the initiative. Then again, it shouldn't have surprised him. Ray had never known where he stood with him but Tommy had a fair idea that he was sure it wasn't in very high standing. Still, as the man had said, he was given this opportunity and maybe it might set him on the road to coaching the seniors, as Ray had suggested.

'I suppose I better give the little fucker the benefit of the doubt this once,' shrugged Tommy just as his phone beeped. He looked at the screen; it was a message from the man himself.   'Jesus, that's spooky,' he said as he scrolled through the text.
Tommy, the club's involved in a community service initiative. There's a lad coming to give you a hand at

training for a while.
What did he do? Tommy replied.
They don't tell you unless it's relevant so it obviously isn't. Anyway, everyone deserves a second chance...
'Prick,' he said aloud as he read the jibe. If it was the last thing he did he would wipe the smug grin off that man's face. He was going to make this Gaelic for Mothers thing a success, even if it killed him.

'Robbie will you put Hayley down for a nap before you go to meet the parole officer?' asked Kim, rubbing him on the shoulder. 'She likes when you read her a little story.'
'Ah luv, I would, only I have to run an errand for Hawk. I probably won't have time.'
'See that's exactly what my ma is talking about,' she snapped.
'What is?'
'You! Dropping everything to run after that fella. What's so bloody special about him anyway?' Robbie scooped up a forkful of beans and burger and popped them in his mouth.
'He can be very persuasive,' he said between chews. Kim was well aware that Hawk was dodgy but she would have been shocked at just how serious some of his crimes had been. She had only met him once and that was by mistake. One of the other lads, who was supposed to be driving Hawk to court one day last year, got so nervous at the thought of being in a car alone with him that he'd overdosed on Valium. He had to go get his stomach pumped. Robbie and Kim had been moving into the flat when he got the call. Kim had insisted on going with him when he said he had to give Hawk a lift into town, saying she could

drop into Hickeys and get the curtain material she had ordered. On the drive in, Robbie had got so stressed trying to steer the conversation away from the real reason Hawk was in court, which was for GBH and not a parking fine as Kim had assumed, that he triggered one of his episodes. He had spent the next three days racing around the place painting the flat, changing his mind about the colour then painting it again. He did that four times before Kim realised on her day off that it wasn't that he couldn't decide on the colour, but that he was having a hypomanic attack. When he had one of them his mind would race and he would act all hyper and on top of the world one minute then be an irritable pain in the arse the next. 'Anyway,' she continued, 'this parole guy is supposed to be helping you to sort yourself out. You said he was working on getting you a job so why don't you tell Hawk that you're going straight.'

'Yeah luv, I'll try and have a chat with him so,' he lied.

'Ah thanks Robbie. And you'll read the story to the little one won't you? I'm going to have a bath. I want to relax on my day off.'

There was more chance of Kim discovering a long lost civilisation in her belly button fluff than him being allowed to go straight. As long as that nut job Hawk was looking at the grass instead of its roots, he wouldn't let Robbie out of his clutches alive, he knew too much about *Hawk Enterprises*, the type of information that could put it's owner away for a long time. Robbie looked at the clock on the wall in the tiny kitchen. 12.30 p.m. The kid went for a nap normally at one. He had to get out to Howth and get into position so he could send the message to detonate the bombs. If he didn't do that the only bits left of him going straight would be the body parts they fished out of the canal. The kid was going to get a very quick story. That's the best he could do.

'Hayley. Where are you hiding? Uncle Robbie's going to read you your story,' he called out.

'She's in the front room,' Kim shouted out from the bathroom. 'She was playing with your new phone.'

'FUCK.'

Robbie sprinted from the kitchen and through the hall to the sitting room in seconds. The phone Martin had given him to set off the detonators was in the hands of a curious toddler. All she had to do was hit send. The little girl was holding the handset to her ear, chatting away nineteen to the dozen. She had only recently started to form full sentences and delighted in using every word she knew whenever she had a chance. He watched in slow motion as she lowered the phone from her ear and looked at it, her index finger hovering over the SEND key. 'Jesus, there's no fucking password,' he cursed. 'Hi Hayley,' he said, lowering his voice, not wanting to startle her in case she tried to leg it, thinking it was a game. The clock was ticking. Just like the bombs.

'Fucking maspurd,' she said smiling up at him.

'Nice little girls don't say bad words,' he said, creeping up alongside her and reaching for the phone. Like shit from a goose she shot across the room and headed for the kitchen. Robbie vaulted the couch to get after her. Just as he did she came scurrying back towards him screeching with excitement at this fun new game. There was nothing for it. He stuck his foot out just as she scampered past and splat! Down she went like a wrestler. He grabbed the phone, ran to the kitchen, got a chocolate bar and had it shoved in her mouth before the first cry came out. Bundling the child up he called to Kim in the bathroom. 'I'm going to read this to her now and then I have to split, alright?'

'Whatever,' came the sleepy response from the steam filled bathroom. Grabbing the first book he could see, Black Beauty, he tucked the little girl in to her temporary bed. The dark brown eyes that looked up at him from the pillow sparkled with anticipation of the story. Robbie checked his watch. 12.45. Fuck.

'Once upon a time there was a horse called Black Beauty. One day he galloped out onto the road and got hit by a double decker bus. The end.' The little girl stared at him, perplexed. Then she shrugged her shoulders and turned her attention back to the chocolate bar.

Chapter Eleven

The sound of crashing made Lorcan jump but he continued typing up his report on the laptop. It was always best to leave his wife alone when she was having a disaster in the kitchen. She had been chopping peppers and onions for a curry when he'd gone upstairs to his little office. The unmistakable sound of crockery smashing to the tiled floor suggested she may be having a meltdown. He sighed and clicked the screen icon to save the document that was urgently needed by the company's financial controller for Monday's meeting with the bank. Typical, he thought, telling me about this at six o clock on a Friday evening. The one day I need to get work done at home in a quiet place, Ruth decides to lose the plot. It was one thing her sitting around moping and feeling sorry for herself and eating herself into obesity but he drew the line at destroying all the family possessions. He was going to have to talk to the kids about her. Maybe even suggest that their mother start seeing a therapist. As he raced down the stairs he realised something was different. There was no sound of crying. Maybe she had run out of tears, it was bound to happen eventually. He could hear the low hum of the radio and then a sound he hadn't heard in their house since the kids were small. Thud - Thud - Thud.
'Damn it.'
The tapping of plastic studs on tile. Thud - Thud - Spludge.
'What the hell is going on?' he asked as he pushed through the kitchen doors.

His wife was standing beside the hob wiping curry sauce off her face with a tea cloth. There were bits of spring onion in her perfectly groomed hair and he wasn't entirely sure but he thought it might have been a prawn hanging on for dear life to the pendant that hung around her neck. She was wearing one of the black maxi dresses she favoured since gaining weight. It was pulled up at the bottom and tied to a knot on one side. Instead of the house slippers she normally wore she had on a pair of thick socks and black shiny football boots. Lorcan shook his head, wondering if he had stepped into some sort of parallel dimension. 'Hi, dinner won't be too long,' she said, turning red. 'I just have to ... well, you can see for yourself.' Ruth reached into the bubbling wok and picked up the white Gaelic football that was simmering nicely in the middle of their dinner. She brought it over to the sink and ran it under the tap. 'Tommy told us to get a ball and practise,' she explained.

'In the dinner?' asked Lorcan.

'No, not in the dinner smarty pants. I haven't quite got the hang of it yet. It's only been a week,' she replied. She dried off the ball and bent down to untie her laces.

'Well go on then,' said Lorcan, moving over to stand with his back to the hob, 'give us a look.'

'I will not. You'll only laugh.'

'I swear I won't.'

'You better not.'

She stood in the centre of the tiled floor holding the ball in both hands and raised her left knee slightly before letting the ball drop to her left foot. It made contact alright but then went shooting up to the ceiling, volleying straight back again. Lorcan caught it before it re-joined the prawns. 'I'm useless,' she said, grabbing the ball and walking towards the hall.

'Hold on. You're not useless. You've just got to alter the way you're holding your leg. Here,' he said taking the ball off her, 'I'll show you.' With the ball in one hand he leaned forward slightly and dropped it down past his relaxed straight leg towards his foot which then flicked quickly and returned the ball directly back the same path it had travelled.

'It's alright for you Lorcan, you've been playing since you were five. I started last week. I knew I'd be rubbish, I shouldn't have bought the boots.' The tears were threatening to fall.

'You just have to keep at it. That's what I used to tell our Garry and he ended up playing on the senior team. Tommy was right to tell you to practise at home. Come on, don't give up already. Just try it without bending your knee. I swear to you, it will click eventually.'

'Ok,' she agreed reluctantly as Lorcan turned the gas off under the overcooked dinner. Holding the ball as her husband showed her, she let it drop but this time didn't bring her foot up to meet it. Instead she waited that extra second and just flicked upwards bringing the area between her toes and the laces in contact with the ball which shot back towards her so fast it hit her square in the nose. 'Jesus, are you all right?' He rushed to her side. She held her face in her hands and her shoulders shook yet no sound came from her mouth. 'You didn't break your nose did you love?' Suddenly he felt protective, like he used to. It was a reminder of what things used to be like, before he was pushed away.

The hands dropped and all he saw was the tears. Normal service resumed. Ruth took a deep breath and he braced himself for the wailing that he knew would come next. She gripped the counter as though she was having trouble breathing and emitted a noise he hadn't heard in such a long time, he'd forgotten she was even capable of it. Howls of laughter. The type that start off in a silent giggle but build up to a deafening crescendo. 'Good God, now this is a sight I've missed,' he said with a grin from ear to ear. 'That Tommy Boylan is doing something right with this Gaelic for Mothers thing and that's for sure.' She tried to nod in agreement but took off in another fit of giggles.

'I'm sorry. It's just that the whole thing is so bloody funny. If you saw the state of us all out there the other night and now here I am scoring goals into the prawn curry! I just can't believe I enjoyed it so much. I can honestly say it is the best thing I've done in years. Thanks for making me do it.'

'I didn't make you. I just put the idea in your head. Now hang up those boots and let's pop open a bottle of wine to celebrate.'

'Can't do that. I have training to go to later! I'll dish this up now. Will you turn up the radio for the news? They mentioned something before you came down about a bomb out at sea.' The familiar intro music for the hourly news finished and a sombre sounding man began to relay the day's main events.

'There are chaotic scenes this afternoon in the harbour area of DunLaoire in south county Dublin. Several yachts competing in a Cruiser Class race have blown up in what some eyewitnesses say looked like gas explosions. As yet there are no confirmed

lists of dead or injured however all four boats sank within minutes. Several other yachts in the closely contested race were damaged by flying debris. The coast guard service, rescue and Garda vessels are all on the scene. We will bring you updates as we receive them.'

The newscaster continued on to other stories and Ruth turned down the volume. 'Jeepers, sounds like it's going to be a busy night for those guys. I'd be amazed if no one was killed. You used to sail, what do you think would have caused it?'

'Propane tanks maybe but most racing yachts wouldn't carry them. It's strange though, four of them blowing up at the same time. Hopefully the crews were all ok. If they were lucky, the explosion might have blown the arse off the boat and may not have killed anyone.'

'I wonder was it an insurance job?' asked Ruth between forkfuls.

'Must be. Sure who else would be bothered blowing up a few sailors?'

Chapter Twelve

Tommy checked his watch. There was only twenty minutes to go before his session on the all-weather pitch was due to start but the under-16 boys practice didn't look like it was going to be finished any time soon. Their coach, Billy Murphy, was standing on the far side of the pitch shouting instructions. Tommy put his hand up to get his attention and then pointed to his watch. Billy turned his hands up and shrugged as though he didn't understand. 'Dopey gobshite,' muttered Tommy as he set off around the perimeter to inform the squatter that he was about to encroach on someone else's training slot.

'Are you finishing up there Billy?'

'Finishing? We're only after arriving,' he said without looking. Then he roared at a ginger haired lad with the ball. 'Take your shot Dan, good lad. He's a great player that young lad. Sorry Tommy, what were you saying?'

'I have the all-weather pitch from 9.15 p.m. on Fridays, block booked. Didn't you check in the clubhouse?'

There was a system for logging any training requirements within the club and any pitch time had to be entered on it. The Stillorgan club existed in the middle of what had become a densely populated area and space was at a premium. There were only two full pitches and one all-weather, which meant that finding a free slot was never easy. 'Yeah, I saw that alright. The mother's football is it?'

'Gaelic for Mothers. The new initiative from headquarters in Croke Park,' replied Tommy checking his watch again. 'As I said, we have the pitch booked.'

'Jesus Tommy, would you get your priorities straight. These lads have a big league match on Sunday. It's only a bit of shooting practise. Ray said we could use the pitch as well.'

'Oh did he now?'

'Yeah. So why don't you take your girlies down that end when they arrive and show them what a goal post is,' laughed the smug little man. 'See if any of them can hit it.'

Tommy caught him by the scruff of the neck and almost lifted him off the ground, much to the amusement of several boys who had overheard the exchange. 'There's only three hits you need to worry about. Me hitting you, you hitting the deck and the ambulance hitting 90 kilometres an hour on its way to A&E with you. Now, piss off. How's that for prioritising?'

'Ray's not going to be happy about this Tommy,' he said as he signalled the lads to wrap it up. Tommy was already walking away to set up his training drills. 'Fuck Ray,' he responded but the wind took the words away before they reached Billy's ears.

The aggro on the pitch didn't go unnoticed by Peter Gaughran as he stood waiting for his latest parolee. The man's tough approach wouldn't go to waste having to deal with Robert King, that was for sure. This was one community service stint that should be interesting to follow. He wasn't obliged to inform the club of the full details of the crime committed by the person serving community service. It wouldn't have mattered anyway because from what he'd heard, anyone who dealt with Robert knew bloody well that half the stuff he did was unaccounted for, the jammy little git. 'Tommy Boylan is it?' he called, seeing him setting up the orange cones in a star shape.

'Yeah, Howya. You must be the lad doing the community service,' replied Tommy beckoning the man onto the pitch.

'No, not me. I'm Peter Gaughran, the parole officer assigned to him. He was supposed to be here by now the little shit.'

'Sounds like a lovely lad,' said Tommy with a grin. 'The women will be along in a minute anyway so officially he's not late yet I suppose. What did he do to get community service anyway?'

'I'm afraid I can't give too much information out but suffice it to say it didn't involve any assault on a female.'

'How comforting.'

'He's at your beck and call every Friday night for the next three months. If you have any trouble or if he doesn't show up when you tell him to, you get straight on to me on this number,' he passed a card to Tommy. 'He'll be banged up so fast his feet won't hit the ground.'

The single headlamp of a motorbike cut across the unlit road leading to the back entrance of the grounds. The engine roared as it pulled up alongside the pitch. 'This must be him,' said the parole officer as he walked out to meet the mystery man. Tommy looked the young fella up and down as he got off his bike. He was kitted out in heavy black boots and faded blue jeans topped off by a well-worn black leather jacket. Not exactly GAA standard issue. He had a definite aura about him. Full of confidence. Cocky even. Judging by the look he gave the parole officer it didn't appear like he had much time for him which probably meant he was a right little gouger. Anyway thought Tommy, we've all made mistakes. First name introductions were made and the parole officer explained how Tommy would have to complete a report every fortnight on how Robbie was working out.

'Ok Robert, you know how this works. Any messing and you end up back in front of a judge and we both know that will mean a custodial sentence. Don't forget we have an appointment with a prospective employer at three o' clock tomorrow.' Tommy noticed the lad looked wrecked as he nodded his understanding. This bloke better not be a smack head, he thought as the parole officer disappeared out the exit.

'You look banjaxed,' said Tommy to the young fella at least twenty years his junior. 'Will you last the full hour do you think or will I have to get you a chair?'

'Sorry man. It was a bit of rush getting here like. I had a message to do on the north side. So what's the work that needs doing?' said Robbie, anxious to get the shite over with and fully expecting to be handed a paintbrush. 'Well son, you've now got the prestigious title of assistant coach. You're going to help me whip this lot into shape.' Tommy pointed towards the group of women who had just started to gather at the other side of the pitch. 'But first,' he said, handing Robbie a camera, 'Hang on to this. I want you to take a team photo in a while.' Robbie just stared at the sight before him, 'I hope you have a wide angled lens,' he said looking at Tommy with a glint in his eye. Tommy smirked and waved to the group that was forming. 'Meet the Gaelic for Mothers. They come in all shapes and sizes, mostly large,' he continued, winking at Robbie.

'So I see. It's a good while since I played Gaa and I never did any coaching. I thought I was here to paint some walls or whatever. I haven't a baldy what I'm supposed to do now.'

'You'll fit in grand with them so!'

There was something different about this fella Tommy, thought Robbie. He felt he was accepted as he was; that he wasn't being judged. That was odd given the circumstances under which they were meeting. There had been other occasions, particularly after his mam died and his da kicked him out, when he had done community service sentences and had been treated like something you'd wipe off your shoes. To be fair, he generally deserved it. Like the time he'd spent his nineteenth birthday cleaning graffiti off the gable end of the Bishop's residence in Drumcondra. The Bishop's aide had even asked him when he'd last washed. Dirty bastard was probably a pervert. Robbie got him back when he ended up lifting the entire supply of altar wine. He flogged it later to the kids outside the disco in the rugby club in Donnybrook. He thought it was hilarious that the posh birds drank red wine while all the girls he'd grown up with were happy with Scrumpy Jack cider. The best part was that the girls from the big houses with their fancy tastes and rich daddies were the very ones who wore their knickers like a bracelet around their wrists when they went out clubbing. As a teenager, if you were looking for a bit of skirt you went to Donnybrook where it would be offered on a plate. The bouncers looked the other way as the horny couples got down to it on the stands that overlooked the rugby pitches. There was more rubber left lying around those stands than you would find on the Goodyear factory floor. If you tried to feel a bit of tit in The Salmon Leap Estate you were likely to get stabbed in the nuts with the heel of a stiletto.

'Tell you what,' said Tommy, jolting Robbie back to the present, 'you lay these five bigger cones out for me in a large circle and I'll get them started with their warm up.' Tommy started jogging up to the women. 'I'll be back to you in a minute,' he called back over his shoulder. With his helmet in one hand he gathered up the cones. As he looked out on the illuminated car park he noticed a brand new Range Rover pulling up. A good looking older woman stepped out and waddled over towards the gate. 'I thought the Celtic tiger was extinct,' he muttered. 'Ah,' Tommy said as he jogged up having just caught the gist of his comment, 'but there was a time not so long ago where one of those yokes wouldn't get a second look. Now they stick out like sore thumbs.'

'There were never any toffs playing Gaa where I grew up.'
'Don't judge a book by its cover. Now come on, I'll introduce you to the team,' Tommy nodded towards the women as they struggled to complete their second lap of the pitch, 'before any of them pass out.' Robbie laughed and went over to the side of the pitch to put his helmet down. He shoved his wallet and phone beneath to keep them dry. 'Eh,' Tommy paused 'look, I don't know what you did to get sent here but I know better than anyone what it is to make

mistakes and how hard it is to get a second chance.'
'Yeah?'
'Oh yes. But we're here for Gaelic not history so let's agree not to piss each other off and we'll be grand.' Robbie nodded agreement and followed this intriguing man in a waterproof navy tracksuit across the pitch.

'Ladies,' Tommy called 'this is Robert ...'
'Robbie,' corrected the young fella, looking at the panting line of purple faces. 'Ladies,' continued Tommy with a smile, 'this isn't Robert. It's Robbie.' The subject of the introductions glanced at the coach with a look of amusement while the women all said hello. 'He's going to be helping out at our training sessions for the next while so if at all possible ...' His sentence was cut short by the sound of laboured breathing. Alison had just completed the second warm up lap and stood before them coughing so much Robbie fully expected to see her phlegm filled lung on the pitch at any moment.
'The bloody fags are going to kill me,' she wheezed before looking to Tommy. 'Sorry for interrupting.'
'So, as I was saying. If at all possible can you make sure that none of you pass out or die on me tonight? It wouldn't give a good impression to Robbie here and we don't want to make him do mouth to mouth resuscitation on his first night. And while we're at it, huddle up there while Robbie takes a group photo of us. ' The group laughed as they took their places. An awkward looking Robbie stood in front of them slightly nauseous with thoughts of the kiss of life.
'Don't look so nervous,' said Tracey, posing with her hand on an ample hip, 'we've already eaten.'
'So I see,' muttered Robbie as he took a couple of

shots.

A few minutes later Tommy clapped his hands and upturned the net bag containing the footballs.'Right, grab one each and we'll practise the solo kick.' He turned to the younger man. 'So you played a bit as a nipper did you?'

'Just till I finished with school, I'm not with a club or nothing.'

'So you can solo the ball?'

'Jaysus, sure everyone can do that.'

The last word of his sentence had barely left his mouth when a football hit him in the back of the head while another got him lower down. 'Me nuts!'

'Sorry!' called Naomi as she ran over to retrieve one of the footballs.

'You were saying?' asked Tommy, as the team continued to attempt the technique.

'So none of them can play?' asked Robbie once he'd recovered.

'Think of it as a challenge,' replied Tommy. 'So where are you from anyway?'

'The Salmon Leap Estate, near the canal. So you played a bit of Gaa yourself did ya?' Alison, who was passing behind them, overheard his question and butted in before Tommy had a chance to answer. 'A bit? He's only the best player ever to come out of Dublin,' she called back as she continued practising.

'How the fuck did you end up with this gig so?' asked Robbie pointing to the chaos of misdirected footballs all around them. 'That's for another day,' he said. He blew the whistle and called the team together.

'I want two or three of you behind each of these cones,' he said indicating the circle Robbie had laid out earlier. The women walked in a huddle towards the area he indicated. Robbie started laughing. 'What's so funny?' asked Naomi.

'It's like looking at one of those programmes on National Geographic. You know where the wildebeests are all milling around the side of the river, all terrified to be the first one to jump in.'

'Are you calling me fat you prick?' she challenged.

'Not you, no.' He answered honestly. Alison, observing the situation, called out in a sing song voice, 'You know what they say? Fat is happy.'

'You must be ecstatic so,' he shouted back.

'Ah Jesus,' Naomi couldn't believe her ears.

'I am actually,' said Alison in response to his comment. 'I've been around a long time son. You'd have to try much harder than that to insult me.'

'I'm not trying to insult you, I swear. I just speak my mind is all.'

Tommy approached. 'Are we having a problem,' he asked, looking between Alison, Naomi and Robbie. 'No,' replied two of them while Naomi just threw her eyes towards heaven and lined up behind a cone. 'Ok, let's move on. You're going to hand pass the ball to the left, not to the person immediately beside you, but to the next person. Then run across and join the line you just passed to. As you do it I want you to call out your name, that's a great way to get to know each other. We'll start off with one ball in and see how we get on. Robbie, will you be on standby to get the ball if it goes outside the circle?'

'Grand yeah,' he said as he put the camera down on the side of the pitch and stuck his hands in the pockets of his jeans to escape the cold. The whistle was blown and the drill commenced. 'Naomi.' 'Ruth.' 'Alison.' 'Mary.' They called their names as they passed the ball to each other, each adding, 'Jesus, sorry,' every time they missed target or dropped the football. After a minute or two Tommy picked up another ball.

'Second ball coming in now.' He handed it to Tracey who mistakenly passed it to the person directly opposite who then passed it on and followed its path. 'Sorry!' Tracey called as she noticed her error and ran from one line to the other, crashing into Alison. 'Jesus!' she said as she bounced off her and landed flat on her arse. 'FWEEEET.' Tommy blew his whistle and helped Tracey to her feet.

'Ladies, two things. One, you don't have to keep saying sorry and two, Jesus doesn't play on the team ... more's the pity. Now let's go again.' The drill continued with balls flying through the area like midges on a summer's night, except it was the middle of winter and freezing.

'God it's shocking cold, I'm perished,' said Tracey to the others in the group who readily agreed. She was a fifty year old lady with knees that were indistinguishable from the broadest part of her thighs. Robbie ran back to them with yet another football that had been sent flying down the pitch in error.

'Yis should try running to catch the ball when it's passed a little wide. That would warm you up.'

'Are you joking? At my age I have to break myself in gently,' Tracey joked with the others. 'I don't want to end up with that sudden cardiac death syndrome.'

'You'd have to move to get that luv,' replied Robbie before tearing off after another ball. Tommy checked his watch and blew the whistle.

'Grab a quick drink and then put on the coloured bibs. There's two different colours so just split it evenly.

The best way to learn is by playing a game.' The women huddled near the entrance and gulped down water.

'Jaysus, they're brutal,' said Robbie as he helped clear up the cones. 'Half of them can't even walk fast, let alone run. You'd have your work cut out for you if they weren't doing it for the crack.'

'How do you mean?' asked Tommy. 'You know, if yis had to play a proper match like.'

'That's exactly what we'll be doing. Give it a few weeks and we should be organised.'

'Ah yeah, very funny,' laughed Robbie.

'There's a blitz on in Rathburn,' said Tommy as he gathered up all the balls except one and put them into the large net bag. 'It's not set in stone but it's something to aim for. There are teams from Silvermine, Kilbradden, Rosehill, Moorville and a few other places interested apparently.'

'Fuck me, you're serious!'

'I certainly am.'

'Rathburn? Are we talking about that place on the north side near Lott's Park? They eat their young out there. Are you bleedin mad?'

'Didn't I tell you not to judge a book by its cover? People in Rathburn are the salt of the earth so they are. They love their Gaelic. Aren't they only down the road from Croke Park? They're mammies for the love of Jaysus. How bad can they be?'

'Ask that lad who had his dick hacked off.'

'Who?'

'It was on the news, the poor bastard was having a slash against someone's back gate and this mad bitch came out and took a hatchet to his mickey. By all accounts she was a mammy, had a baby's bottle in the other hand or so they said.'

'Will you stop or you'll have that lot running a mile. I'm not telling them about the blitz till it's confirmed anyway.'

'I'll tell you one thing,' said Robbie, nodding towards Ruth. 'She wouldn't want to bring that shiny new Range Rover of hers over there.'

'Will you stop? There's plenty of robbing bastards this side of the Liffey too by the way. Anyhow, if it does go ahead I'll have to tap the club here for some money to hire a team bus and buy a few jerseys. We'd have to make a good impression.'

'A team bus going out might do but it's an ambulance you'll need coming back.'

'It's Gaelic they'll be playing and as I keep saying to this lot, it's a non-contact sport.'

'It is in me hole,' laughed Robbie.

'Yeah,' winked Tommy as he blew the whistle to resume training, 'but don't tell them that.'

The women sauntered over chatting among themselves. 'Tommy wasn't that terrible about all the yachts that blew up tonight?' said one of them. 'I didn't catch the news yet this evening, what happened?' Robbie pretended not to be paying attention and instead practised a few solos with the ball. 'A load of yachts that were taking part in some race from Howth exploded.'

'Was anyone killed?' asked one of the team. 'Don't know. I did hear that one of the crew, a woman, lost a leg. It's awfully sad. Apparently she was due to get married in a couple of weeks.'

'Did they say what caused it?' asked Tommy. 'No, but it's bound to be just a tragic accident, dodgy electrics or something. It couldn't be deliberate. Sure what kind of person would be bothered blowing up a load of sailors?' Robbie knew the type of person who would do that only too well and for the first time in his life, for reasons he could not understand, he felt a little guilty.

In order to break the women in gently Tommy decided to only play half the pitch. 'In this exercise, when you get the ball you have to hand pass to each other at least three times before you can aim for a goal or a point. If you get possession from the other team you have to play it out to the half way line and back in again. Understand?'

'Yes,' they responded. 'FWEEEET.' He threw the football up into the air. It landed back on the ground with a thud and fourteen pairs of eyes looked at it. 'Eh, is there something we are forgetting to do here ladies?' asked a clearly amused Tommy. The majority of the women that were nearest shrugged their shoulders, one or two started to question each other and then Alison piped up, 'Gosh sorry, I thought you handed it to us to start.' Robbie burst his sides laughing, 'This is the best crack I've had in years.'

'Let's try again. I throw it up,' said Tommy, 'and two opposing team members try to get it first. If you can't grab it then try to hit it over to one of your team mates. Is that clear?'

'Crystal,' said a few of them without any conviction.

'FWEEET.' The ball was thrown high in the air and as gravity brought it back down towards their upturned nervous faces it was suddenly and violently punched out to the wing. The smallest one on the team, Mary, all four feet eleven inches of her had managed to launch herself through the air to make contact with the ball. 'Jaysus!' Tommy's eyes were wide open in amazement. 'Have you springs on those boots there Mary?' The ball hit Ruth square in the knockers which almost sent her flying but she managed to run a few steps and solo the ball before hand passing it to Tracey. The game continued. 'Someone's been practising,' Tommy roared. Tracey passed the ball to a woman who screamed with fright and passed it immediately to Brid who was already red in the face, which Tommy knew, was more from shyness than fatigue. 'I'm free,' roared Naomi from the left wing. Brid fumbled a pass but it hit its target and Naomi caught the ball and lined herself up with the goal. Just as she dropped the ball towards her foot to kick, it was whacked out by one of the other team who started to play the ball back to the half way line. Tommy saw more errors and fouls than he could count but he decided to ignore them because they were having a good time. The game continued for another fifteen minutes and the women looked banjaxed.

The ball was kicked out onto the right wing where Alison, wearing a very snug yellow bib, was loitering with Norma, a girl from the blue bib team. Both women, not being strangers to the local chipper, were crimson red in the face and breathing heavily. 'I'll give you fifty quid if you don't run after it,' said Alison. 'No bribery on the pitch ladies,' shouted Tommy smiling broadly as the two women trundled after the ball. Alison made it marginally ahead of Norma but instead of bending down to pick up the ball she ran straight past it and out towards the gate that led to the car park.

'You alright Alison?' called Tommy after her, hoping

she hadn't taken offense at his comment.

'Need to pee ...' Her voice trailed off as she ran faster than she had all night towards the changing room toilets.

Before he had a chance to comment, two others followed after her. 'Sorry, can't hold it a second longer,' they whimpered as they shot past him. Tommy could do nothing but shake his head. 'We might as well finish up ladies. It's time to stretch and warm down anyway.' The team gathered around and began to follow Tommy's moves as he led them through a serious of stretches just as Alison and the others returned.

'Bloody typical,' she said in all seriousness to the other girls, unperturbed by male ears. 'I almost managed to control the farts tonight and the flipping pelvic floor just about collapses.' Robbie caught Tommy's eye which held a look that told him to shut his mouth. He bit his lower lip as the conversation continued.

'I know it's desperate, I've been leaking the whole fecking night,' said Tracey. 'I wouldn't mind but I do those exercises squeezing down there every night religiously while I'm watching my soaps.' Robbie felt blood on his tongue and his face had started to turn quite red.

'Should you wear one of those pads do you think?' asked Alison, farting mid-sentence as she bent over to stretch out her hamstrings.

'Ah God no, sure those things would be shocking uncomfortable for running around. Anyway, it's only a dribble, it'll be grand.'

Unable to hold it any longer, Robbie doubled over and fell to his knees clutching at his stomach.

'You alright there?' asked Tommy, a knowing look in his eye. 'Grand yeah,' he managed to squeak, 'bit of a stitch.' The women started to make their way off the pitch saying goodnight to everyone as they went. Robbie checked around the pitch for any leftover cones or footballs so didn't hear his phone ring beneath the helmet. Tommy felt a hand on the small of his back as he bent to count the footballs in the bag. 'Naomi,' he said, looking behind him. 'You looked good out there.'

'Not as good as I feel,' she grinned, raising one eyebrow. Tommy blushed and wished for one of those American sinkholes to swallow him before he made a bigger twat of himself. She walked away leaving the slightest spark of tension behind. Tommy's eyes stayed on her for a few moments longer than necessary before another voice interrupted him.

'That was so much fun, thanks.' Ruth smiled shyly and pulled self-consciously at her large sweatshirt.

'I see you have been taking my advice on practising your solos at home,' he said, recovering quickly and smiling with encouragement. 'I have yes, although it has caused a few broken dishes and a peculiar addition to the evening meal,' she replied. 'Worse things happen at sea,' said Tommy before suddenly remembering the events from earlier. 'Oh God, that was in bad taste, sorry.'

'What was?' asked Robbie as he joined them, acutely aware that he hadn't had as much of a laugh in years as he had in the last hour or so.

'Me cracking a joke about worse things happening at sea considering those poor sailors earlier today.' Tommy looked contrite.

'Shit happens.' Robbie was trying to brazen it out, a thing he had never had to do before. Something had changed in him tonight and he was fucked if he knew what or why.

'Is that your phone that's been ringing?' asked Tommy as it started off again.

'I didn't hear it,' he said walking over to check it. 'Probably the bird checking up on me.'

He lifted the helmet up and retrieved the phone just as the floodlights switched off. He tapped the screen and saw three missed calls and a single text all from the same number. The Hawk didn't like to be ignored. Robbie opened the text message and grimaced as he read it. *Be at the warehouse at 10.30 and don't fucking ignore my calls again.*

'Shit.'

'Everything alright?' asked Tommy.

'Yeah, yeah, look I have to lash.'

'Listen you did great tonight, see you next week then ok?'

'Grand yeah, see ya.' Robbie sprinted out the gate not noticing his wallet on the ground where his helmet had been. He didn't know if he'd be around to see tomorrow let alone next week. Hawk was angry and that only ever meant one thing.

Chapter Thirteen

'You're bleedin joking me!' Robbie roared inside the helmet as the Fireblade began to stall less than a mile away from the Gaelic grounds. No shagging petrol. He had been running on the reserve tank earlier. This was like another nail in his coffin because Hawk was already pissed off. This would send him into orbit. He had to get juice and fast. He revved the throttle causing a wheelie as he went into a petrol station. Still sitting on the bike he stuck the nozzle into the tank and took out his phone to text Hawk as the petrol flowed.

'Excuse me. You can't use a mobile phone in the forecourt when you're filling your tank.' Robbie turned his helmeted head, visor half up, towards the voice. A man of Indian origin stood between him and the exit, pointing to a sign which gave the same information in picture form.

'Fuck off.' Although his voice was muffled by the helmet, the gentleman understood.

'Sir, there is no need for such vulgarity. I must insist you adhere to the rules of the premises.'

Robbie reached into his pocket to get his wallet so he could pay and get his arse over to the warehouse. Nothing. He patted both sides of his jacket, no tell-tale lump. He felt his jeans, nothing there either. Shit, he thought, I must have left it on the pitch.

'Sir, you will also have to remove your helmet to pay for your petrol inside.'

The man with the sing song voice and the death wish was the only thing standing in the way of his getting to the Hawk. He only had one option. He removed the nozzle, replaced it in the pump and calmly closed the petrol cap on the tank before turning the key in the ignition. The little man in the red tank top and white shirt started to jump up and down and wave his arms.

'You cannot steal. It is not allowed. I will get the police.'

He thought about head-butting the annoying little prick but he didn't have time. He aimed the bike directly at him and opened the throttle. The bike shot up in another wheelie and headed straight for the attendant's head. He dived out of the way and smacked head first into one of the pillars that held up the roof, splitting his lip open in the process.

The bike roared out of the station and on to the dual carriageway. It didn't matter if they got the reg on CCTV because the bloke who actually owned the bike could prove it wasn't him driving. It was already after 10.30 and the warehouse was at least twenty minutes' drive away. In all the years he had been with Hawk he'd only been late once before and that was because he'd been doing an exam in school. At the time, he was too naive to realise that when Hawk said he wanted to see you, it meant immediately. Robbie hadn't got the message till after the exam because his phone had been taken by the supervisor. When he had tried to explain that to a very irate Hawk he was rewarded with a baseball bat to the hand and three broken fingers. That was when he decided that leaving school might be the safest option. Racing across the city through every junction, he finally arrived at the laneway leading up to the warehouse. He cut the engine and had a quick look at his watch which showed him he was in deep shit. 10.55 p.m. The grill on the metal door opened just as he was about to bang on it. Butch's eyes were alive with the expectation of carnage, like a hyena shadowing a lion on an imminent kill. Robbie was well aware that the stooges that protected his boss were jealous of the close relationship he seemed to enjoy with him. At that particular moment Robbie would have gladly traded places. The door opened and he entered. The sound of Johnny Cash wormed its way into his ears from deep within the warehouse. The only light came from the cord hung metal light fixture at the back which swayed gently throwing a dull hue of illumination across a tarpaulin covered mound. Robbie strained to see anything of significance that might reveal what it was. The Hawk maybe? No way. If anything happened to him his cronies would be long gone. His violent streak was the only thing that kept them all together.

A knuckle duster festooned fist met the side of his face with such force he thought he felt his eyeball come out. The blood, no longer confined by tissue, spread across his face filling his eye socket which had already started to swell. He braced himself for what would surely follow; to fight back would mean death. A hand caught him by the throat. The grip pushed up beneath his lower jaw like eagle's talons preparing to puncture the blood vessels of its prey. This was no eagle. This was the Hawk. He looked at the scarlet patterns on Robbie's face with indifference. It was hard to keep the one good eye open now because the blood had started to flow into it. It trickled down over the hand that was still squeezing on his throat. The song playing was something about twenty minutes left to live and Robbie hoped to fuck that Hawk wasn't going to take the song too literally. 'Who the fuck do you think you are?'

Guessing that it was meant as a rhetorical question, Robbie kept his gob shut.

'Am I working for you now, is that it? Still he didn't move. 'I asked you a fucking question you prick.' His grip tightened as their faces almost touched. His eyes were wild now. The smell of blood was in his nostrils. 'No,' Robbie just about managed to croak.

'Where the fuck were you?'

'Community service.'

The blow to the gut winded him. He would have bent double except his head was still in the hand of the Hawk. 'Why didn't you answer the phone? The truth this time or I might lose my temper.' The irony of his words would have amused Robbie if it were someone else getting seven different shades of crap beaten out of him.

'It was ... under ... my helmet ... on the ... pitch.' Every other word was interrupted by a gagging sound.

'What fucking pitch?'

'The Gaelic Pitch.' Finally the grip around his throat was released but only so the hand could be used to punch him again, this time in the kidneys. Hawk moved to the front again.

'So which is it that was more important than answering my call? Community service or football with the lads?' 'The Gaelic is the community service,' Robbie replied, slightly bent over and wishing he could put ice on his face.

'Bollix.'

'I'm serious. I have to help out in a club in Stillorgan,

training a bunch of mammies,' said Robbie, pain pulsating through his body. 'But I did the job in Howth like you asked.'

'See that's what I want to talk to you about,' the Hawk said, walking back and forth between Robbie and the black tarpaulin menacingly.

'But they went off Hawk, I saw it myself. It was all over the news and all. Some bird lost a leg they said.' The words were scarcely out of his mouth before the shark eyes were boring into his one open eye.

'Do I look like I give a flying fuck about some young one's leg? She's a bleedin sailor. Stick a wooden peg under her and a parrot on her shoulder for all I fucking care.'

'Sorry.'

'It appears someone might have tried to get one over on me today.' He spoke from the corner of his mouth as he lit a cigarette with a flip-top silver lighter.

'I swear man. I don't know anything about that.'

It was worse than he thought. Someone had obviously tried to double cross Hawk and now he was looking for a bloke to blame. The wall of muscle walked back over to the tarpaulin and whipped it off in one movement. The barely recognisable face of Macker, one of Hawk's henchmen, was looking back at Robbie. His eyes were wide with terror. He was sitting in a chair with his mouth covered with thick tape. His arms were tied behind his back and several yards of thick robe secured him to the seat. Both his legs were strapped down. The chair was on top of a large flat trolley normally used for transporting heavy items around the warehouse.

'I know you didn't Robbie, because this prick here told me everything. Didn't you Macker?' Hawk grabbed the man's hair roughly and shoved his head forward and back in a nodding fashion. 'Seems Macker here thought he might make himself a few quid by tipping Carcass off to my plans for his cocaine shipment. He was planning to fuck off to Ibiza to do a bit of snorkelling. I never knew Macker was into that shite, did you?' Robbie just shook his head. 'You think you know someone wha? I called round to his gaff to have a little chat about my suspicions and there he was with the missus, packing his bags. She's a right feisty one is his missus. At least she was.' Macker's head slumped forward. Robbie could well imagine what had happened to her. 'What happened the cocaine?' he asked, aware now that the beating he got was purely because he missed the phone call.

'Oh we got it alright. Carcass didn't get a chance to do anything about Macker's tip off. One of the screws in the Joy let me know what was going on. The same fella told me that Carcass had a bad fall in the shower. Seems he fell and slit his throat on a knife. Dangerous fucking places them prisons.'

'Yeah,' laughed Robbie nervously.

'Anyway,' said Hawk 'I thought Macker here should really get to know Irish fish before thinking about any of them foreign fuckers.' He reached down to a small bag on the floor and removed a scuba diving mask and placed it on his victim's face. He pulled the rubber over the back of his battered head and let it snap sharply into place. 'Wouldn't want the salt getting into the eyes would we Macker, eh? Robbie, give us a hand here will ya.' He threw a large coil of rope to the floor in front of him.

Hawk pulled a large anchor from behind the

chair and lifted it effortlessly up onto the seated man's lap. 'Secure it to him good and tight now. I want to turn up the stereo.' Hawk sauntered over to the shelving unit at the side and turned the dial up. He warbled along to his favourite song, 'I hear the train a comin ...' 'Can't bleedin beat old Johnny. The man in black,' Hawk called before shouting to Butch to bring the van. Robbie grinned in false agreement and wrapped the rope around the blubbering man on the seat trying not to look at his face. It didn't work. Macker managed to catch his eye as he tightened the anchor to his chest. The man knew he was going to die. That was a given. The inside of the mask had started to mist up with the sweat coming from his pores. There was no way out. The terror in his eyes seemed to reach out and pull at the seedlings of conscience that were starting to grow in Robbie's mind. He looked away quickly. What the fuck was he supposed to do anyway, untie him? Ah bollix, he thought as he made eye contact again. Stealing a look to check no one was watching he pulled the rope tight and instead of tying a knot he looped it back beneath Macker's arse. He'd still probably drown but Robbie's conscience would be a little clearer.

A white van sprayed to look like a Dun Laoire Rathdown county council vehicle was reversed down through the building. No-one emerged for a few minutes as the driver's door seemed to be jammed but when it eventually opened Butch climbed out. The three of them pushed the trolley that carried the marked man over to the open double doors. Butch operated a hydraulic lift to raise the trolley to the same level and then all three climbed up and pushed it inside the dark interior. Hawk jumped out and looked back at Robbie who was expecting to be sent to dispatch Macker to his scuba lesson. 'Piss me off again, this will be you,' he said pointing at the trussed up man. 'Butch, get rid. Robbie, follow me. I have a job for you.'

Chapter Fourteen

'That's not funny Tommy,' said Ray clambering out of the cupboard while sweeping brushes and cleaning products fell all around him. 'You know I suffer from claustrophobia.'

'I find that hard to believe considering how much time you spend stuck up your own arsehole.'

'What's that supposed to mean?'

'Isn't it obvious? You're egotistical and self-obsessed.'

'No I'm not.'

'Yes you are. You always have to be right. You never accept that someone else might be more informed on a topic than you.'

'That's rubbish. I had a conversation just last week where I was proved wrong.'

'You did?' said Tommy, incredulous.

'Yeah, well I found out later I had been right as it happens but you take my point.'

Tommy shook his head in despair. It had been this way ever since he had agreed to train the Gaelic for Mothers team or 'Gaa for Ma's' as he now termed it. He was prepared to put up with their lack of fitness, farting and running to the jacks during training. He was even OK with the fact that he had learnt more than a gynaecologist about floppy pelvic floors. The rush of projectile vomit that careered up his oesophagus whenever the women discussed gory childbirth stories was beginning to subside. Tommy was trying to create something lasting here, a desire to be strong on the pitch as a team. Then this prick thought it would be OK to tell the under-16's coach

Billy Murphy that he could train on the astro turf during the 'Gaa for Ma's' slot. If he hadn't shoved Ray into the cupboard he might have been sorely tempted to give him a punch. The smug git would have just loved that because then he would be able to tell all and sundry that he'd been right about Tommy—that a leopard doesn't change his spots.

'You'd want to watch yourself pal. Do you not think you're biting the hand that feeds you with this kind of attitude?' Ray wiped down the front of his club jersey.

'Ask my arse.'

Tommy had his back to him now looking out over the all-weather pitch which was now in darkness. He made a mental note to go back down and lock the gate. He had spotted Ray's car just as young Robbie took off like a bat out of hell on his motorbike. If he didn't say anything about the earlier pitch invasion now it would just be taken as submission by Ray. Then before he knew it, they'd have the whole shagging club trying to muscle in on his time slot.

'I don't know what your bloody problem is anyway. It's only a bunch of mammies Tommy, not the Brogan brothers. They don't give out the Sam Maguire to a crowd of pot wallopers looking to shed a few kilos. When they start representing the county then they can call the shots on training times.'

For the second time that night Tommy had to count to ten in his head to avoid boxing the guy. 'I'm entering them in a blitz,' he said suddenly, turning around.

'Are you having a laugh?' Ray couldn't believe his ears. He pulled a chair out from behind his desk, sat down and folded his arms.

'I'm deadly serious.'

'I've seen them training. That lot can barely run one lap around the pitch. What makes you think they can keep going for a whole match?'

'Well, as you pointed out they are not expected to play at county level so the matches are only ten minutes a side. There will only be ten players so we'll have a few subs. What I need from you is a kit for them to wear and the use of a team bus.'

Ray clicked his fingers. 'Hey presto! There you are. One fully kitted out team and a bus ... In your dreams. The same dream has the committee of this club agreeing to spend precious funds on that lot.'

'But you said the powers that be at Croke Park were willing to give extra funding to promote Gaelic for Mothers.' Tommy was suspicious now. Ray looked smug. 'I prefer to interpret it as them giving money to clubs that got involved in the initiative. I didn't see any instruction that specifically said the money was solely for the mammies. Besides,' he continued, 'didn't I provide you with footballs? The rest of the money has been allocated to the senior squad so there is nothing left to talk about really.' Tommy stared at the floor, not trusting himself to speak. He could feel the nerve endings firing around his body but he was in control. He was going to have to work this frustration out of his system if he was to have any chance of moving forward. Standing up, he wordlessly moved to the door before turning back to Ray at the last second. 'You're a real prick, you know that don't you?' He didn't wait for a reply.

The car park lights were off and the enclosed all-weather pitch they had been using earlier was in darkness. As all the balls and cones were cleared away he knew it would be safe to use as a running track. Ten or twelve quick laps would be just what he needed to sort his head out. Tommy leaned his hands against the sturdy metal railings that surrounded the pitch. He placed one leg back and bent the other leg slightly at the knee. After holding the stretch for twenty seconds and repeating it on the other leg he was ready to run. He set off slowly at first going in an anti-clockwise direction around the enclosure in the dark. Ray was making a right fool out of him and probably not for the first time either. Tommy had been suspicious over the years that Ray had known a bit more than he let on about his being shunned by the club but he'd never been able to prove it. When he returned from England he had decided to let sleeping dogs lie. No doubt the lads had a great laugh taking the piss out of him for training the mammies. He couldn't blame them. The women were great to give it a go and he had to hand it to them, they turned up full of enthusiasm. That, however, didn't take away from one simple fact. They were brutal. He could forgive the lack of technical expertise because hardly any of them had ever played the game. The thing that really went against them was their fitness or lack of it. He would have to address that or they really would need to have an ambulance as their team bus. The blitz was only a couple of weeks away and while he fully expected them to be pulverised by the other teams, he wanted them to do the best they could.

Anger started to well up in him again and he picked up the pace a little. Ray was so fucking stubborn. Would it have killed him to agree to get jerseys printed up with the club crest and sponsor on it? Well fuck him, thought Tommy, he'd find a way around it. 'I'll get my own bloody sponsor,' he said aloud. He knew people after all. Running at full sprint now he berated himself for not pushing right out to the edge of the pitch on his first lap. 'No cutting corners,' he scolded himself. It felt good to run at this pace in the dark, strangely liberating actually. Tucking in his head he dug deep for extra energy. The next second saw him flying through the air, fully aware that he was going to land right on his snot and being powerless to stop it. He tumbled forward and landed on his back, totally winded. He'd tripped on something. He got onto his hands and knees and started inching his way back to where he had tripped. The little finger on his right hand was the first to touch the square leather object. Peering through the rain, he saw that it was a small black wallet. The rain was getting heavy so he slipped the wallet into his pocket and decided to call it a night. Locking up the enclosure he hurried to his car and jumped inside cursing the inclement weather. The rain beat against the windscreen which was already starting to steam up. For a split second he hoped the wallet might be Naomi's. He checked himself. What on earth was he thinking? What would he have done if it was? Opening it quickly he flicked through the contents – a durex, cash, a few cards and a license. The name on it was Robert King. The address was Harold's Cross. A quick look at the clock on the dashboard read 11.15 p.m. which was way too late to call to the young fella's house. It could wait till tomorrow. Tommy didn't work weekends because the schools were closed and he thought there would be a good chance Robbie would be home on a Saturday morning. If he had a phone number for him he could've at least put him out of his misery. There was nothing worse than losing a wallet and having to spend ages retracing your steps.

Robbie was an enigma as far as Tommy was concerned. He was obviously a bit of a rogue otherwise he wouldn't be doing community service in the first place. The lad seemed to have a good sense of humour and he was bright. Tommy drove through the deserted streets and wondered if Robbie had finished school. The chances were he hadn't, given that he was in trouble with the law and seemed to be familiar with the system. Most of the women on the team seemed happy enough to accept him even if he did push the accelerator on his voice box before he put his brain into gear. It genuinely didn't appear as though he was deliberately trying to be insulting. The lad just said whatever came into his head, even if it was politically incorrect. Truth be told, Tommy loved that. There was far too much pussy footing around topics nowadays. It was much better to call a spade a spade.

Glancing out the window towards the car park, Ray O'Toole watched as Tommy drove away in the pelting rain. He held the glass of brandy to his lips and gulped it down. The prick had rattled him tonight. While locking up his office he'd noticed the pitch allocation chart outside on the wall. Tommy had put a note on it in very large block capitals—EVERY FRIDAY 9.15 G4M TRAINING – NO PITCH SHARING. Typical, thought Ray, the man was as subtle as a scorpion in your jockstrap. He would show that prick once and for all. The rumour that had been circulating recently had finally been confirmed that evening, just before Boylan came in throwing his weight around. The GAA had been approached by Gaelic Park in New York. They wanted to host an international Gaelic Football tournament. The Irish were flung all over the world nowadays and as a result, there were GAA clubs in the most bizarre locations. Representatives from Gaelic Park were visiting GAA boards all over the place to select the teams they wanted to take part in the tournament. If the Iona Gaels' senior men's team was, as he expected, picked to represent Leinster at the tournament, it could mean only one thing, sponsorship. Recession or not there were plenty of companies out there that would give their eye teeth to have their logo emblazoned across the team's jerseys, especially if the rumours of a TV documentary were true.

That had been an unexpected development. The powers that be in Croke Park had let it slip that a production company was interested in making a programme about how the diaspora were frequenting Gaelic clubs world-wide to keep in touch with their roots. The tournament in New York would serve as the ultimate finale to such a programme. So the bottom line was, if the club got that kind of sponsorship, he could take great pleasure in telling Tommy Boylan to shove his unfit, flabby arsed shower of mammies up his hole. The only bloody reason he had agreed to the whole ludicrous suggestion in the first place was to get his hands on the additional money from the GAA headquarters. There wasn't a snowball's chance in hell of him actually committing to such a ridiculous proposition in the long term. Whatever about giving up valuable pitches to a crowd of wasters, it was a whole other ball game having to put up with Tommy Boylan for any longer than he had to. Ray never had any time for him. Back in the day when they played together he had been such a pain. The way he used to go around the place treating his body like a sacred temple. Jesus, there were cows in India that were treated with less respect. The man was ridiculous. And, if it wasn't bad enough that he maintained such high standards for himself, it started to rub off on the other lads in the team and then the coach got stuck in. Before they knew it they were on strict diets and training twice a day, seven days a week. That was when Ray said fuck it. If he was totally honest he wasn't in the same league as some of the lads but that intensity just put him right off. It wasn't long before his arse started to mould its shape into the subs bench, a fact that he was slagged about relentlessly. That prick Boylan didn't care though, as long as he was cock of the walk. All the young fellas in the kids teams looked up to him, chased him around the place looking for his autograph and all that celebrity shite. Like the cat that got the cream he was, till it all went tits up that day in Croker.

At the beginning a lot of the team and the coaching panel sided with Boylan. Not Ray though. He saw it for what it was, an opportunity to push the king pin off his pedestal. He spent weeks talking to everyone individually, bringing them around to his way of thinking, that Boylan had disgraced the club and brought the entire game into disrepute. It took a while and was touch and go with a lot of them for quite some time, especially the lads who had grown up playing with Tommy, but eventually Ray started to convince everyone that Boylan shouldn't be part of the team set up in any fashion. When the case had come before the courts and Tommy had narrowly avoided a custodial sentence, there were some who began to question whether banishing him might be a bit too harsh, especially as the whole episode had been so out of character. Ray was particularly proud of how he got around that one. At the time he had been a mentor to the under-21's team which was partly the reason he didn't turn up to all his own team's training sessions. He bribed Lorcan Sheehy's son Garry and two other players who were mad keen to be part of the Senior squad. He promised them selection if they did a little something for him and kept it quiet that he had asked. In the middle of a friendly match against another local rival club, the lads created a situation which caused a penalty to be given against them. It was a complete replication of what had occurred in Boylan's last match. When the referee gave his decision, the lads started beating the heads off the other team's players. Ray himself was even shocked at the ferocity of the attack, but then he had promised them their places on the first team, and to a lad of that age that meant everything. When they were interviewed after the fracas they all admitted they wanted to show they could be like Tommy Boylan. It took less than twenty four hours for Ray's plan to work. Boylan was asked to stand down from the team and told in no uncertain terms that his help wasn't needed in any present or future coaching roles. He had pissed off to England within a week. Garry Sheehy and the other two lads were so thrilled to be on the senior squad, they would never admit it wasn't pure talent that put them there. Ray placed the empty brandy glass on the counter and left the clubhouse with a smirk on his face. He'd managed to handle Tommy Boylan then and he would do the same again. No bother.

Tommy pulled up the driveway of his house and got out of the car. Although he was still pissed off that he'd let the little prick get to him, he had finally managed to calm down after his spat with Ray. He stripped off his waterproofs in the hallway and placed Robbie's wallet on the narrow table beside his keys. The house was just as it had been when he left earlier, quiet. Was it ever any other way? Well yes he thought, it was actually, when his parents were alive and he was young. There was a different culture back then. People visited each other's houses without texting ahead to check if it was alright to call. There used to be great fun in the Boylan kitchen, everyone singing and telling jokes. That was a lost art. No-one knew how to tell jokes anymore; instead they just handed around their phones and told people to scroll down. Tommy filled the kettle. He missed all that crack and it wasn't that people had more money or anything back then, quite the opposite in fact. When he was growing up recession was so normal it didn't even make the news. People valued the simpler things in life like humour. Then the Celtic Tiger roared and society took itself on the trip of a lifetime up its own arsehole.

The house echoed with emptiness as he made his cup of tea. He wondered if Naomi was still awake and what she might be doing. He couldn't help it. Like Robbie, he thought there was probably a lot more to her than met the eye. She was fun, of that he was sure. What he wasn't so confident about was whether or not she was flirting with him. Then again, he'd been so long out of the game she would need to print *I'm interested* on a cricket bat and smack him straight in the face before he would cop on. Smiling he realised that the thing that made her so intriguing was that she would probably do just that. The few women he had dated in recent years were all into bloody mind games, pretending they weren't interested if they were, smiling and chatting to blokes they had no interest in just to make some other bloke jealous. It was a bloody minefield that Tommy hadn't got the mental armour to step through. It used to be hard enough for him to pluck up the courage to chat someone up, if his attempts could be called that, than to be faced with all that head wrecking stuff. Naomi was different. She seemed straight up and honest as well as vibrant and passionate, very much as he had been as a youngster. Football had been his driving force. He wondered what it was that got her out of bed in the mornings and whether there was anyone left in it when she did.

Chapter Fifteen

Kim was going to kill him when he got home, whatever bleedin time that would be. He'd been told there was a job that needed doing but was then left sitting on his hoop while Hawk showered bits of Macker out of his hair.   Robbie heard the power shower stop and subconsciously sat up straighter in his seat. His eye felt like a ball of cement. He'd managed to see his reflection on the surface of the shiny steel kettle. There would have to be some good excuse for Kim. Suddenly it came to him! He could say he got kicked in the face with a ball at the training earlier and that Tommy had brought him to the hospital to get it checked out. Deadly, that was sorted then. It wasn't like she would meet Tommy and suss out Robbie had been bullshitting. He tried to grin at his master plan but only managed it on one side of his face.   Hawk emerged from a cloud of steam in jeans and a shirt. He spent so much time at the warehouse he had converted two offices into a bedroom and a luxury bathroom. The land and buildings were only zoned for industrial use but so far no one from the council had dared to tackle him on it. The dulcet tones of Johnnie Cash edged into Robbie's ears like creeping lava. He wondered whether Hawk would have it piped into his casket when he popped his clogs. Not that it was something that was likely to happen any time soon, worse luck he thought.

'You had something you wanted me to do?' he asked as Hawk boiled the kettle and tore the wrapping off a camomile teabag.

'Yeah, I'll tell you now in a sec. I just need a cup of

this to help me calm down.'

Robbie stared at the man's back while tentatively touching his battered eye socket and wished the loony fucker had drunk one earlier. Lighting up a smoke Hawk took it and his tea and plonked down in an armchair opposite. 'That'll be a nice one,' he laughed, pointing to the side of Robbie's face that was beginning to resemble the elephant man. 'Yeah,' laughed Robbie as though it was a longed-for gift from Santa Claus. 'The haul I liberated from Carcass needs shifting,' said Hawk abruptly.

This was something new. He had never directly used Robbie in the drugs side of his empire before now, preferring instead to utilise his talents in procurement. 'With the commotion you managed to cause at sea the lads were able to land the stuff safely enough. But then didn't the fuckers decide to bring the shaggin' sailors to the hospital in Dun Laoire. Apparently it was like an episode from Casualty out there with all the poxy ambulances.'

'Where's the gear? Back on the boat is it?'

'No, there's a small holding area for stuff that's already passed through customs. I have a bloke on the inside so we managed to get the code for the gates.'

'So am I to head out there when Butch gets back with the van?'

'No, the coke will be stuck there for a while. It's the safest place while all this forensics shite is going on. I don't want to attract attention. My bloke on the inside told me that stuff is left there for a minimum of four weeks before customs try to push for it to be collected.'

'Fair enough.'

'The load is in a container marked LBD-1701. The

coke is packed in boxes on a pallet numbered BD-TS11. Make a note of it because when I decide to shift it I want it moved fast ... and Robbie?'

'Yeah Boss?'

'This time, when I ring you'd better fucking answer. Get it?'

'Got it.'

'Good.'

Robbie managed to extricate himself from the warehouse quicker than normal because Hawk was expecting some female company and didn't want an audience. There was an understanding with a few pimps in the area. They were allowed to operate on his turf so long as they provided him with horizontal jogging partners from time to time. He called it a service level agreement but in truth, he was the only one who got serviced. It wasn't surprising that the bloke had to pay to get his end away. What normal bird would want a head banger like him porking them? Not that he wasn't good looking, Robbie conceded. Kim had thought so anyway, but looks wouldn't stand for much if he was sitting across from a girl at dinner talking about which inflicted the best fracture, baseball or cricket bat.

It was agony trying to pull the helmet on over his swollen eye and cheek. He knew he would gladly sleep with it on when he crept into bed beside Kim. 'Shit, my wallet,' he said remembering that he had most likely left it behind on the pitch. He swung his leg over the bike and kick-started it, leaving it idle for a few moments while he considered what to do. If he went all the way back to the club and it wasn't there he'd be pissed off because it meant someone either nicked it or he'd dropped it while driving the bike. He was too tired for a wild goose chase. Between Kim's niece robbing his phone and nearly blowing up half of Howth and the training which had him pegging up and down the pitch retrieving balls, he needed his kip ... and his Kim. Everything was alright when he had her beside him. He was looking forward to a nice lie-in because the next morning was Saturday. He didn't have to meet the parole twat about the poxy job till three. 'The fucking cheek, making me work on a weekend,' he mumbled inside the helmet. But then he remembered that Kim had mentioned something about her sister coming to collect the sprog and bringing her mother with her. Lunch had been discussed which inevitably meant he would have to do it. His own ma had been a great cook and passed on all her tips and tricks to him whereas Kim knew shag all about food. One time she even served up raw prawns in a sauce thinking they were sushi. Robbie had only eaten one before he realised the mistake. He'd still spent the whole night puking interrupted only by having to check if there was a hose stuck up his arse pumping in more vomit. She had been banned from their kitchen ever since although he did relent for tea and toast which even she couldn't get wrong. If the almost mother-in-law was coming with the sister who was trying to outdo Angelina Jolie with all the kids she was spitting out, then it suited him just fine to say he had to go see a bloke about a job. It was bound to be some shite stacking shelves in Tesco but if he refused it he'd be breaking parole. If that happened he'd be tossed into the Joy and wouldn't be able to shift the drugs for Hawk, and well, that just wasn't an option. So if he was told he had to scrape shit off a toilet bowl in McDonalds he would just have to get on with it.

Pulling up the borrowed Honda outside the apartment block he looked up to their flat to check if any lights were on. The place was in darkness. Lifting up the seat of the motorbike he took out a heavy chain and looped it through the wheel before securing it to a metal railing. It was dead handy having the bike. He made a mental note to visit its owner in the Joy when he next got a chance. The entrance door to the complex closed behind him with a dull thud. Bracing himself he took the helmet off as gently as he could but it still hurt like fuck. He took the stairs two at a time, desperate to get his head down. The flat was quiet as he opened the door, relief coursed through his knackered body. The last thing he needed was for the rug rat to wake up and start bawling. Taking off his boots he tip-toed towards the jacks to see if there was anything in the medicine cabinet he could use to lessen the swelling and bruising to his face before morning. The moonlight from the window wasn't really bright enough to see what he was doing as he fumbled his way through packets of Tampax and cans of Lynx.

The light switching on almost made him scream which would have totally ruined his street cred. 'Robbie?' mumbled a very sleepy sounding Kim.

'Go on back to bed luv, I'll be in there in a second,' he answered, careful not to turn towards her.

'Sure I'm awake now, how did it go at the Gaelic yoke? How come you're so late?'

'It was grand yeah, I've just got a bit of a headache,' he replied avoiding the second part of her question. He was really hoping to avoid the topic of his bashed eye till he'd managed to get some kip.

'Let me grab some Nurofen, I've a stash in the press. Here let me look.' She stepped past on the good side of his face and pulled the mirrored cabinet door fully open to search. 'Ah here we go,' she said pulling out the small packet before closing over the door and looking up.

'Jesus!' she shouted in fright, dropping the box to the floor. 'What the hell happened to your face?'

'It's nothing, relax.'

'Are you crazy? Half your face is swollen up like a balloon and you tell me to relax. Did you get into a fight Robbie?' Seeing his reflection in the mirror he saw for the first time the extent of Hawk's handiwork. His eye was totally closed over and the eyelid looked like a slug. A massive gash stretched from the side of his head to the centre of his forehead. Blood had congealed in thick red lumps mixed together with his eyebrow. The cheek bone was no longer distinguishable and the whole area was beginning to turn the darkest shade of black he'd ever seen. 'I asked you if you got in a fight. You'll end up in prison, is that what you want, is it?'

'You know it isn't. Look I didn't get in a fight, it was just an accident.'

'What sort of accident?'

'At the community service placement.'

Kim's face scrunched up in confusion. 'I thought it was a Gaelic football club you had to go to, not a boxing ring.'

'It was a football club. I have to help out a bloke. He's trying to train a clatter of mammies to play Gaelic.'

'Just how exactly does that involve you getting your face smashed in?' she asked while taking out some medical wipes from the cabinet. 'Sit down on the toilet lid. That has to be cleaned up,' she added, indicating the wound. 'Now go on, tell me what happened.'

'Well this bloke, Tommy his name is. He's coaching a gang of women who I'd say have an average age of a hundred and twenty. Hardly any of them have played before and one of them kicked me in the face.' Kim looked at him in disbelief. 'How the hell could some old granny lift her leg that high?'
'Ok, maybe I exaggerated their ages slightly. They're all in their forties or fifties I'd say, although one of them is a bit younger.'
'That still doesn't explain how you got kicked in the face Robbie.'
'As I said, none of them know the rules of the game and during the match at the end of training I reached down to pick up the ball like this.' He demonstrated by bending down to pick up an imaginary ball so that his hands were almost on the floor and his head was level with his knees. 'Yer one came along and tried to kick the ball while I had my hands on it and she missed and got my head. See you're not supposed to kick it if someone has their hands on it on the ground,' he added, standing up and pointing to his injury, 'for obvious reasons.'
'If it was a women's team why were you playing?'
'There was an uneven number is all. I just played to make up a team.'
'And nobody offered to clean it up or bring you to the hospital? I'd say that might need a stitch.'
'Tommy offered but I said no. I didn't want any fuss.

Anyway, it's far enough from my arse so I won't have to sit on it eh?' he winked with his good eye and sat back down on the toilet seat. She smiled at his cheekiness. 'What am I going to do with you?' she purred as she gently cleaned the wound.

'I'm sure I can think of something,' he answered, pulling her down onto his lap.

As Robbie drifted off to sleep some time later, Kim lay awake beside him. She knew he had to meet his parole officer the next day and she was worried about what he'd think when he saw the state of Robbie's face. And here he was, yet again in the middle of another stint of community service. The fresh start that she hoped and hoped for just never seemed to happen. She wished he would cut ties with the Hawk. A lot of the kids in the estate they'd grown up in had been part of his gang in one way or another over the years. Most of them were either smackheads or in prison now as a result. She and Robbie had been in the same class in school; she knew he was clever. She'd always had to work to get results whereas he seemed to do as little study as possible and still romped home in exams. It had been such a shame when his mother got sick. The cancer had riddled most of her body by the time they discovered it. Mrs King had been well liked on the estate. She'd always had time for everyone, always believed you should make the best of the cards you'd been dealt. That must have been the reason she stayed with Robbie's da, couldn't have been love. No-one could have affection for a brute like him. Kim still remembered the day of Robbie's Ma's funeral. No consoling hug for his son or younger daughter. Kim had cried that day when she saw Robbie become both mother and father to the younger girl. Sheila had only been ten years old but her brother was her hero. He had to leave school then to earn money to take care of her. His father made no secret of the fact that he wasn't going to do it. Only days after the funeral he kicked Robbie out of the house but the up side of that was the end of those beatings he'd endured for years. As soon as his sister was old enough Robbie encouraged her to apply for a US green card. She secured one on the second round and Robbie sent her off for a new life in New York. Even though they didn't get together for a few years after that, she knew that the day of the funeral was the day she fell in love with him. She turned her head and looked at him sleeping soundly beside her. Gently she touched his dark hair, careful not to wake him.

Hunger woke Robbie the next morning at ten. After making love the previous night Kim had promised she would take the rug rat out to the playground in the morning so Robbie could rest. She also liked to be out of the house when he was preparing food which he had to do early because her lot were coming for lunch later on. It was typical he thought, he'd been totally banjaxed the night before, then she appeared and gave him the horn so he had to give her a good seeing to. He wasn't long getting off to sleep after though which was great. And now he'd managed a bit of a lie-in too. He got up out of the bed, farted while scratching his balls and wandered into the bathroom for his morning slash. Stripping off his boxers he stepped into the shower and hit the power button sending what felt like boiling arrows straight into his face.

'FUCK,' he roared. In his bleary state he had

forgotten about the injury. He finished washing while taking care not to touch his face. There was zero chance of shaving, he wasn't a total masochist. He threw on some clothes and went into the kitchen. After a quick coffee he opened the fridge and started to pick out the ingredients he needed for lunch. Kim had bought it all the day before armed with the shopping list he'd prepared. He was happily chopping up garlic and rosemary to baste the small leg of lamb he planned to roast when he heard the door of the flat open and the sound of Kim's voice. It was the other voice he heard that almost made his heart stop. For a few seconds he wondered if he was actually really awake. 'What the fuck is he doing at the flat?' he asked himself. 'And what might he have said to Kim?' Dropping the knife he practically sprinted to the hall.

'Tommy, what are you doing here?' he asked.

'I just came by to give you back your wallet. You left it behind you last night, what with the commotion and all,' he indicated Robbie's busted up face and winked at him from behind Kim. The sigh of relief was audible from the younger man. 'How did you know where I lived?' he asked.

'I checked your wallet. Your address was on the license.'

'That's deadly. I hadn't missed it yet actually,' he lied. 'So,' said Tommy stepping up to have a closer look at the injury, 'that was some clatter that ball caused.'

'I thought you said one of the women kicked you in the head,' said Kim although not with any element of suspicion. 'Well yeah,' Tommy interjected quickly, 'but both she and young Robbie here were going after the ball at the time so that's how it happened.'

'Jaypers, I never realised it was such a rough sport,' Kim said innocently.

'A few digs wouldn't be unheard of. Isn't that right?' Tommy asked, looking eye to eye with Robbie. 'Ah yeah, I'll just have to take better care of where I put my head next week.'

'Sounds like a plan,' Kim laughed. 'Anyway, I'll leave you to it. I'm going to give the young one a bath before her mum comes to get her. I think there's an inch of muck on her from the playground, kip of a place.'

The two men were left alone in the kitchen. Robbie closed over the door. 'Jayzus man, nice save there. I bleedin owe you one.'

'No problem. I only found it because I tripped over it in the dark when I was running.'

'I'm not talking about the poxy wallet you dipstick!' Robbie said laughing while pointing to his swollen face. 'Oh right. Your missus saw me outside checking the names on the bells. Once she copped who I was she started to thank me for trying to help you after one of the women kicked you in the face. So do you want to tell me what really happened? You drove out of the place like you were on fire after you checked your phone.'

'It's nothing important,' replied Robbie going back to his chopping. 'Anyway, what were you doing running in the dark?'

'I had words with Ray O'Toole. He's the director of football at the club. Smarmy little shit he is too. I'm trying to get a few bob for the team. You know, to get jerseys and maybe rent a team bus.'

'What and he won't give you a dig out?'

'There's more chance of a bat flying out the eye of my mickey,' said Tommy. 'So what happened to you anyway?'

'Seriously, it's nothing to worry about. Just the boss getting a little cranky, that's all.'

Tommy's eyes narrowed with suspicion. 'I thought your parole officer bloke said he was bringing you to meet someone about a job today?'

Robbie looked a little shifty. 'Yeah, that's right.'

'So, what? You went early and got boxed for your trouble?'

'Look, I do a bit of work for a bloke and he wouldn't have the best temper.'

'Was he the reason you ended up having to do community service?' asked Tommy, curious.

'Fuck no. That was for beheading a rooster,' laughed Robbie.

'You don't strike me as the cruelty to animals type.'

'I'm not but he was a noisy little bollix,' said Robbie unwrapping the cling film from the leg of lamb. 'Do me a favour Tommy?' he asked, changing the subject while handing him the meat on a plate. 'The bathroom is out there Tommy, run that around the inside of the jacks will ya. The mother-in-law is coming for lunch.'

Chapter Sixteen

'Tenerife? Who the hell gets married out there at this time of year?'

This was the last thing Ruth expected when she answered her mobile phone in Tesco. It was one of those new smart phones that were more intelligent than their owners, which in her case at that moment wasn't difficult. She had been in the shop for the best part of a half hour and so far her trolley consisted of a can of chicken soup and a packet of Brillo pads. Not exactly haute cuisine. It was just the weekly shop. What was so flipping difficult about that? Now this phone call from Lorcan had put her into a total tailspin.

'It's one of the young lads from the office, Eric. I promoted him last year. I think he feels obliged to ask me.'

'You don't have to go surely. There's a recession on. Can't you use that as an excuse? Everyone else does.'

'I own the company Ruth. I think the staff know we have a few quid. Anyway, I've already booked the tickets. We fly out Sunday.'

'But ...'

'Come on, live a little. Let the hair down. I'll chat to you about it over dinner, got to go.'

Just like that he was gone. Off to broker some million euro deal or other and here she was still looking at chicken soup con Brillo for the evening meal. Tenerife in October? For the love of God. She would have to get a swimsuit and clothes for warm weather. This was a bloody nightmare. Jesus, she realised, she was going to need an appointment at the

beauticians to get her underarm and legs waxed. Oh God. If there were going to be colleagues of Lorcan's around she couldn't risk looking like a burst mattress in her swimming togs. The thought of having the bikini line wax almost made her faint on the spot. Scrolling through the contact list on her phone, she tapped on the number for the salon. 'Hello, Ultimate Beauty, how can I help you?' the chirpy female voice said. 'Hi, my name is Ruth Sheehy. I was wondering if I could book an urgent appointment for today for leg, underarm and bikini line waxing with Marie?'
'Sure we can. Could you come in at four?'
'That's great, see you then.' With one last look at her meagre trolley she shoved it up against the fruit stand and walked out of the shop. Takeaway would have to do for dinner. There was too much to get ready for this trip and she only had a few hours.

When Ruth finally pulled up outside Ultimate Beauty she was raging she hadn't booked a facial or massage as well. After the frantic pre-trip shopping she was a ball of stress. The relaxation would have been welcome. Entering the salon she gave her name to the girl behind the desk. 'Oh Mrs Sheehy, I'm very sorry but Marie had to rush home. One of her kids was sick. I've managed to slot you in with another one of our therapists or I can swap you to another day next week?'
'I'm going away on Sunday so I have to get it done today actually.'
'OK, if you'd like to follow me through then please.' The girl led the way through a little warren of corridors and alcoves and opened one of the rooms to lead her inside. A white terrycloth robe lay on the plinth. 'If you'd just like to undress and pop that robe

on, your therapist will be along in just a moment.'

The door closed behind her and she raced to get undressed and covered back up again. This was always the worst part. Fearing some stranger would wander in just as you were bending down in your nude to pick up a sock or something. Her husband hadn't even seen that much with the light on for donkey's years. Sitting up on the plinth she felt her heart racing, due in no small part to the speed she'd got undressed and back into the dressing gown. God I'm ridiculous, she thought. Why couldn't she just relax? A light tap on the door told her the girl had arrived. When she didn't voice any objection to her entry, the door opened. The beautician had her head bent slightly as she manoeuvred a small trolley through the door. Lifting her head up to acknowledge her client a broad smile spread across her face.

'Ruth!'

'Oh my God.'

'No, it's just me. God failed the waxing module of the course.'

'Sorry Naomi. I didn't mean to sound rude,' replied Ruth, pulling the garment even tighter around her. If a large hole full of gurgling acid had opened at that second on the floor she would have dived straight into it.

'Marie had to leave early so you have the pleasure of my company instead. So let me check I have it right. It's leg, underarm and bikini line, correct?'

'Well maybe I might just go for leg and underarm.' Her face was so red it was threatening to give off steam. 'Don't be silly. You've seen one, you've seen them all. Was it just bikini or would you try something a bit fancier?' Naomi asked with a wink.

'Fancier?' Ruth prayed she wasn't going to whip out a style book showing the various *Do's* one could get done *down there*.

'Well there's Hollywood, Brazilian, French or the regular bikini one.'

'I'm not sure I want to know the difference,' said Ruth wincing.

'I suppose it depends on the occasion,' Naomi replied as she began working on Ruth's legs, spreading the hot wax over the shin area with a small flat wooden stick.

'Occasion? Oh, it's a wedding in Tenerife,' Ruth replied in confusion.

'You lucky wagon! I'd give anything for a bit of the four Spanish S's.'

RIP! The first piece of cloth was pressed on and torn off.

'Do I want to know what the four S's are?' asked Ruth, wishing she had either gotten drunk or taken a pain killer before she came in.

'Sand, sea, sun and shagging. Bet you and the other half will be doing lots of that. Weddings always make me fierce horny.' RIP! 'Jesus Ruth,' Naomi held up the cloth to show her. 'It's like an animal pelt and that's after only two peels.' RIP!

        The sound of a slight sniffle caught Naomi's attention. She turned her head to look and to her shock Ruth was crying. 'Oh I'm really sorry, was I a bit rough? Do you want to take a break for a minute?'

'It's not that,' she sniffed.

'Oh God. Me and my big mouth. I've gone and insulted you. Please don't make a complaint, I really need this job. It's just that I thought with us playing Gaelic and all ... you know ...'

'What? That we were like friends?' Ruth finished the sentence for her.

'Well yes, I suppose I did.' Naomi shrugged.

'I'd really like that. I'm sorry for blubbering, ignore me.' Ruth dabbed her eyes. 'Lorcan's always giving out about it.'

'Is that your husband?' asked Naomi as she began to stir the wax. 'Is it okay to continue by the way?'

'Yes, go on.'

'So what has you upset then? You can treat this room like the confessional. No secrets leave here.' Ruth wiped away another tear and smiled.

'I wish I could be like you.'

'No you don't. You wouldn't be driving around in a brand new Range Rover on my wages for one thing,' Naomi laughed.

'What you have is worth more than all the money in the world. Confidence.'

'A lot of people call it arrogance.'

'Only the jealous ones. I'd give anything to be able to walk into a group like you do. I bet you'd have no problem getting into a swimsuit in front of your husband's work colleagues.'

'Is that what's bothering you?'

The tears started again. 'I don't even undress in front of Lorcan anymore. Not since I piled on the weight. I wouldn't relish the task of cleaning the vomit off the rug.'

Naomi sat on the seat next to the plinth and rubbed Ruth's arm. 'Has he said something to you?'

'No, but look at me. I'm not exactly Cheryl Cole am I?'

'That skinny wench? If she stood sideways and stuck out her tongue you'd think she was a zip.' Ruth burst out laughing even as the tears kept falling. 'Look, you can't change your weight dramatically before you go to Tenerife but you can change that.' Naomi tapped her forefinger on the centre of Ruth's forehead as she spoke. 'If you want to be confident, you've got to make it happen. No one else can give it to you. When's the last time you straddled that husband of yours and bounced up and down on him like a pogo stick?'

Ruth was scarlet. 'We haven't had sex for a long time, well over six weeks. God, I can't believe I'm even telling you this.'

'Is there any chance he is seeing someone else?' Ruth looked aghast. 'I don't think so. He's either at home or at the club every night.'

'Right then.' Naomi clapped her hands together. 'Then it's a medical emergency.'

'What is?'

'If a man hasn't shot his load in that long he's either dead or suffering some sort of blockage. I'm going to give your lady garden a makeover. Then you're going to do a Chelsea flower show of your very own in your bedroom tonight. And you the one with the degree in horticulture!'

'Excuse me? My what garden?'

'You know. The aul triangle, downstairs. We're going to make it jingle jangle enough to make the Dubliners rise up.'

'Oh I don't know Naomi.'

'Trust me. You'll be a new woman! I wouldn't recommend it if I didn't have one myself.' Naomi winked as she took out several jars of brightly coloured Swarovski crystals.

'What are they for?' Ruth asked cautiously.

'My friend, prepare to be vajazzled.'

'Va what?'

'We are going to mow the lawn down there and redecorate it.'

'Oh sweet divine Jesus.'

'That's what your fella will be roaring later when you tie him to the bed and rattle the bones off him.'

'So how does this work then?' asked Ruth.

'Well first I wax the area in the Californian style.'

'Which is?'

'Bald as Kojak.'

Ruth turned pale.

'Then I'm going to glue these babies on.' She rattled the colourful crystals. 'You can be thinking up what designs you might like.'

'What, like an arrow or something?'

'Ruth luv, no man I ever heard of needed directions. Now, let on you're at the dentist. Lie back and open wide.'

Chapter Seventeen

'Are you taking the piss?'

'Certainly not.'

'You want me to drive around in that yoke wearing a hat with two horns on me head?' Robbie stood at the north side of St. Stephen's Green staring at a bright yellow boat on wheels.

'It's a bit more than that. The Viking Splash is a big tourist attraction. Last summer comments about it were trending high on Twitter. Do you tweet Robert?'

'Tweet? Do you see any fucking feathers?' The bloke was really beginning to give him a pain in the hole.

'You know,' replied Peter, his parole officer, 'you could try to be grateful for a change.'

'Yeah,' shrugged Robbie, lighting up a smoke, 'and you could fuck off with yourself.'

'Would you rather a job washing dishes in The Joy?'

Robbie looked up the street at another one of the amphibious vehicles making its way down the street. It was full to the brim with roaring tourists in wet gear and Viking helmets. 'I have a choice then?' Peter's deadpan face was answer enough. 'So what exactly do I have to do?' asked Robbie with resignation.

'The Viking Splash tours run every day from ten to three thirty in winter. They give the tourists a bit of a feel ...'

'You mean tit like?' Robbie interrupted with his trademark cheeky grin.

'As I was trying to explain, they give the tourists a feel for medieval Dublin. Each tour takes an hour.

They go into the water at George's Dock.'

'Fuck me. I thought the boat thing was only for effect. You mean they actually float?'

'Absolutely. Tell you what,' he replied pointing to a man approaching them, 'here's the lad who runs it. He's going to bring us for a private spin and explain it all to you.'

'G'day. How are you going?' Seemingly unperturbed by the state of Robbie's face, the big Australian stuck out his hand. 'I'm Craig, welcome to Viking Splash.' Typical, thought Robbie, even the shite jobs are going to foreigners. 'Hop on board,' said an annoyingly exuberant Craig. The two men climbed the steps and clamoured into the vehicle. The inside had rows of red plastic seats with two raised slightly at the rear. 'Sit up the back there mate, so you can get the authentic tour. It's the best way to show you what you'll be expected to do. We can go through the boring stuff later.' Robbie wasn't so sure there was a distinction. The engine shuddered to life. Craig tossed plastic helmets with two large white horns on either side back to them. Peter put his on, turned to Robbie with a big stupid grin on his face and indicated that he should do the same.

'I will in me bollix,' said Robbie.

'Sorry mate, it's the uniform for the job,' shouted Craig, still beaming from ear to ear. Clearly he was high on diesel fumes, thought Robbie. 'Is the offer of the job in Mountjoy still on the cards?' he asked shoving the helmet on his head as they moved off slowly from the kerb.

The boat on wheels turned right onto Dawson Street and drove on down before coming to a stop at a set of lights at the side of Trinity College. A double decker bus pulled up alongside and Robbie caught sight of his reflection in one of its windows. 'I look like a fucking twat,' he mumbled. He pulled up his collar and slouched down as far as he could in case anyone he knew saw him. Meanwhile Craig waffled on through the microphone about medieval Dublin and how the Vikings who arrived on their long boats settled there. Robbie stared ahead, a bored look on his face. 'You know what really happened don't you?' he said, turning his head slightly towards his parole officer.

'No. What?'

'The horny bastards rowed up the Liffey alright. But the stupid fuckers got out on the wrong bleedin side. They rode the arses off all the local young ones and got themselves riddled with the pox. Then they were too scarlet to go home with their Mickey's glowing like Darth Vader's light sabre. So they stayed.'

'That's probably not the version you should give the tourists Robert.'

'I dunno. Let's ask Skippy there what he thinks,' he nodded towards Craig.

'Let's not.'

'You're no crack.'

'I'm your parole officer not a comedian.'

'No shit.'

Robbie looked around the peculiar hybrid vehicle. There was nothing to it really. It felt like a boat even though they were driving on the road. A thought occurred to him and he shouted to Craig. 'If this yoke goes into the water, how come there's no lifejackets?'

'They're stored in the hold,' he said, pointing to a large hatch on the panel behind their legs. Robbie did a quick calculation of the number of seats. 'Must be a fair bit of space down there,' he noted.

'That's right mate. More than you would think. These are deceptive little buggers.'

Robbie smiled. An idea for how he could repay Tommy for not dropping him in the shit with Kim was beginning to form in his mind. They turned into George's Dock from Pearse Street and Craig came back on the microphone. 'Hold on to your helmets, we're going in.' The vehicle drove down the slipway and made the transition from land craft to sea faring vessel.

'So can this yoke go out in the open sea or what?' asked Robbie as the water in the calm dock area lapped up against the side of the boat.

'It most certainly can. They are modelled on the Higgens boats used in the D-Day landings.'

'So why do you only fart about in the docks then?' asked Robbie.

'Insurance mate. Open sea costs buckets more.'

'Fair enough.'

'So what happened to your face?' asked Craig eyeing the bruised area suspiciously.

'Walked into a door,' replied Robbie.

'You'll have to wait till that fades before you can start working on the tours.'

'That's fine by me.' He wondered if it might be worth boxing himself in the face on a weekly basis to avoid having to look like a fucking eejit. 'Don't worry though, the boats have to be hosed down and cleaned each evening. We can start you on that. They are stored each night at a garage in Ringsend. You can

start today if that suits.' Robbie opened his mouth to protest but his parole officer got there first.
'That suits fine thank you.'

Chapter Eighteen

Tommy blew his whistle. 'Right you lot. Pay attention. I've been asked if we'd play a match.'

'I hope you told them to shag off,' laughed Alison.

'Why would I do that?' he replied.

'Well let me see. One, we don't know the rules. Two, we can't run to save our lives and what was the last one? Oh yeah. Three, we're totally shite.' The rest of the squad squealed with laughter.

'You're not totally shite. Little Mary there has a jump on her like a flea.'

'Any chance of a nicer analogy?' the frizzy red haired woman chirped. 'And stop calling me little Mary, I'm officially one inch above a midget so feck off and think of another name.'

'Stretch,' Robbie called out as he took cones out of a bag.

'You might have noticed Robbie, I'm four foot eleven.'

'I know,' he chuckled. 'The other team won't have a rashers who we're passing to when we shout you the ball. Besides, you nearly double your height the way you jump. It's genius.'

The women chatted among themselves coming up with various nicknames for each other. In the week since they had last trained more of them had bought proper football boots. Tommy was seriously impressed. 'So who wants to play us then Tommy?' asked Naomi breaking away from the group and walking towards him. 'Knockvicar,' he answered.

'Knock the crap out of yis more likely,' Robbie muttered in his ear.

'Knockvicar? As in Roscommon? We have to go all the way up there?'

'Well, actually no.'

'Oh so they're coming here?' asked Ruth, looking unusually vibrant and sun kissed.

'Not exactly,' replied Tommy. The team, curious now, gathered around.

'What's the story?' Even Robbie stopped laying out the cones.

'There's a replay of the ladies intermediate All-Ireland Final on Saturday week.' A sea of blank faces looked at him as he spoke. 'They want to have an exhibition match at half time to showcase the Gaelic for Mothers initiative.' The buzz of nervous chatter began. 'So where do we have to play it?' asked Naomi realising before the others the connotation of it being played during an All-Ireland final. Tommy caught her eye and with his own dancing brightly gave them the big news.

'Croke Park.'

'Mother of Jesus.' Brid caught hold of Naomi for fear she was going to faint. 'Ah Tommy, you can't be serious.'

The newly christened Stretch looked up at him, fully expecting him to laugh and say Got Ya! But he didn't. Instead he gave them the lowdown on their first ever fixture—playing in a 72,500 seater stadium. The headquarters of Gaelic games in Ireland. 'It's only going to be six minutes a side. It'll be over before you know it.'

'This is so exciting. I think I'm going to pee.' Alison beamed while crossing her legs.

'So we haven't long to prepare,' Tommy continued. 'I think we need to do a bit of extra running.'

'Extra? Why?' asked one of the women.

'Well it's just that ... how do I put it?' Tommy struggled to find the right words. Robbie stepped out in front and looked around the group. 'Yis are fat.' Tommy jumped out beside him, not sure whether there might be an assault. Nobody moved.

'What he, eh ... means is,' Tommy stuttered, 'we have to get our fitness levels up.'

'No. What I meant was yis are a herd of fucking elephants.' He nodded at Stretch, 'Well except you,' then he looked at Naomi, 'and you.' Naomi's stone faced expression changed to a smirk as she extended her hand and raised her middle finger to him. 'Ah Jaysus, would you go easy?' Tommy said, hoping the women wouldn't all start bawling. He looked anxiously towards Ruth who was the most emotional. To his shock she stepped forward and raised her arm. Robbie ducked. Instead of the slap in the face he'd expected she clapped him on the shoulder.

'Robbie's right girls. Most of us,' she smiled at Naomi 'came here because we wanted to do something to get active. I for one have been having a ball. What about you guys?'

'Me too.'

'It's great fun.'

'Better than I expected.' The women all gave their various opinions. Naomi, with her hands on her hips, stood and stared in amazement. The vajazzle must have done the job because the woman, who only a week ago had been a sobbing mess, was standing there full of confidence. A natural leader. 'Tommy, let's face it, has his work cut out for him. Robbie just calls a spade a spade. What was it the young sax player fella said in The Commitments?'

'I'm black and I'm proud,' Stretch piped up.

'Yes that was it. Well I knew I was fat but I never thought I could be this proud. I've never felt this good. We're a team,' she said giving Robbie a squeeze, 'all of us.'

'Right then.' Tommy clapped his hands together. 'Let's decide on positions. After that speech I think there is only one name for captain.' He looked around the group for agreement as he pointed to Ruth.

'Absolutely!' Naomi shouted.

'Any takers for goalie?' asked Tommy next.

'Put Alison in goals,' said Robbie. 'She'll fill the fucking thing and besides, she's got some boot on her for clearing the ball away.' The woman in question put her arms out to the side and shook her body. The layers of flab jiggled and bounced.

'Nothing's getting past this baby.' The rest of the team whooped and cheered.

'Naomi, you're centre field. You're by far the fittest of the group.' Tommy hoped he wasn't going red. The expression he'd used had a double meaning in his mind. Turning to the next person he caught Robbie's eye. There was an unmistakeable glint as the young fella raised one eyebrow. He had twigged it, the little bollix. He continued going through the team, appointing them to their various positions on the field. When he got to Tracey she put up her hand to stop him.

'I have a confession to make.'

'Please say you're a retired county player who's been hiding her talents,' Tommy joked.

'I'm not really a mammy. I don't have any kids so maybe I won't be allowed to play. Is the initiative really just for women who were able to have children?' Robbie piped up. 'Well I suppose technically it's called Gaelic for Mothers. But somehow I don't think Tommy is gonna be asked to check your cervix to see if you've actually given birth like.' Tracey burst out laughing. 'Although maybe he'd be happy to take a look,' he joked. 'For the love of the game of course.'

Tommy split the women into two groups and handed out the separate coloured bibs. 'We'd better get moving ladies. Croke Park awaits.'

'Jesus, imagine it,' Ruth beamed. 'Our very first match ever and we're playing in Croker! Wait till I tell Lorcan.' She bit her lower lip in anticipation.

'There're lads up there,' said Tommy, pointing to the club house bar illuminated in the darkness, 'who would have smothered their mothers to get to play in Croke Park's hallowed ground. Some of them still would.'

'I've never even been there. How will we get to it?' asked Brid. Tommy took a deep breath.

'That's a bit of a problem actually. We might have to get the number 11 bus. It goes all the way across the city. But let me worry about that. I'll figure something out.'

'No need man,' said Robbie, grinning with mischief. 'It's sorted.'

'Do I want to know how?' Tommy asked suspiciously.

'Probably not,' he replied.

'Will it involve us being arrested?' Robbie put his hand on his chest over his heart. A look of indignation crossed his face. 'Tommy. Would I?'

'How'd you manage to convince yer man to give you jerseys by the way?' asked Robbie as they were clearing up after the training session.

'Who, Ray?'

'Yeah, when you came to the flat you made out he wouldn't give you the steam off his piss.'

'He wouldn't.'

'So where are you getting the kit for this exhibition game?'

'It's being supplied by Croke Park thanks be to Jaysus. If it wasn't, the lot of them would be running around in their nude,' Tommy laughed.

'I think I feel sick,' replied Robbie, picturing the scene.

'I'm going to have to come up with something for this blitz in Rathburn though.'

'This Ray fella must be a right bollix if he's not willing to give you any dig out.'

'He said the women could buy their own jerseys in the club shop or I was welcome to go out and get my own sponsor.'

'I might know someone who can help with that.'

'I don't know, setting up these sponsorships can be a very complicated process. Lots of negotiations and shite. How well do you know this person you're going to ask?'

Robbie grinned. 'I only sleep beside her every night.'

'Kim? Who does she work for then?'

'Some English crowd. They make lots of different cleaning shite and healthcare stuff. She runs the marketing department so she decides on any sponsorship they do. I'll have a chat with her.'

Chapter Nineteen

Robbie eyed up the framed diplomas from some obscure college in America that were hanging on the wall. Definitely bogus, he thought. He looked across the room at the counsellor who was clearly irritated.

'I'm here now amn't I?'

'But you missed your last appointment. By rights I should report that to your parole officer.'

'Come on man, what do you want from me?'

'What I want, Mr King, is for you to take these sessions seriously.'

'I am,' Robbie lied.

'Clearly that is not the case. For instance, you don't have anything to show me from that exercise I gave you.'

'What exercise?'

'The Barbie doll.'

'Oh that.' Robbie had fucked it in the canal as soon as he'd left their last session, but not before yanking the head off it first.

'So what excuse do you have for not completing the exercise?'

'I've got a dick.'

'Excuse me?'

'It's meat and two veg I have in my jocks pal and in my world blokes don't play with fucking dolls, alright?'

'The point of the exercise was not to play with it but to take care of it. Keep it clean and tidy. Have you managed to achieve that?'

'What do you think?'

The counsellor sat back in his seat, folded his arms

and sighed. 'Well that doll is the property of this office and I expect it returned before your next session or I will report this incident.'

'Alright, alright. Will you relax about the poxy doll? I'll sort it.'

Fucking muppet, thought Robbie as he slammed the door shut behind him. The more time he spent in that flute's company the more he wanted to punch his lights out. Anger management me arse. He checked his watch, almost 11 a.m. Perfect timing. Hawk skidded to a stop and he jumped into the car. He pulled out a smoke and lit it. They were heading over to have a chat with the bloke who brought the grievous bodily harm charge against Hawks oul one. The case was due before the courts later that day. 'So what's the story with this lad we're going to see anyway?'

'Seeing how he and me ma were the only ones in the bar when she battered him, he's the only witness.' Robbie looked at an open bag in the back seat. A lump hammer and masking tape were among several other items that could be used to bring the bloke around to Hawk's way of thinking.

'Will he take much convincing do you think?'

'He has a young bird,' Hawk replied ominously. Fuck, thought Robbie. He wasn't about to batter some young one. 'You can take the girlfriend for a spin while I chat to her fella. I'm just going to suggest to him that she'll be on a day trip just long enough for him to withdraw his statement.'

'What the fuck do I do with some kid?' Robbie was terrified at the prospect.

'How the bleedin hell would I know? I don't have any, as the ma keeps reminding me.'

'Putting you under pressure is she? Jaysus and I thought it was only the women that got that on account of their biological clock 'n' all.'

'Listen Robbie pal, when it comes to becoming a granny, my ma's clock is Big fucking Ben. Do you get my drift?'

'You'd better hurry up and get married so,' laughed Robbie.

'Married me bollix. I just need to knock up some young one.'

The sound of a mobile ringing came from Hawk's jacket. He took one hand from the wheel and retrieved the phone from his pocket. 'Yeah?' His face betrayed nothing as he listened to the caller. He glanced at Robbie quickly as he began to speak. 'Fuck. Right then, my man will be out there whenever you give the all-clear. Give me the nod when you're good to go and I'll send him over.' It had to be his contact in customs in Dun Laoire. Hawk put the phone back in his pocket and confirmed Robbie's suspicions. 'That was yer man out in the depot. Seems there's some sort of training happening next week so he's afraid they'll be demonstrating how to use those dogs that smell shit like bombs and drugs. He doesn't know for sure but the stuff will need shifting just in case. He's not down to work the weekend but he's going to swap with someone. He'll give me a shout once he knows what day he's on.'

'Grand yeah,' Robbie nodded. It would be just his poxy luck that it would be Saturday when he was supposed to give Tommy's team a lift to Croke Park for their game.

Chapter Twenty

'Tommy? I thought it was your voice.' Naomi came through the reception as he stood awkwardly behind the counter with a bunch of twenty euro notes in his hand. Her colleague who had only recently started at the salon was fumbling over the screen trying to put the sale through. 'I'll take for it Linda, if you want to start closing up.' She noted the voucher on the counter and her heart contracted. The fact that Tommy might have a woman hadn't actually entered her head before now.

'Someone's birthday?' She asked, hoping her voice didn't betray any emotion.

'What? Oh no. There's a teacher leaving from the school and the Principal asked me to pick up a voucher for a present.'

'Oh that's OK then.' She smiled as she tapped the screen to process the sale. Tommy stared at her. Had he heard her right? The silence owned the moment. Naomi could feel his eyes on her. What was it Ruth had said? That she wished she had her confidence. The tables had well and truly turned on that one anyway. Looking up quickly as she handed him the change she noticed an ever so slight red hue from his skin. Jesus, she thought, he's bloody worse than me.

'So you work here then?' he blurted out, thankful that his real thoughts hadn't tumbled out instead. Like 'You're gorgeous,' or 'Any chance of a snog?' 'No Tommy,' she said with a smirk. 'I just wander in off the street and they let me play with the customers.'

'Lucky them,' he replied, surprising himself with his bravery. With just the counter separating them they looked into each other's eyes. No words were needed. Naomi could hear her pulse racing as desire engulfed her. Tommy felt his throat tighten. 'I've locked up the back so I'll get off now, see ya.' Linda marched into the reception oblivious to the sexual tension in the air. Naomi just nodded and followed her to the door to see her out, shutting it behind her.

This was it. If they didn't act on the obvious attraction now, God only knew when, if ever, it would be the right time. Thinking of all the advice she had given Ruth she took a deep breath and turned. If her intuition was wrong that would be the end of the football, she would be far too mortified to continue. Tommy had turned around. His back was to the counter. He let his eyes take her all in—the vibrancy of her face, the shine of her hair and the curves of her body. She wanted him too. He saw it. It had been so long since he felt anything remotely like this. Big match nerves were nothing compared to it.

'Right. That's it.' He pushed himself away from the counter and walked towards her. Naomi held her breath. Jesus, they were like a pair of teenagers. Everything seemed to take forever. He stepped one foot in front of the other and then he was almost there. She moved toward him. He would be face-to-face with her in a second and then ...He brushed past her. No! No! No! That wasn't supposed to happen. Not bearing to turn around she heard the sound of the door opening and shutting. 'Better lock this,' he said turning the key. 'I've thought about this moment for too long to be disturbed.'

Naomi turned to see a beaming Tommy striding towards her like a prize stallion. Moving in unison, the sexual energy peaked as their lips sought one another. Neither one of them had ever known a hunger so fierce. Her fingers gripped his hair as she pressed her body to his. Their tongues explored each other's mouths and she felt him harden as he pushed her up against the counter. Naomi thought about leading him to one of the rooms so they could lie on a treatment bed but she wasn't sure it would take their combined weight. Crashing to the floor would definitely ruin the moment. He had to lead this. She didn't want to scare him off by appearing like a cheap tart. Hopefully there would be plenty more opportunities to take the lead and show him some of her tricks. His hands were on her covered breasts now and she longed to feel his skin on hers. She pulled his jacket off and he started to unzip her tunic. 'Are you sure this is OK?' he whispered, his breathing heavy. 'I want this Tommy. I want you, now.' He pushed the tunic off and her bra fell to the floor immediately after. She fumbled with the buttons on his shirt, found it was taking too long and ripped them open. The thick hair on his chest added to his masculinity. He pulled her over to the couch and slipped off the rest of her clothes. He stopped when he removed her thong. A look of surprise crossed his face but it didn't last long. He was a man on a mission.

Chapter Twenty One

'What's going on over there?' Alison pointed to the main pitches where an under-12 boys blitz had been in full flow. Instead of four games being played simultaneously, all the kids and their parents were crammed up against the chain-link fence. Adults strained to balance on their tiptoes in order to gain a precious millimetre or two in height as they looked out over the sea of bodies. The children risked a permanent pattern of the chain-link on their faces as they pushed as far forward as the steel fixtures would allow.   People were pointing and laughing at something further down the avenue. From where Tommy and the rest of the Gaelic for Mothers team were standing on the all-weather pitch, the view was blocked by the club house. The sound of a horn broke through the roars of laughter coming from across the car park. The kids' teams had now abandoned their match totally and were all running up the avenue to get a better view of whatever it was that they could see but Tommy couldn't.

'Maybe they've organised to bring the Sam Maguire Cup to the club today. That's about the only thing that would get that sort of reaction.'

'Not at all. I reckon they're practising their welcome for when we come back later on from our inaugural match in Croker,' Naomi suggested.

'That's probably it alright,' said Tommy, winking at her. 'Sure you might as well dream here as in your bed.'   They had seen plenty of that in the past few days. The chemistry between them didn't go unnoticed by Ruth who sidled up to Naomi.   'I suspect there's a bit of news you need to share and I want ALL the gory details.'

'What on earth are you suggesting?' Naomi teased. 'Come on you! Stevie Wonder could see the spark between you pair. I bags the seat beside you on the bus.' Catching only the last part of her comment, Tommy added, 'If Robbie ever shagging gets here.'

As if on cue, the subject of the children's attention finally came into view. 'What the fuck ...?' Tommy's eyes nearly fell out of his head as he took it all in. A bright yellow boat about twenty five feet in length and on wheels rounded the gable end of the club house building. Sticking up on either side of the front of it were two large white horns about four feet each in height. It came to a stop in the car park just next to the all-weather pitch. In vibrant blue letters it read VIKING SPLASH TOURS on the side of the vehicle. Tommy shook his head and laughed. The women, more curious now than the kids, began to spill out for a closer look. There was a high pitch tone as the microphone was switched on and a beaming Robbie stuck his head out from behind the Captain's wheel. 'Howya girls. Your team bus awaits.'

'I'm afraid to ask,' said Tommy climbing aboard for a better look.

Alison's body quivered non-stop as she stood bent forward with her hands on her knees. The combination of years smoking and her sheer bulk made her laughter sound like it was piped through gravel. Her face was scarlet as she struggled to speak. Every time she looked up at the 'team bus' a new wave of giggles started. Robbie glanced over as he jumped down off the amphibious vehicle. 'You all right there blobby?' he asked, clearly enjoying her amusement. She just nodded, knowing there was no chance of forming words. 'Right so. Load her up. There's plenty of space.' The women climbed the few steps up onto the deck and took their seats. 'We'd better get going soon or we'll be cutting it a bit fine,' said Tommy, checking his watch.

'Will you chill your pits. I know a shortcut.'

'There's no shortcut to Croker, at least not for drivers. You have to go through the city or over by the east link bridge. There's a show in the O2 arena so the roads will be jammed that way.'

'Who said anything about roads?' Robbie hopped aboard and started the engine. 'Wait!' Ruth shouted. 'Tracey isn't back yet, she went into the loo.'

'Is she alright?' asked Tommy. 'She's been in and out of there all morning.'

'It's just the nerves. Here she is now.'

Robbie turned to see Tracey approach. 'Oh good Jaysus.' She looked like an elephant dressed up for one of those Indian weddings. She wore bright pink shiny leggings which did nothing to hide the extremely visible knicker line. On top she had squeezed herself into a luminous green sweater. The words Samsung Night Run were overstretched across her immense chest.

'Did you forget to turn on the light when you got dressed this morning Tracey?' asked Robbie. She didn't hear him. She was too busy chattering to the women already on board. Ruth caught his arm. 'Go easy on her. Her husband recently walked out,' she whispered. Looking over the strange attire one more time Robbie asked, 'Did he take all the fucking mirrors?'

Tommy sat beside Robbie up the front as they pulled out from the club car park. Ray O'Toole was desperately trying to put order back into the blitz by ushering the last of the young boys back onto the main pitches. It wasn't going well. He stared as the Viking Splash bus made its way onto the avenue.

'I might have known you'd be involved. You just have to cause a scene wherever you go, don't you? Setting a great example to the kids once more.' He directed his words at Tommy. The object of his ire unfurled a smile in tandem with his middle finger which he held up to a very pissed off looking Ray. 'Guess you should have rented me a proper team bus,' said Tommy. 'Then I wouldn't have to rely on my mate here.' Robbie grinned and let out a roar as he threw a large black sack towards the group of boys. 'Here lads, have a helmet.' Chaos ensued as pre-teen boys pushed and shoved each other out of the way to get their hands on one of the Viking replica helmets. Robbie sounded the horn as he drove away.

'Who's yer man? He looked like he was going to self-combust just now.'

'That's the bloke I told you about before. Ray O'Toole. He's in charge around here.'

'I'd say his name suits him. I'm guessing he's not your biggest fan then?'

'The feeling's mutual, I can assure you.'

Tommy tried to ignore the bemused faces of the people on the pavements as they drove down past the crowded Shopping Centre and turned right at the dual carriageway instead of left as he expected. 'What the fuck are you doing?' he asked. 'We're supposed to be in there by two o'clock.'

'Jaysus,' said Robbie, 'have you been getting nagging lessons from the oul wans back there. Would you ever relax?'

'Robbie, Croke Park is that way,' replied Tommy raising his thumb to point behind his shoulder.

'You've got serious trust issues. Do you know that?'

Tracey squeezed her way to the front of the bus and tapped Robbie on the shoulder. 'Are there any facilities on board?' He turned to look at her, one eyebrow raised. 'Ah shite Tommy,' he said, his voice steeped in sarcasm, 'I forgot to collect the off duty air hostesses.'

'I meant a toilet,' Tracey replied, clipping him on the ear for good measure.

'No luv, no jacks on board. Sure anyway, you just went. I nearly drove off without you.'

'I can't help it. I suffer from a very nervous tummy. It has a terrible effect on my bowels.'

'Well then tuck those leggings into your socks just in case you shit yourself all over me bus.'

'I thought it was a boat,' said Tommy through gritted teeth.

'Bus, boat, whatever the fuck. Just squeeze your arse good and tight Tracey luv. We'll be there in less than a half hour.'

'We will in my hole.' Tommy had begun to get seriously grumpy.

'Didn't I tell you to relax?' said Robbie as if he were speaking to a child.

'How can I relax? I'm trying to get back in with GAA headquarters. Instead of turning up to play as *invited guests* in an exhibition match, what are my team doing? We're going on a magical mystery tour of south County Dublin in a poxy yellow boat on wheels.' Robbie grinned and turned the wheel to the left following a sign for Dun Laoire. Tommy took out his phone and started frantically scrolling through his text messages. He was trying to locate the number of the Croke Park co-ordinator to tell her he was going to have to let her down. The sound of the women shouting made him look up.

'Jesus Robbie, what are you doing? Can this shagging thing float?' The Viking Splash boat tore down the slipway next to Dun Laoire pier on its wheels and floated out into the harbour. People walking their dogs stood and stared as the girls on board squealed in delight. Robbie grabbed the microphone. 'James Bond came out of the sea in an Aston Martin. This is bleedin Dublin so yis can make do with a floating lorry.'

'So where's Daniel Craig then Robbie?' shouted Alison from the back.

'He took one look at the Bond girls on this yoke and threw himself overboard. That's him breaking the world record at the doggie paddle to get away from you shower of mutts. Anyway, yis have Tommy here.' 'Somebody has,' Ruth teased as Tommy went puce and Naomi grinned mischievously. The girls all turned in an effort to glean the gossip on this exciting development. Robbie turned to Tommy and raised his eyebrows. 'Naomi, right?' Tommy just looked ahead as the boat made its way around the headland and headed for Dublin port. There was the faintest hint of a smile on his face. Robbie looked ahead too. 'Tommy Boylan, you're a dirtbird.'

'Listen Captain Birdseye, you just concentrate on getting us to the game on time. How are you planning to get us back onto dry land anyway?' Robbie whipped out his mobile and dialled a number. As he waited for the call to be answered he replied, 'I know a bloke.'

A very relieved Tommy smiled as they pulled up outside the player's entrance to Croke Park. He had managed to make contact with the organiser of the exhibition game and she stood waiting for them with her official's pass hanging around her neck by a lanyard. She looked no more than twenty years old. 'Tommy Boylan I assume?' she approached with her hand outstretched. 'My dad was a huge fan of yours.'
'Thanks,' replied Tommy with a smile that hid the fact that the comment made him feel old. 'Louise isn't it?' He shook her hand.
'That's a pretty unique team bus you've got there.'
'Yeah. There was a bit of a mix up over our transport, but we got here in the end.' The women all gathered around. The nerves were palpable. Everyone strained to hear in case they missed something vital. 'We better get you changed. The kit is all laid out for you inside the dressing rooms. We have plenty of sizes available if what I put in there doesn't suit. You'll be on at half time so we'll call you down from the stands about ten minutes before that. Just give me one second to get security to open the gate for your bus then we can go in.' She walked to one side and spoke into her walkie-talkie.

Tommy turned to the group while Robbie drove through to where the girl had indicated, much to the amusement of supporters arriving for the main match. 'Ladies, this is it. How are you all feeling?'
'Like I'm going to puke,' replied Tracey. Tommy and the team followed Louise through the player's entrance. Their faces were a mixture of excitement

and dread. They walked through the vast area beneath the stands where the team buses were parked. Two large intercity size coaches were lined up neatly side by side. The next bus was a smaller version with the name Knockvicar GFC emblazoned on the side. 'The opposition are here,' shouted Tommy from the front of the line. The silence behind him made him stop and turn. 'Oh good,' he said. 'For a second there I thought you might have all legged it.'

'We would,' replied Ruth, looking around the immense stone structure, 'if we knew how the hell to get out.' 'Come on the girls,' roared Robbie as the crowds in the stands above their heads started to cheer the start of the main event. Louise led them through a door and indicated a large changing room to the left.

'You can get changed in here. It's the senior men's dressing room. I'm afraid the main teams playing today are in the ladies ones.' They all walked into the pristine room with its white walls and immaculately varnished benches. Tracey sprinted past shouting, 'Where's the toilet?' She skidded to a halt at a bank of silver urinals. 'Please tell me I don't have to use them,' she pleaded with the co-ordinator. 'I have to do a number two.'

Louise laughed. 'Just go around to your left there.'

'Thank God.' Tracey's voice called out over the sound of a cubicle door banging shut.

Alison bent down to take her football boots out of her kit bag and let off a fart that threatened the foundations of the stadium. 'Jesus girls, I'm awful sorry,' she said as the last stragglers made their way into the dressing room. 'It's the nerves.'

'It's the greasy fry-ups you mean,' shouted Robbie

through the open door. 'Get out you!' Naomi slammed the door in his smirking face. The kit was packed in brown cardboard boxes. Shorts, jerseys, even socks were supplied. The newly designed G4M, Gaelic for Mothers logo was printed in shocking pink across the front. Sizes were swapped around until almost everyone was sorted. All except Alison who was struggling to get shorts on. 'This is hopeless. The large doesn't fit. Are there no XL's in the box?' Naomi rummaged through the remaining garments. 'Nothing above large I'm afraid.' 'Would one of you go and ask the girl if she has one somewhere?' asked Alison. Ruth opened the dressing room door and spotted Louise. She explained the predicament. 'Come with me,' Louise said to Robbie who had been leaning against the wall outside chatting to Tommy. Two doors and a corridor later they were outside another changing room. Louise knocked and went inside. With the door slightly ajar he caught a glimpse of the other team.

'Good Jaysus.' He said aloud. The co-ordinator emerged with something the size of a parachute hanging from her arm. 'Are they the shorts or did you grab a tent to keep us dry from the rain?' She laughed and threw them over to him.

'Can you find your own way back? I have to bring these guys out to the stand. I'll be around for your team in five minutes, okay?' Robbie ran back to the changing rooms and forgetting to knock, barged straight in. Alison had just that moment dropped her hair bobbin on the floor and was bending down to retrieve it, her back to the door. He saw nothing else except immense mounds of bare skin with the faintest hint of material sticking out as her thong disappeared up the crack of her arse.

'Hope that's not the team gone up your gicker,' Robbie said from behind his hand. He kept it in position to catch any sudden rush of vomit and threw the shorts on to the bench with the other. Alison turned around. With the confidence borne of many years on the planet she strode over to him and grabbed him in a bear hug. The rest of the team gathered around, cheering. 'You want me Robbie, I can tell,' she joked, mushing his face into her pendulous jersey-covered breasts. His muffled cries made the team fall about the room in convulsions.

'I want me ma!' he screamed.

A rap at the door and the sound of Tommy's voice cut through the joviality. 'Right girls, we've to go out to the stands.'

Robbie burst out through the doorway looking like he'd just had all the blood drained from his body. 'What was going on in there?' asked Tommy.

'That lot were ganging up on me so they were.'

'If you dish it out you have to be able to take it,' Alison said as she came out, now fully dressed. She pinched his bum as she passed. His face flushed red as half the team followed suit. 'Did you see that Tommy?' said Robbie, incredulous. 'That's sexual harassment that is.'

'I didn't see a thing,' replied Tommy. Louise met them at the entrance to the tunnel.

'I recognise this bit from the telly,' Ruth whispered to Naomi as they walked up towards the pitch. The towering stadium loomed into view with each step forward. 'Where's the other team?' asked Alison. 'They're already in their seats,' replied Louise as she led them out to the side of the pitch and up a set of concrete steps. A group of women looked up as they approached. They were all dressed similarly to Tommy's bunch but with different coloured jerseys. 'Knockvicar is it?' Tommy extended his hand to a man in a tracksuit who he assumed was their coach. 'Jesus, Tommy Boylan? I didn't know you were involved in Ladies' Football.' The man took Tommy's hand and shook it, 'I'm Mick Lehane.'

'It's only a recent development Mick,' said Tommy, following the women into the row of seats behind the Knockvicar team. Robbie sat beside him and took out his packet of smokes. 'You can't light up here.'

'Wha? Tommy I've just been violated. I'm bleedin traumatised so I am.'

'What did they do to you anyway?'

'It was bad enough the first time. Don't be asking me to relive it.'

The Iona Gaels mothers' team ignored the banter between the lads. Instead they sat and simply stared at the other team. Their mouths hung open in shock. Naomi, who was sitting on the other side of Tommy, nudged him. He turned to look at her. 'Are you sure it's Gaelic Football we're playing today? That lot look like they could take on the All Blacks in rugby.'

'We'll be grand,' he reassured her without conviction.

'We'll be killed,' she replied.

Louise appeared back almost immediately. 'OK Knockvicar and Iona Gaels, it's time to go. We'll be going around to the other end of the stadium and following the Artane Band out onto the pitch. They'll be playing throughout your match on the north end of the pitch. You're only out there for twelve minutes in total so you'll have to get stuck in straight away.'

The two groups stood up and followed Louise's lead, Knockvicar going first. They went back through the tunnel and were once more in the bowels of the stadium. The sound of boot studs on concrete reverberated off the grey stone walls as they made their way around. The crowd roared. Someone had clearly scored a goal in the main match. Tommy walked back towards them and pointed to one of the opposition. 'Would you say she was a bottle-fed baby?' he joked, trying to relax them with slagging, an ancient Dublin tradition.

'She wasn't born. Something that size could only be made in a factory,' said Alison. 'And you call ME an elephant?' she continued, looking directly at Robbie.

'You should apply for one of those rural resettlement scheme yokes,' he said. 'Set yourself up in their neck of the woods. You'd be like yer one from that 90's girl band in comparison to them. What's her name? Skeletal spice.' The rest of the women laughed among themselves. Robbie and Tommy fell behind slightly.

'Fair play, I think you have them more relaxed.'

'It's going to be carnage Tommy. You realise that don't you.'

'I recognise their captain,' he replied, not getting drawn by the question. 'She used to play county football for Cork. She must have moved house.'

'Probably more bulls for her to practise her tackling on in Knockvicar,' said Robbie. 'Christ, I thought most of our team were big women. But this shower? They're not women, they're beasts.'

The two groups lined up next to each other behind the marching band. Tracey called out to Louise, 'Excuse me, but is there a toilet I could use before we start?'

'Sorry. The nearest toilets are back in the dressing rooms. You don't have time.' Tracey looked horrified,

'But ...'

Her words were drowned out by the booming sound of the big bass drum. The Artane Boys Band began to march out onto the pitch. 'Best of luck,' shouted Louise over the din.

'Tommy I really need ...' Tracey attempted to talk to him.

'It will be over before you know it. Now come on.' His hand was on the small of her back. He gently pushed her out and ran up to the front of the line. It had been over twenty years since he'd lined out on this pitch. He hoped today's event would have a less violent end. Knockvicar's goalie went to the right-hand side goal. Tommy pointed Alison to the other one and the rest of the girls got into position. 'Shite,' he said to Robbie. 'They have us playing into the sun. The girls won't be able to see shag all.'

Naomi was centre field and lined out against her opposite number who held her arms aloft. The ref threw up the ball. Naomi leapt into the air and straight into the elbow of the other player who shoved it back with brute force. 'Hey!' she shouted as the girl whacked the ball out to one of her team mates. A woman came up the left flank and the ball was passed out to her. She ran up the pitch solo-ing the ball effortlessly. Tommy was sure he felt the ground vibrate. To his delight his women closed in around her. Seeing she was out of options, she hand-passed to her left. Naomi, having read the game correctly, barrelled through and intercepted the pass. She punched it out of the other girls reach and got a box in the mouth as payment from one of their forwards. The referee, facing the other way, saw nothing. Ruth was looking up the field with her eyes squinting. The ball hit her square on the nose and sent her flying on her arse with the shock. She sat dazed as the game continued. Naomi intercepted another ball and one of their players went on her snot in the process. She stopped for a split second to check on the girl. 'Sorry, are you alright?' she asked before the ball was knocked out of her hand. Tracey was sweating but not from exertion. She was playing in a forward position and hadn't yet seen the ball up close. All she could concentrate on was the time. The sooner she got to a toilet bowl the better. Her insides were bubbling up like a volcano. She didn't know which end would erupt first. Ruth had recovered and Tommy roared at her. 'Give Naomi a hand, she's going to get a chance to intercept again.' Ruth ran up the field. Before she realised it she was on the ground again thanks to a heifer of a woman with a streaky false tan. She was still getting back on her feet when Knockvicar scored yet another goal.

The Artane Band played alongside the pitch as Tracey was clutching her stomach. 'How does she have a stitch?' Robbie asked Tommy. 'She hasn't bleedin run a step.' Tommy wasn't paying attention. He was listening to the stadium announcer. 'And ladies and gentlemen if I'm not mistaken, we have Tommy Boylan on the pitch as coach of the Iona Gaels Gaelic for Mothers squad.'

Don't say it, thought Tommy. Don't bloody mention 1985. The booming voice continued. 'Tommy was a member of the Dublin squad in the early 1980's. But

of course he will be best remembered for ... Oh my.'
The announcer stifled a laugh.

The sound of retching made Tommy whip around to his right. 'Oh Jaysus,' shouted Robbie. The French horn player from the band looked on in horror as Tracey stood before him with a hand on either side of the rim of the instrument. The projectile vomit filled the horn's cavity in seconds. The jubilant sound of trumpeting suddenly changed to choked gurgling as the last bit of air in the wind instrument got swallowed in a puke tsunami. Robbie fell to the ground, his face purple with uncontrolled laughter. Tommy felt time slow down around him. One by one, the rest of the players copped on to what had just occurred. The game slowed as everyone strained to see. Snapping out of his trance-like state, Tommy ran to Tracey just as the full time whistle blew. 'Let's get you back inside.'

'I'm so sorry Tommy. I let you down. I don't know what happened. I sometimes get the runs when I'm nervous but this is the first time I've ever done this.'

'Well, I'm not a betting man,' he laughed, giving her a reassuring hug as he led her away towards the dressing rooms. 'But if I was? I'd put money on that young lad preferring to rinse out puke rather than scraping out your shite.'

A tall man stood looking down at the scene from behind the window of a corporate box. His tanned hand reached out to pick up his pint. He took a long drink. 'Worth coming home for,' he said in a thick New York City accent.

'What is? The Guinness or that display?' asked another member of the group. 'Both,' he replied with a smile. 'Doesn't compare to the men's seniors games you saw during your trip I bet,' asked a man wearing an official GAA blazer. 'No, you're right there,' the American replied. The GAA man smiled in a self-satisfied way before his guest continued. 'It was a breath of fresh air.'

Chapter Twenty Two

'Robbie? We're on,' said the voice on the other end of the phone.

'What? Now?'

'No, fucking yesterday. Yes now. So get a move on. Yer man is only on till five o'clock.'

Robbie looked around quickly as Hawk gave his instructions. The team hadn't yet emerged from the dressing room where they had been nursing their wounds. He reckoned they were trying to coax Tracey out because she was totally morto after her performance. 'Where am I bringing the stuff?' he asked. His mind was shooting off in every direction, wondering how he was going to get rid of the women. 'It has to be cut. A bloke will be waiting in a red van at the Carrickmines retail park. His name is Micko. Do the handover and he'll take it from there.'

'Jaysus Hawk, are you sure? A car park? That's a bit open isn't it?'

'Who died and left you boss?'

'Sorry. I was wondering about the risk is all. It's a big stash you said.'

'Yeah and the plastic bales are packed in cardboard boxes. You'll look like any other delivery van dropping stuff off.' Not quite, thought Robbie, looking at the Viking Splash vehicle. As subtle as a sledgehammer in the nuts it was.

Tommy emerged from one of the corridors. He was shaking hands with the leader of the band. 'So are you sorted? The van will be here for you,' Hawk continued. 'Get your arse out to Dun Laoire and get the gear. I gave you the container and pallet number before. Yer man will have the cameras off until five so get in and out quick. And don't fucking draw attention to yourself by getting into any rows.' That's rich coming from him, thought Robbie hanging up. You'd swear he was Mother bleedin Teresa. The sound of subdued chatter spilled out into the bus parking area as the team emerged. One by one they climbed up into the boat.

'Tommy, are all the teams as rough as that lot?' asked Ruth.

'You guys were just taken by surprise, that's all. Playing into the sun didn't help either.'

'We were beaten up. At least I feel like I was anyway.' Ruth rubbed her aching limbs to prove the point.

'It was our first match,' said Tommy. 'The nerves would have played a part.'

'Who are you telling?' Tracey whimpered, still scarlet at the memory.

'Look on the bright side,' ventured Robbie. 'It gave you a taste of what to expect in Rathburn. You know what they say—nothing focuses the mind like a hanging.' Tommy shot him a dirty look unnoticed by the women.

'Rathburn?' Several of the girls piped up. 'What's that all about?'

'Whoops.' Robbie ducked his head down into his collar and started the engine.

'What's going on Robbie? What's happening in Rathburn?' Alison moved up through the vehicle towards him. 'Tommy will explain. I've to concentrate on driving this yoke,' he said. He stared straight ahead to avoid eye contact with a glaring Tommy. 'You and your feckin mouth,' Tommy whispered as he went back down to sit and inform the girls about the upcoming blitz. Robbie checked his watch. It was three o'clock. He had time. Just. He'd drop the girls back to the club and then dump the Viking Splash boat back to the garage where he'd liberated it from earlier. He could be over to Hawk's warehouse in twenty minutes on the Honda. The van would get him out to Dun Laoire in half an hour if he put the boot down. 'Back the way we came is it?' asked Tommy reclaiming his seat at the front. 'Yeah. I've to pick up some parcels for the boss so I better get a shift on. I'll drop this lot back to the club but then I have to split.'

'I was kind of hoping we could have a bit of a debrief. Maybe a drink in the bar to talk about the blitz, now that you shagging well dropped me in it.'

'How did they take it?'

'Listen to the silence. Doesn't that say it all?' Tommy glanced behind. 'I said I would go over some points about today's game too.'

'That wasn't a game. It was a massacre.'

'It could've been worse,' said Tommy unconvinced.

'What's worse than no poxy scores? I take it you have told them that getting goals and points is the object of the game?' Tommy pulled a face.

'They were shell shocked, that's all.' Robbie looked back at him with a dead pan expression.

'They were shite.'

'Oh, were they now? Mr GAA know it all. Well let's see how shit hot you are.'

'How do you mean?' asked Robbie.

'I've a funeral to go to on Friday. An aunt died in America and she's being buried back here. You'll have to take the training session till I can get back. I should make it by 9.45 p.m. at the latest.'

'Would you go and shite.' Robbie said with a disbelieving look. 'They don't bleedin plant people in the dark Tommy.'

'I know that smart arse,' he replied as the truck slowed to a stop behind a long line of traffic. 'The funeral is at three and the burial will be straight after. It's down in Cork though so unless you have a mate with a chopper?'

'You're not seriously going to leave me alone with that lot?'

'As you said to me so often earlier,' said Tommy, grinning, 'would you ever relax?'

The traffic was at a standstill. It was almost 3.30 p.m. and they hadn't moved more than a few feet in the last five minutes. Robbie was beginning to get anxious. If he didn't get to the docks soon he wouldn't have a prayer of making it to the pick-up on time. Not if he had to drop this lot off and then get the van. Fuck, fuck, fuck. They were more than a mile from the entrance to the docks but Robbie was out of options. Traffic on both sides of the road was stopped. 'Must be a hold up on the bridge,' shouted Alison. 'Sometimes they lift it up if there's a tall ship or something big coming up river.' Robbie started to sweat. 3.40 p.m. If he messed this up he was dead. He touched his still slightly bruised eye as a reminder of the least he could expect. Tommy noticed how tense Robbie was becoming with each passing minute. 'So this fella you're collecting the stuff for. Is that the bloke that gave you the hiding?' he said, pointing to the side of Robbie's head. Robbie nodded and lit a smoke, inhaling deeply. 'I have to collect some gear for him before five.'

'Gear? You don't mean drugs do you?'

'No way man. I don't deal drugs. It's just some parcels is all.' Robbie answered without looking him in the eye. 'Where do you have to collect it?'

'From a depot in Dun Laoire.'

'So what's the big deal? Once we get to the water you'll be back there in no time.'

'I need a different van,' said Robbie, chewing on his thumbnail.

'Why? I thought you said it was just some parcels. The girls would put them on their knees.' Robbie tapped the steering wheel anxiously.

'Eh, no. I don't think so.'

'Only trying to help.' Tommy stretched his legs out.

The traffic began to move. 3.55 p.m. Fuck this, thought Robbie. I'm going to have to take my chances collecting the gear in this yoke. He knew there was no way he'd have the time to collect the van now. Hawk said his contact would have the CCTV off till five. That gave him shag all time to get there and get the stuff loaded. A shriek of laughter from the back of the vehicle made him look in the rear view mirror. Suddenly he had a plan. It wasn't ideal but it was the best he could manage under the circumstances. He hadn't wanted to involve them but logistics was not proving to be his strong point. When they finally rolled down the slipway into the water his watch read 4.00 p.m. Cursing the lack of a speedboat motor he pushed the lever to top gear. 'So tell me about this boss fella then. What's his name?' Tommy asked, seeing a different side to Robbie. He was extremely agitated.

'Hawk.'

'Where?' Tommy looked skyward. 'I didn't think

they could be found round here'. He'd always fancied himself as a bit of a bird watcher. It had helped occupy him during his wilderness years in the UK.

'No you twat,' said Robbie, following Tommy's gaze. 'Not a bird. Hawk is his name.'

'That's a stupid bloody name,' he laughed.

'Funny, no one has thought to tell him that,' Robbie said, pretending he was giving it consideration. 'So this Hawk fella, what's he into?' 'A bit of this and a bit of that. You know yourself.' Robbie was offhand in his response, hoping Tommy would get bored and change the subject. He didn't.

'No. Enlighten me.'

'He's a kind of wholesaler.'

'Of what?'

'Just stuff. Now leave it will ya Tommy for fuck's sake. You're wrecking me head.'

Tommy did as he was asked. Robbie was rattled. Not surprising when you considered the beating he'd received just recently. Warning sirens were going off in Tommy's head but if Robbie said he wasn't dealing drugs then he would give him the benefit of the doubt; at least for the time being. The boat motored along at a steady pace despite Robbie's impatience. Alison trailed her hand out in the water.

'The bay's much cleaner than when I was a young one. Back then you could have walked on it; it was so full of shite.'

'It's probably all the radioactive waste chucked in it that's keeping it clean,' laughed Naomi. After less than thirty minutes the boat neared the slipway and Robbie flicked the lever from sea to land craft mode. The wheels caught a grip on the sludge covered slipway and spun a few times. 'Come on, come on!'

Robbie spoke through gritted teeth. The vehicle lurched forward as the heavy tread tyres finally made contact. Robbie put his foot down and they tore up the small incline. He grabbed his phone and used his thumb to flick through the screens. Their pace didn't slow as they shot through the car park, following signs for the depot. Tommy had visions of a couple of late afternoon pier fishermen ending up as hood ornaments if Robbie didn't pay attention. Finally the vehicle slowed as he approached a set of large metal gates.

A man in a yellow anorak with CUSTOMS & EXISE printed on it in black appeared from the gate post. 'Paperwork please,' he said, viewing the Viking Boat on wheels with suspicion. 'I thought my boss had sorted it,' said Robbie eyeballing the man. 'What's the company name?' The official asked the question as he walked alongside the boat looking each woman up and down. Robbie turned to see what the bloke was looking at. He had been so concerned with getting to the depot on time, he hadn't noticed it. One of the team had obviously found the bag with the tourist goodies. Alison's big head grinned back at him as he looked around. She had a Viking helmet on and a plastic club in her hand which she used to bop the bloke on the head as he passed. 'Eh, company name?' he repeated ducking to avoid another clatter off her. 'Hawk Ltd,' replied Robbie. He hoped to fuck this tosser was the contact and he hadn't missed the pick-up. It was barely discernible but it was there. The quick look of recognition on the bloke's face told Robbie he had made it on time.

'The arrangements for pick up are still as outlined to your boss. The depot closes at five,' he said, checking his watch. 'You have thirty minutes.'

'Ah Jaysus man, come on. Thirty minutes? How am I going to load it that fast?' pleaded Robbie. 'Can't you delay things half an hour?' The official on Hawk's payroll was unmoving in his resolve.

'Half an hour is what you've got. It's not my fault you were late. If you run over that, you risk being locked up for a long time.' The double meaning of his words was lost on everyone except Robbie. 'The containers are clearly marked,' the man said as he walked away. 'You're on your own from here.'

'We'll help you load it,' shouted Alison from the rear as Robbie revved and drove through the now open gate. 'Yeah, we'll all get stuck in. You'll be done in no time,' agreed Ruth. It wasn't ideal, thought Robbie, but neither was having in-built air conditioning in his head courtesy of a bullet.

'Here Tommy, go into the notes icon there will ya.' He handed his phone over. 'There's one marked depot. Call me out the container number.' He continued driving slowly past large burgundy freight containers. He remembered the first bit of code was LB something.

'I found the note called depot but there's just two lines of letters and numbers. It doesn't say which is container and which is the pallet.'

'What?' said Robbie in disbelief. 'Give it here.' He grabbed the phone and looked at the screen. He tried to shake the imaginary sound of a big clock ticking in his head. His pulse quickened and pushed the blood through his veins almost as fast as the sweat came out his pores. 'I don't fucking believe it,' he said after reading the note aloud. He checked his watch. Twenty seven minutes before the cameras would be turned back to full operation.

He hit the accelerator and careered down the centre aisle. His head snapping left and right reading the container numbers as he drove. When he saw it he hit the brakes so hard the helmets shot off several of the women further back. BD-TS11. That was one of the numbers. He jumped down and ran to the container door. He wriggled the lever free and with Tommy's help, pushed it open. Several of the team had climbed down and followed them inside. 'How do you know which number is which?' asked Tommy.

'I don't. The other number is 1701. If we find that then we have it the right way around I guess.'

'There it is,' Naomi shouted from behind them on the left. LBD-1701was clearly marked. It contained twenty five large brown cardboard boxes. 'Are you sure this is the stuff?' asked Tommy. 'No,' replied Robbie, picking up the first box. 'But I haven't time to find out.'

'Here,' called Ruth stepping towards a box. She was pulling nail scissors out of her bag. 'I'll open one and you can check if they contain what they're supposed to.'

'NO,' shouted Robbie, diving to block her way. 'We've to be out of here in less than twenty minutes. I'll have to take a chance.' The last fella who tried to interfere with this gear was hugging a ship's anchor on the sea bed. Tommy organised the women in a line to speed up the process. Robbie shook his head as he watched a bunch of fairly well-to-do women and a Gaelic Football legend load five million euros worth of pure grade cocaine onto a stolen Viking ship. He couldn't have made it up.

Chapter Twenty Three

'Here mister, how much for de tour?' A ginger haired kid about nine years old roared up. Robbie looked down from the Viking Splash bus.

'There isn't any tour.' He replied curtly as he looked around. He had come here as arranged to meet Hawk's contact after he'd dropped the girls off. He was starting to get anxious. There was no bleedin sign of yer man and shoppers laden with bags were staring at him and the bus. The kid was undeterred. 'De sign on de siade says you can hop on anytime but.' He spoke like a Dublin pure breed, using two syllables were only one existed.

'Well you can't.' Robbie answered without even looking at the child. He took a long drag of his smoke.

'Why not?'

Robbie stood up and turned to face the boy who was really beginning to piss him off. The little carrot top head strained to see up into the boat. Thick green snot cascaded out of his nose and had started to form a crust on his top lip.

'Jaysus, you look like Kermit had a shit on your face.'

'Come on mister,' he whined, ignoring the insult, 'Giz a go on the tour.'

'It's bleedin dark out. I don't do tours at night, right?' He checked his watch, 6.15 p.m. and still no sign of yer man.

'Ah go on mister.'

Robbie had enough, 'Which part of fuck off do you not understand?' The young lad stormed off shouting, 'Them tours is only for nerds anyways.'

Robbie couldn't argue with that. He checked his watch again, 6.20 p.m. Something wasn't right. The bloke who was supposed to be meeting him wasn't new to this game. Hawk had used him to cut coke before. There was no way he'd leave five million in cocaine like a sitting duck. The cars started to empty out of the car park one by one. From his elevated position Robbie could see all the way out to the main road that ran alongside the retail park. He spotted it out of the corner of his eye: the tell-tale blue and white of a Garda car. He held his breath as he watched its progress. If it turned in he was fucked. He was well known to the Guards even if they had never managed to pin anything major on him. And he was sitting in a borrowed Viking ship. Although it was possible that the Aussie hadn't realised it was gone yet because it was one of the spare vehicles from the depot. If the cops spotted him they would be on him like flies on shite. If they found the cocaine they'd get a bleedin hard-on they could pole vault with. The squad car slowed as it approached the roundabout just before the car park's entrance. Robbie bit his lip and kept his eye on the car. If it turned in he would have to leg it with the gear. There was no other option. The car slowed even further. Robbie turned the key in the ignition, ready to bolt. The cop car sped up, flicked on its siren and disappeared off down the road. Robbie blew out the breath he'd been holding. 'Fuck this for a game of soldiers.' He picked up his phone and flicked to Hawk's details. The man answered in one ring.

'Is it done?'

'No, yer man never showed up.'

'What do you mean he never fucking showed up?'

'I've been here forty five minutes and there's not a sign of the prick. The fucking pigs passed by a few minutes ago, nearly gave me a bleedin heart attack. I can't stay here any longer. It's too risky.'

'Shut up will ya, let me think.' Hawk went quiet.

'Will I bring it to the warehouse so?' Robbie asked quickly, keen to get moving somewhere. Anywhere.

'No you fucking won't. It's too dangerous. I'm not there anyway. You'll have to bring it to your gaff.'

'My gaff?' Robbie didn't know which would lead to his demise quicker. Telling Hawk to piss off or telling Kim to shift the couch so he could stack a shit load of cocaine in their living room.

'Yes, your poxy gaff Robbie. The bleedin cops would be all over me if they saw a big delivery like that coming in. You'll have to sit on it till I find out where that prick got to.' 'Ok.' Robbie knew resistance was futile and potentially life threatening. Anyway he needed to stay alive, if only so Kim could murder him later.

It took almost an hour to unload all twenty five boxes from the hold of the Viking Splash. If ever there was a time he missed having a lift in the building, this was it. Lugging the boxes up one at a time meant he'd had to climb up and down the stairs fifty bleedin times. Now he was banjaxed and he still had to drop the poxy yoke back to the garage. Kim wasn't home. She was probably at her ma's. Even so, he had to check that she wasn't going to wander in and start rooting around the boxes before he got home. He tapped out a text and hit send. *Howya luv, what time u back*? She responded immediately. *Not sure, why*? *Had to store some stuff at flat*. His finger flew across the keypad; *just for a couple of days. Ok,*

she replied, *so long as it's not in the way. C U later x.*
Robbie looked at the scene in their living room. The boxes were packed five across and five high blocking access to the rest of the room. Fuck it, he hadn't time to sort it now.

The phone went just as Robbie put his key in the front door later that night. Looking at the number he pulled the key back out and slid his finger across the phone's screen.

'Howya.'

'Did you stash the gear?' Hawk didn't waste time on salutations.

'Yeah, it's at my gaff like you said.'

'You know what will happen if you fuck me over on this don't you? Only Butch said you never collected the van today.' Hawk's statement hung in the air like a noxious fart.

'I was delayed at the fuckin' community service yoke. They had me driving the Gaelic football team to a match.' Hawk laughed. Jaysus, you couldn't read the man at all.

'I thought you were a soccer man Robbie. Still, I suppose a GAA team bus is the last thing the cops would suspect of carrying drugs.' Robbie thought it best not to mention he'd driven the gear half way around Dublin in a stolen bright yellow boat on wheels.

'So did you find out what happened to the bloke I was supposed to meet?' he asked, still standing outside on the street. He couldn't risk Kim overhearing the conversation if she was home, which he hoped she wasn't.

'The gee bag got done for knocking the head off his missus. When they arrested him they found a shitload of gear. One phone call they allowed him and who does he bleedin ring?'

'Dunno.'

'Me! The fucking eejit. Now the poxy cops know there's a link between us. They'll be watching me like a bleedin hawk.' Robbie sniggered. Hawk didn't. 'That wasn't supposed to be funny.'

'Sorry boss. So what's the story then? With the gear I mean.'

'You're going to have to sit on it. Make sure not an ounce goes missing, do you hear me?'

'Yeah. Loud and clear.'

Kim was a woman and Robbie was a chancer with questionable taste in mates. That, coupled with a new cardboard box dividing wall in her living room meant that she was going to be curious. If she got any hint of what the boxes really contained he'd be out on his arse. Maybe she wouldn't be back yet and he could think of a proper excuse. His illusions were shattered as soon as the door to the flat closed behind him. 'Robbie!' The shout came from the living room. 'I'm stuck.'

He ran to her voice and skidded to a stop when he took in the scene before him. The neat wall of boxes he'd constructed had collapsed and at least half of them had split open. Kim lay pinned on the ground by a combination of boxes and spilt contents. 'What the hell have you got yourself into Robbie?' she roared at him. 'I could be dead under here. What is all this stuff?' He barely registered the earbashing. He was too busy concentrating on the fate of Hawk's stash, now scattered all over Kim and the carpet. He was dead when Hawk found out.

'ROBBIE! Stop gawking and help me out of this lot.'

'Wha? Sorry. One second, let me move some of it.'
He reached down and pushed the boxes that hadn't
split off Kim. Then both of them started scooping
armfuls of the stuff and throwing it to one side.
'Well?' snapped Kim. 'Do you want to tell me why
there are a few thousand bloody Barbie dolls in my
living room? And while you're at it, you can explain
why the invoices with them clearly state they are the
property of Smyth's Toys.' She was spitting mad.
She would have gone into orbit totally if it was pure
cocaine she was covered in instead. 'Clear it up and
get this stuff out of here Robbie.'
'It's kosher, I swear.'
'Oh, you bought over Smyth's Toys did you?'
'No. It's just a mix up is all. This lot must have got
mixed up with Hawk's shipment of ... stuff.'
'Look I know you feel obliged to keep doing work
for that Hawk fella because he helped you out when
your ma died. Don't you think you've paid your dues
at this stage? I don't like you hanging around him.
You know that.'
'I know. I'll sort it out, okay?'
'He's holding us back Robbie. I want us to move on
with our lives but I'll not have you at that bloke's
beck and call.'

Robbie sat on the couch when they were
finished and tried to figure out how this had
happened. The container and pallet numbers! He
hadn't noted which was which when he put the details
into his phone. He knew at the depot he was taking a
risk but he hadn't the time to check it then. Anyway,
what fucking thicko uses the same number for two
things? It was just as well the bloke never turned up
to take the coke earlier. Otherwise Hawk would know

he'd made a balls of it and right about now he'd probably have a fish swimming through his ear hole. 'What are you going to do with it?' asked Kim. 'You could bring it up to Smyths. They're open till ten most nights as far as I know.'

'Yeah, that's a good idea. I'll just lash out and get the van.'

Three hours later he had jimmied the lock and disarmed the alarm to the small office in Portobello. It was heavy work, lugging the boxes of Barbie dolls up two flights of stairs for the second time that evening. Instead of stacking them neatly he used a letter opener from the fancy desk to slice open the boxes that hadn't split earlier. One by one he emptied the contents all over the floor of the pristine office. Just as he was about to leave he spotted a miniature statue of Michelangelo's David on a shelf. He put it down in the centre of the desk, reached for a Barbie and flicked his lighter. Holding the flame in position over the doll's mouth, he waited till a hole had melted away. Then he positioned the doll's head neatly onto the dick of the statue and walked out, closing the door behind him. 'Sound theoretical principles, my hole!' he muttered as he started up the van.

Chapter Twenty Four

Naomi sat on a stool in the salon's kitchenette and drank her coffee. She was still sore from the football match two days before. Well, if she was totally honest, her muscles had even more of a workout when she got home that night. Not to mention most of the next day. Shona's granny had taken her to a relative for the weekend so Tommy had filled the gap—both figuratively and literally. Once he realised he didn't get his willie for stirring his tea there was no stopping the man. He told her he had a lot of catching up to do. She had been with other blokes over the years who were only interested in sex. That suited her fine but it never took long for her to lose interest. Mainly because they were the type of blokes who could only hope to keep one major organ fully functioning at a time. The brain normally lost out. With the best will in the world, even she couldn't shag nonstop without some sort of verbal interlude. If that was all she wanted to do she could buy one of those rampant rabbits and an endless supply of Duracell batteries. She had no issue with the use of sex toys. In fact she quite liked them. But they were much more fun if the partner came up with some novel uses for them, and that required speech.

Tommy was different. She could see he was most comfortable in a football environment and she loved that he was so passionate about their team. He truly believed they could make something of themselves. It also hadn't gone unnoticed to him why a lot of the women had joined up. He was approachable and Naomi had been proud of him when they all went for a team drink after Robbie dropped them off. Alison for all her bravado just wanted to be welcomed by the group. She had opened up to Tommy over a pint at the bar. Apparently she had always been big, even as a toddler. Throughout all her years growing up and out she had been bullied about her weight. Because of her size, she had never felt able to join any of the school teams and she had only recently come to terms with how marginalised it had made her feel. It had taken her a long time to accept herself as she was. Years spent on various fad diets lost her nothing but money. Naomi had been almost moved to tears the way Alison described meeting Tommy for the first time. How he had accepted her straight away and not made any assumptions as to her ability. Even Robbie, with his very direct approach, had given her a sense of belonging that you only find in the bond of a team.

Naomi had to give in and admit that Robbie was a bit of crack. He was easily the most politically incorrect person she had ever met. He was a gouger, pure and simple. Tommy knew that Robbie was no angel but he hadn't given him any problems to date so he was prepared to leave well enough alone. Poor Tracey had been almost ready to leave the team until Tommy had a chat with her in the bar. Nobody could have blamed her if she decided to go. Puking your ring up into a French horn in front of thousands of people was not exactly something you posted on Facebook. He had slagged her about it saying that even if it showed up on YouTube it wouldn't matter. She'd had her head stuck so far down the instrument no one would have seen her face anyway. It was such a unique thing, thought Naomi, Irish people only slag people they like and admire. Tracey was worried that if she was always as nervous as that she would end up doing Technicolor yawns on half the Gaelic pitches in Ireland. Luckily her sister had phoned to say she'd been sick too. It turned out the restaurant they'd eaten in the night before the game had served dodgy meat. Over sixty people were affected and it had even made the news.

Of all the team Ruth was the one Naomi had bonded with most. It was typical. The two people with the most diverse backgrounds had formed the closest friendship. It seemed that the simple advice she had given Ruth had worked wonders. She told Naomi later that having the vajazzle done was like having this big shocking secret. She felt it empowered her. It had taken Naomi to point out that a husband who hadn't sought sex elsewhere after the drought she imposed must seriously love her. Ruth had left for her holiday in Tenerife a different woman. But not before she swapped numbers with Naomi who had insisted on getting feedback on the reaction to her most artistic vajazzle yet. Ruth eventually surfaced after two days abroad. She sent a text saying that her husband had almost screamed in delight when he saw the sparkling crest of his beloved Chelsea FC. Naomi had burst out laughing when she read the next text. *Missed the wedding ceremony because Lorcan was so happy with the vajazzle. He went down more times than Drogba!!!* By the end of their short trip Ruth said she was well convinced that Lorcan didn't care about her weight. He just wanted her to be healthy so she would be around for a long time. The door buzzer went. Naomi finished off the last of her coffee and went out to greet her first client of the day. She could hear her in reception chatting animatedly with Marie, another member of staff. 'Hey there,' said Ruth. 'I was just checking with Marie here that there wasn't going to be any fisticuffs between you two.' Marie, who had always looked after Ruth in the salon, just laughed and put her hand on Naomi's shoulder. 'I taught her everything she knows.'

'Well then I owe you both,' smiled Ruth vibrantly, 'because this girl gave me back my life.' Naomi showed her into the treatment room.

'You did this yourself you know. Look at you, you're positively sparkling.'

Ruth picked up one of the jars of Swarovski crystals and shook it. 'Not as much as I'm going to be,' she laughed.

'Jesus,' said Naomi beaming, 'I've created a monster.'

'So how was the rest of your weekend with Tommy?' asked Ruth as she assumed the position.

'Tiring,' replied Naomi with a wink. 'I think I need to see a doctor.'

'Oh my God, you're not pregnant?' Ruth shot up into a sitting position almost knocking the hot wax into unchartered territory.

'No! I just need some horse strength vitamins to keep up with Tommy. He's a very fit man. Imagine what he must have been like in his hay day?' Ruth lay back down. 'Lorcan said he never really had time for girls back then. He was married to the club. Till it divorced him.'

'Well he's making up for it now, he's got me in a right state,' said Naomi with a devilish glint in her eye. 'I have to do some remodelling of my own,' she added with a wink. 'What?' asked Ruth. 'You can't be planning to wax anything else surely? Your eyebrows must be about the only body hair you have left.' Naomi shook her head and held up a picture from a magazine.

'The Rampant Rabbit? I'm guessing this is a sex toy then?' Ruth went slightly red as she spoke.

'Oh yes indeed, it's the big daddy in the self-stimulation department,' replied Naomi excitedly.

'If Tommy is sorting you out, why do you need it?' Ruth was perplexed.

'I can't have Tommy staying over all the time till I know it's serious. My little one would just get attached and she's seen enough change as it is.'

'Has Shona met him yet?' asked Ruth.

'No. She's with her gran till tomorrow. So tonight is our last night until I can get away again. Hence the need for the rabbit.'

'God, you can't go a couple of nights without sex and there I was happy to go over six weeks.'

'And now?' Naomi asked with her eyebrows raised. She already knew the answer.

'The way I feel now, Lorcan would be lucky if he got a rest for six hours.'

'That's the spirit baldy,' laughed Naomi as she perused her handiwork.

Chapter Twenty Five

Tommy pulled into the marked area in front of the small row of shops. Although it was early days with Naomi he hoped she was interested in a relationship. The sex was outstanding but even if there hadn't been any, he liked her as a person. He could be himself around her which was a very unique experience for him. She was so exuberant and God, how he needed that. After the Croke Park fiasco the other day he had made an executive decision. He was going to get on with his life. What had happened in the past had happened. No amount of soul searching was going to change it. He was looking forward to the evening ahead. Naomi had explained that her little one, Shona, was coming home the next day. It was going to be weird not waking up next to her after tonight. They had spent all weekend in her house. Actually, since that first explosive encounter in her salon they had spent every available minute together. He hadn't met her kid yet but was happy to. If she was anything like her mother she could only be adorable. He pushed open the door of the shop. For some reason he half expected that it would be a woman serving. He was a little surprised to find a man of about twenty behind the counter. He had tattoos and a piercing in his lip. Fair enough, thought Tommy. It's not like it's Harrods or anything.

'Excuse me?' Tommy ventured. The young man looked up from his magazine with a bored expression. He didn't speak. Tommy, not used to being in a shop that sold this stuff, didn't know where to begin looking for the item Naomi had asked for.

He thought it was an unusual request, seeing as though they had only just started seeing each other. But then Naomi wasn't what you would call the shy type. 'My girlfriend,' he began and paused smiling. Was that what she was? He hoped so. 'My girlfriend asked me to buy her a rabbit.' 'Which type?' replied the assistant.

'There's different ones? Jaysus son, in my day a rabbit was a rabbit.' The young man pushed himself off his stool with what appeared to be massive effort. 'Follow me,' he said in the most uninviting voice Tommy had ever heard. They passed rows of shelves with all manner of toys and peculiar items. When the bloke stopped he pointed to his left.

'As you can see, there are various options. It all depends on your girlfriend's taste. Did she express any preference for colour?'

'No, she never mentioned it,' said Tommy, looking at the variety of colours available. 'What about size?' asked the young lad. 'All she said was she wanted a big rampant rabbit,' said Tommy shrugging his shoulders. The young man reached over and picked an enormous black one up. 'Better give her what she asked for so,' he said. 'There's one or two other things you can get to go with it.'

'Yeah?' said Tommy.

'Well I've always found that people who buy the rabbit like to get extras' replied the assistant.

'Is that right?' Tommy, clueless at this stage, handed over his credit card. He hadn't known they made rabbits this size. He just hoped it wouldn't be too big.

Tommy pulled up outside Naomi's place and buzzed her doorbell. She opened the door immediately. 'I brought dinner,' he said, holding up two small brown bags from the local Indian takeaway. He followed her inside and put the food on the kitchen counter. She threw her arms around his neck and kissed him hungrily. 'Did you manage to get the other thing I asked for?' she asked with a playful giggle. 'Or did you think it was too much of a girlie thing to buy?' 'I beg your pardon,' he said, pretending to scold. 'Not only did I venture into the shop to get it but I also purchased a few extras.' 'Oooh!' she squealed. 'I can't wait to try it out, or maybe you could control it for me?' Tommy hadn't a rashers what she was on about, but then there was a good few years between them. 'I'll just lash out to the car and get the rest of the stuff.' Naomi opened a bottle of red wine and poured a couple of glasses. She was busying herself serving up the food when she heard Tommy come back. He seemed to be struggling to get something through the door frame. 'What in God's name is that?' she asked. He was carrying a large rectangular container made from a wooden frame and wire mesh. 'It's a hutch.' He spoke in a matter of fact tone. 'For what?' Tommy opened a hard plastic animal carrier. 'For this guy,' he said as he pulled out the biggest black rabbit Naomi had ever seen. 'What the fuck is that?' She screeched, her eyes nearly popping out of her head.

'It's a rampant rabbit. Technically he's called a buck, and he's only rampant if there's a few young ones around. Rabbit young ones I mean.'

'Why would you buy me a bunny?' she asked, baffled.

'Did you bump your head at the match on Saturday? You asked me later that night to buy you one. Don't you remember? You said we could both play with it. To be honest, I thought you were pissed.'

She looked up at his face and laughed. The big innocent head of him. 'Not a rabbit you gobshite,' she said, nodding toward the bunny. 'I meant a Rabbit, you know?' Tommy looked utterly baffled. 'Oh Jesus Tommy. Don't tell me you haven't heard of the Rampant Rabbit? I thought it was England you lived in for all those years, not a shagging cave in Afghanistan.

'I thought all rabbits were rampant. Isn't that where the expression "riding like rabbits" comes from?' She laughed and went to the shelf in the corner. Picking up a magazine she found the same advert she was looking at earlier with Ruth. She held it up for him to see. When the penny finally dropped a few seconds later, he started laughing so much he couldn't catch his breath.

'So the bunny is no use then?' he managed to say after a few minutes. 'Not unless he's a Duracell bunny,' she said, wrapping her arms around his neck, 'because they just keep going and going and going. Just the way I like it.' When they finally stopped laughing at Tommy's misunderstanding she spoke with her head leaning on his chest. 'I suppose I could keep it for Shona as a present. She's been nagging me for a pet for ages.' 'That sounds like a great idea,' he agreed. 'Actually,' she said, pulling back slightly and looking up at him. 'I've a better idea. Why don't we say you bought it for her as a present when you come to meet her?'

'You're sure about that are you?' Tommy understood how protective she was of her daughter's feelings.

'Well if you'd prefer not to we can just bring it back

to the shop tomorrow,' she replied quickly pulling away. 'Naomi, stop.' He caught hold of her and wrapped his arms around her waist. 'I think it's a fabulous idea, especially since I plan on being a big part of her mother's life. I have to get the seal of approval from the boss.' She knew the words forming in her mind were coming way too early in their relationship but she did nothing to stop them. She was nothing if not impulsive. 'I think I love you Tommy.' They were just six simple words, but to him they meant everything.

Chapter Twenty Six

The text had just read – *meeting in club at 8.30pm. All coaches and mentors to attend. No training tonight*. It was from Ray O'Toole. The first thought that came to Tommy was that the pitches would be free. He had confirmed that with a quick call to the club house. The blitz in Rathburn was on that coming weekend. Any extra training the girls could do would be great. He had put out feelers to the team in a group text earlier to see if they were available. All except one had replied saying they were happy to train. The next hurdle he had to overcome was convincing Robbie to take the session. He recalled the conversation. 'I have to go to a meeting with all the coaches tonight,' he had said. 'So there's pitches available.'

'You have your goo,' Robbie had replied in his thick Dublin accent.

'I haven't even asked you yet.'

'Good. Keep it that way.'

'Come on Robbie. I wouldn't ask you if I didn't have to. They really need the extra work so they won't be killed in the blitz.'

'You already asked me to take Friday's training. Now you want me to do this one as well?'

'You owe me after you let it slip about the blitz anyway.'

'I do in me hole. Ok, tell you what. I'll do it if I can teach them some survival tactics.'

'Ok,' Tommy had laughed. 'Just don't give them any weapons.'

As he drove into the club car park he laughed

thinking back on it. He saw the women starting to congregate at the all-weather pitch. He jumped out to explain that they would have a different coach for the evening. From the corner of his eye he saw Robbie taking a box from some man in a small van. Tommy wondered what he was up to. 'Hi ladies, I appreciate you coming out tonight. The pitches hardly ever come up like this so I wanted to take advantage. I have to go to a meeting in the clubhouse so Robbie is going to go through a few things with you. Don't give him a hard time,' he said with a grin pointing at Alison. 'The poor fella is still traumatised after you lot surrounded him in the changing rooms.'

'He loved it,' laughed Alison. 'I bet he was at himself all night after it.' Robbie stood just outside the pitch fence. 'I'm not coming in till you throw a bucket of cold water on yer one. She's like a bleedin rhino on the pull.'

'They promise they will be nice, don't you girls?' asked Tommy. The team sniggered in response, nodding at the same time. 'Anyway,' he continued, pointing up to the bar, 'I'm only up there. You can make a run for it if they get out of control.'

'Yis better go for a few laps to warm up,' said Robbie holding the whistle tentatively to his lips.

'Can you be trusted with that yoke?' asked Alison.

Robbie laughed as the women all filed past at a slow jog. To be fair to them they had all improved in fitness, albeit moderately, in the weeks that they'd been training. Much and all as he slagged them off, he had to admire their balls. These women, who were the furthest thing from athletic, turned up every week. It didn't matter what the weather was doing. He'd seen Tommy train them in howling winds and flogging rain. Robbie couldn't help but be impressed. Let's face it, they were a herd of hippos, well a good few of them were at least. Yet they went through the training without a word of complaint. He wasn't a fool, Robbie had overheard a lot of the chat the girls had in training. He knew all about the lack of sex and the fellas who never picked up their jocks. He'd heard about Ruth's fella who went for pints on a Thursday night and then farted out something that smelled like rotten trout all the next day. Alison's bloke insisted on cutting his fungus filled toenails into the empty bath just before she ran it. She told Robbie she half expected a call to the door from the Lancet Medical Journal, investigating the only woman in history to get athlete's fanny. It was funny he thought as he watched them struggling to complete the third lap of the modified pitch. He had learned more about how women think in the last few weeks than he had in years with Kim. The irony was that she'd be the very one who would benefit from all of this, without ever having met these women.

The best thing he learned was that women read so much into little things, like how you reacted when they came down the stairs in a new outfit. Or what you said when they came in from fighting through the aisles for the grocery shopping, or worst of all, what you did straight after sex. He only realised in the last week how shit women felt if you just turned your back after a ride and went to sleep. It was only from eavesdropping on the women's chats that he began to realise that sometimes the woman's need was greater. That had been a big revelation. Well, that and the fact that these birds actually got their hole an awful lot. The last of the team were jogging, or as close to it as they could, up to the top of the pitch. It was time to give this lot a dose of reality. 'Right you lot,' he shouted. 'Yis got fucking hockeyed at that match in Croke Park. We're going to learn some shit to set the record straight. Are yis in?'

'YEAH,' came the unified shout.

'What way do you want to lay out the cones then Robbie?' asked Ruth.

'Fuck the cones. You lot need some assault training.'

'Assault? That sounds a bit rough,' said Ruth. 'Gaelic is a non-contact sport isn't it?'

'It is yeah. And Ireland have a world class soccer team,' replied Robbie sarcastically. 'So what's with the assault training then?' asked Naomi. 'Tommy said we were just unlucky meeting Knockvicar. He said the other teams wouldn't be the same as them.'

'No, he's right there. They'll be ten times worse. Do you even know where Rathburn is?'

'Isn't it where the famous street light is? What's it called? Oh yes, the High Lamps,' said Naomi.

'That's right. And do you know what the mammies in Rathburn do if their sons act the maggot?'

'No.' The girls crowded around to hear.

'They hang them from the High Lamps by their bollix. So what do you think they'll do to a crowd of posh birds from the suburbs?'

'Oh Jesus,' whispered Ruth.

'Look, you lot just need a bit of extra help. It's not in your nature to be devious so that's where I come in. Let's start at the beginning.'

Robbie got the girls to split into two halves and positioned them as though they were starting a match. 'Right. The first problem is the throw-in.' Naomi and Stretch stood next to each other in front of

Ruth and Tracey. 'Now I want to see digs from behind,' he said to the back pair. 'Well, when I say see I mean I don't want to see it but I want you to give her one ... so to speak.'

'I'm confused,' said Ruth.

'The ref will be at the front so it will be hard for him to get a good look. The person at the back has to give a good fucking box into the kidneys of the girl in front from the other team. Elbow is better that fist. You can get your back into it. Anyway you don't want to injure your hands because you'll need them later for giving the slaps.'

'My God,' said Ruth. 'You're serious. What does Tommy think?'

'You'll see what he thinks when he watches you all in action. This team means everything to him. Some more than others of course,' he winked at Naomi. She smiled sweetly while raising her middle finger to him. 'He'll be over the moon if you even get a score so we owe it to him to at least try to win.'

'Ok. What else do we need to know?' asked Alison.

'I want at least one dirty tackle out of each of you. So break into groups of three and I'll show you how it's done. The one in the centre has the ball and the other two have to try to get it off her. Right, let's go. Give it a lash.'

The ladies did as instructed. Naomi, Ruth and Alison started the drill. Alison had the ball. She stepped left and then right to try to get past the other two. For their part they waved their arms about and generally tried to get in her way. Robbie watched them all going through the motions. He blew hard on the whistle. 'What in the name of Jaysus are yis at?'

'We're doing what you said,' replied Alison, panting.

'What's the problem?'

'The problem Blobby,' he said putting his arm around her shoulders, 'is that you are not playing a fucking tiddlywinks blitz. This is football and you have to get stuck in.'

'How?'

'Bulldoze your way through. Some of you could fell a tree if you leaned against it. Use your size. Now go again. And this time don't be so bleedin polite. Actually, that reminds me. If you do send someone on their snot in a match don't be stopping to say sorry and help them up. Score the fucking point first. Then go back and do your Florence Nightingale bit if you still want to.'

Ruth, Naomi and Alison got into position. The whistle blew. Alison tucked the ball under her left arm and stuck her right elbow out. She shoved it right into the left tit of Naomi who almost puked with the impact. Next Ruth came in trying to knock the ball out of Alison's possession as she went to solo it back into her hand. A shoulder into the windpipe knocked her flat on her arse. Alison ran four steps, bounced the ball and took a shot at goal. It hit the back of the net. Robbie clapped his hands. 'Aw thanks Robbie, that's my first ever goal,' beamed Alison.

'Good on ya. But that's not what I am applauding,' he replied. 'This is.' He pointed to his left to where Ruth and Naomi were bent over still trying to catch their breath. 'This is what I'm talking about. Now we just have to work on our technique.'

'Thank God,' said Ruth, relieved. 'I can handle practising hand passes and solos.'

'Not that technique you gobshite. I mean the practise of fouling without getting caught. Some say it's an art form. You have to use your shoulder like a battering ram. Just don't let the ref get a look at you. Now on your feet and go again. Swap the ball around so you all get a turn.' Tracey and Brid stood on either side of Stretch. She looked up at them quickly before darting left then right. She bounced the ball with her left hand while simultaneously punching Tracey in the gut with her right. Robbie shouted encouragement, 'Lovely play Stretch,' as Tracey buckled and fell to her knees. He watched as the other groups followed suit and began to perfect the art of foul play. It was the only thing that would get this lot through a match. It was time to add to their arsenal. He blew the whistle.

'Ok. Now, it's possible the ref might be more on the ball than we'd like so here's something else. You all have proper boots with studs, right?' The women all nodded. 'Grand, well every time you feel the opposition is getting ahead of you, I want you to stamp on their feet or lash out across the shin area. Like this.' He demonstrated the move slowly on Ruth. 'What about the ball?' asked Stretch.

'Don't mind it, take out the player,' he replied. 'Just make it look like you were aiming for the ball. The other thing you can do is lean on the person marking you when you are both chasing the ball. Use them to steady yourself as you're running and then give them a good shoulder shove at the last minute when they're getting ready to kick the ball. It will fuck up their balance and if you're lucky the ref will think they slipped.'

'Clever,' said Naomi, smiling. 'Oh, one more thing,' said Robbie. 'Will you remember not to all bleedin crowd around the ball when one of you gets it.

Otherwise you've nobody to pass it out to. In future when I roar SPREAD, I want you to all run as far from each other as you can.'

'Yes sir!' they shouted.

'Do you want to get a quick game in before we finish? To see if you can put some of this stuff into practice.' The women looked at each other and reluctantly agreed. The two sets of bibs were dished out and Robbie threw in the ball. Ruth was on the blue team and Naomi on the yellow. As the ball came back down through the air Ruth slipped in behind Naomi and jumped for the ball. With her knee firmly stuck into the small of the back she shoved her out of the way and grabbed the ball. 'Jesus Ruth, you nearly knocked my vajazzle off,' she shouted as the others barrelled past her on the ground. 'Your what?' asked Robbie, dragging her up. 'Nothing,' she replied laughing and ran to chase down the ball.

Robbie stood in the middle of the pitch with his arms folded. Pride spread across his face. He watched as bodies went flying left, right and centre. They were quick learners to be fair. By the time he'd finished with them next Friday they'd be ready to take on Mike Tyson, never mind Rathburn. 'Ow!' Stretch was holding her mouth. 'What happened to you?' asked Ruth, jogging up alongside. 'Brid gave me an elbow in the face. Almost knocked my fillings out.' 'Nice one,' shouted Robbie, giving the culprit the thumbs up before blowing the whistle. 'Actually, that reminds me. Tommy said to tell you that GAA rules state that everyone has to wear a gumshield during matches.'

'Where do we get them?' asked Stretch still tending to her mouth.

'You can pick them up in any sports shop. The kids all wear them,' replied Alison. 'They're just plastic yokes. You drop them in boiling water for a few seconds then put them in your mouth and bite down.'
'Sounds like a normal Saturday night then,' laughed Ruth to the surprise of everyone on the team except Naomi. The session ended with the usual stretching exercises. It was standard practice now for the farting to ring out louder with each more adventurous stretch. It had become almost routine. No one even commented or laughed anymore, much less apologised. Even so, Robbie, for all his years in the shallow end of the etiquette pool, couldn't get used to it. Kim would rather die than let one off in public like that. Alison, noticing his discomfort shouted over. 'Better an empty house than a bad tenant eh?'
'So do you think we might have a better chance in the blitz if we use our new skills then?' asked Ruth.
'Absolutely, but I've one or two things up my sleeve just in case,' he grinned back.
'Like what? You're going to give us machine guns?' laughed Naomi.
'No, I'm thinking of something entirely different. A bit like the way you rely on insurance when all else fails. You just leave it to me. But look, before you go, I brought you all something as a gift.' The girls crowded around as Robbie carried over a large cardboard box he had stashed earlier at the pitch side. He opened it up and handed each of them a bottle of wine.
'Jeepers Robbie! Thanks very much. What's this in aid of?' asked Alison.
'It's a two-sided thing really. I thought you all deserved a treat after getting the shite kicked out of

you in Croker. But more importantly, when you finish the bottle you can use the corks to plug those arseholes.'

Robbie ducked as gloves and water bottles clattered off him.

Tommy looked down on to the pitch from the bar as Robbie trained the girls. A descending mist made it difficult to see them properly. He thought he would have been able to get down before they finished up. He was wrong. The meeting dragged on for ages, mainly because Ray liked the sound of his own voice. There was a short break now but it was going to resume with the main agenda items shortly. 'That was probably a waste of time for you Tommy.' The voice belonged to Mick Murphy, the men's senior's coach. 'Why would you think that?' asked Tommy, his voice friendly yet defiant. There had been some minor club business to attend to at the meeting but the main item on the agenda was the exciting news about the Gaelic Park contingent scouting for teams to take part in the international Gaelic Football tournament in New York. The opportunity for some serious sponsorship was not lost on any of the members. 'Well to be fair,' Mick continued, 'the Yanks are hardly going to come all this way and then decide a bunch of mammies are the best Leinster has to offer are they?'

'Why not?' replied Tommy without looking at his colleague. Mick followed Tommy's gaze and watched as two of the women stopped running at the top of the pitch to pull their knickers out from the crack of their arses. 'Eh, you really need me to explain that comment?'

'I don't see any reason why we wouldn't be in the

running as much as anyone.' Tommy was determined not to show anything other than complete faith in his ladies.

'You're a funny man, that's for sure.' Mick laughed as he went to join Ray on the other side of the room as the meeting was about to recommence. For all his bravado, Tommy knew there was more chance of him becoming the next Dublin team manager than his lot being selected to go to New York. Still, wouldn't it be fantastic he thought. If only to see the look on Ray O'Toole's face.

Chapter Twenty Seven

'Howya. It's Anto out at the depot.'

'Yeah? What's the story?'

'I think your lad fucked up.' Anto whispered urgently into the phone. 'Why?' Hawk reached out to turn down the stereo. An act that proved the man on the phone had Hawk's full attention. 'A van arrived from Smyth's Toys this morning to collect a couple of pallets of gear. Only the pallets were empty.'

'So Robbie helped himself to some clobber.' Hawk relaxed a little. 'He's an enterprising fella. Although he'll get a hiding for lumping it in on my job.'

'No that's not it. The container number and pallet were the same, only swapped around.' Anto replied.

'Explain.' One word was all Hawk could manage as a nasty realisation started to creep into his mind.

'Your stuff was in container LBD-1701 on a pallet marked BD-TS11. That load is still here. It looks like your lad took stuff from a container marked BD-TS11 and a pallet market LBD-1701. He mixed them up.' Anto's voice was breathless, like he'd just run a marathon. Nobody liked to give bad news to this man.

'So what you're telling me is the gear I have is not my bleedin gear? What the fuck is it so?'

'Barbie dolls.' Anto replied, glad he wasn't face to face with the man who he knew was very close to self-combustion.

'He left five million in cocaine and he took FUCKING BARBIE DOLLS?' Hawk roared.

Anto held the phone away from his almost ruptured eardrum and prayed that Hawk wouldn't want to shoot the messenger because he had more to tell. After the initial outburst the silence was smothering. If still waters ran deep then Hawk at this moment was a chasm. 'Hawk?'

'Where's the gear now?' The barely controlled voice continued. 'It's still here but ...'Hawk cut across him. 'Disarm the cameras at five tonight and make sure you are still on duty.'

'But I finish at three. Anyway ...'

'You fucking finish when I tell you, got it? And get rid of any other cunts hanging around.' The depot man steeled himself. 'But that's what I've been trying to tell you.'

'What is?'

'There's an inspection this afternoon. It starts at 2pm.'

'What sort of inspection?' Hawk felt his blood turn cold.

'The drug squad. They're bringing in the dogs.' Hawk said nothing. He clenched his teeth as he took this all in. He had five million euro worth of cocaine that he'd got for nothing and it was all about to land right in a copper's lap. The depot would be crawling with customs men getting ready for this inspection. There was no fucking way he could get it out. All Anto could hear was the sound of angry breathing. 'I'm going to kill him.'

'Who?'

'Robbie King. That's who.'

Robbie was at a loose end. The Viking Splash tour operators hadn't seen the funny side when he delivered their vehicle back earlier in the week. They had parted company, but not before he reminded them that he was a criminal with contacts. He knew his parole officer would get on his case eventually but for now he was free. He walked up the side of the canal heading towards the city centre. The plan for the evening had been to cook Kim a nice dinner. He was still in the dog house with her over the Barbie doll incident. When he rang to suggest it to her she hung up on him. She only did that when she was raging. If it was just a normal strop she was throwing she would shout and roar and occasionally give him a smack. This was different, serious even. All vision and no sound was the worst scenario. At least if she was talking he could figure out what she was thinking. He knew she was unhappy with him doing work for Hawk but what could he do? As far as she was concerned Hawk was a bit of a scumbag, a lad from the wrong side of the tracks. Robbie wasn't about to tell her the truth. She'd leave him for sure if she knew he was working for a fella who handled drugs and had people killed. He decided to try a text. She would give in eventually, she always did.

Hi luv, I'm heading 2 town 2 pick up something nice for dinner 2 say sorry. What do you fancy? The reply came back immediately. *Don't bother. I'm staying with my mam tonight.* Fuck. She was really pissed off. *Ah Kim. Don't be like that. I'll sort it.* He hit send as a nagging feeling began to claw at him. She had warned him often enough. Maybe she really was reaching the end of her tether. *I've heard that before Robbie. Now leave me alone. I need time to think.*

Robbie knew texting back would only make her angrier. He tucked his head down against the cold winter wind and strode off towards The Barge on Charlemont Street. It was only half five in the afternoon but he needed a pint. He had some thinking to do himself.   As he rounded the corner onto Charlemont Bridge he bashed straight into a man coming the opposite direction. He also had his head bent towards his chest with a big scarf around his neck to keep out the cold. 'Why don't you look where you're going?' The man spoke gruffly and Robbie noticed he was wall-eyed. Neither eye looked straight ahead; instead they were turned outwards to each side. He couldn't resist. 'Why don't you go where you're looking?' He replied chuckling to himself. The man grumbled a response that Robbie didn't catch. Someone else had spoken first and it distracted him.

'Have you no home to go to?' He looked up. 'Tommy! How's it going?'
'Grand thanks. Are you off into town for a bit of late evening shopping?' he replied.
'Me? No, not unless you know a shop that sells big white flags,' said Robbie, sounding a little glum.
'You've lost me.' Tommy shifted a heavy looking shopping bag from one hand to the other.
'It's Kim man. She's pissed off with me. I was just going for a pint. You don't fancy one do you?'
'It's a bit early isn't it? It's not even six o' clock.'
'Fair enough. I'll see you after I take YOUR training session AGAIN tomorrow night.' Robbie started to walk away, having made his point. 'I didn't say no you flute,' Tommy called after him, but he was already gone. He watched as Robbie crossed the road and entered the pub. 'Grumpy little bollix,' he muttered as he transferred the bag again and followed.
'Make that two,' he called to the barman who was

pulling a pint of Guinness for Robbie when he entered. 'Bad row then was it?' he asked as the two men sat staring as the pint's liquid whirled and spun itself from brown to black. 'I don't have a good feeling about this one,' said Robbie sadly.

'She'll come round, they always do.' Tommy tried to sound like an authority on women, which he certainly was not.

'I dunno. She's gone to her mam's. That's never happened before.' Robbie looked morose. 'Jaysus,' laughed Tommy, trying to lighten his mood, 'your ears will be scalded off you with all the talking they'll be doing about you.'

'I know,' said Robbie, picking up his pint. 'That's what I'm worried about. Her ma would rather she was going out with the Yorkshire Ripper than me. Now she has Kim's undivided attention. She'll be laying it on with a trowel.'

Tommy looked at Robbie's pint compared to his and wondered if there was a hole in his glass. He ordered two more and picked up his own to catch up. 'I only met her the once,' said Tommy between gulps, 'but Kim struck me as a girl who knew her own mind.'

'She is. She's great but she has a very close relationship with her ma. If it wasn't for her we'd be married by now. Maybe even have a young one toddling about.'

Robbie stared into his pint as he spoke. He knew what was happening. He'd forgotten yet again to take his medication. The combination of that and his lack of sleep recently meant he was starting to have one of his downers. It was part of the condition he had. He was either high as a kite or totally depressed, sometimes both within the space of an hour. 'Does your Kim want kids then?' asked Tommy, desperate to lift the mood. There had been so much talk about depression lately and only the other night he'd seen a documentary about suicide. They said if someone was down that talking was the best thing to do.

'Kids? Yeah, eventually like. But she won't even think about that till we're married.'

Tommy looked to the door as a gang of après-work types barrelled in, some cracking looking birds among them, all scantily clad. 'For the love of God,' said Tommy. 'Would you look what they have on. I'd wear more than that getting into the bleedin bath.' Robbie looked towards the source of the noise but turned away disinterested. Tommy persisted. 'So why does her ma hate you so much anyway?'

'That's a long story' he replied.

'Better get another in so,' said Tommy, beckoning the barman over.

'Here, it's my round.' Robbie rooted for his wallet and threw a twenty euro note on the counter. 'Have you to go anywhere later?' he asked.

'No. I've just got to get this yoke into a freezer,' Tommy replied, kicking the heavy plastic bag he'd carried in with his foot.

'Grand so. Because I've a ferocious goo on me for a belly full of pints.'

'Well I've no work tomorrow so I suppose it would only be my Christian duty to keep a miserable scrote like yourself company.' He rubbed his hands together quickly. 'Jaysus, it's been ages since I went on the batter.' 'I'm starting to feel better already,' said Robbie, visibly perking up. 'So go on. You were going to tell me why her ma has it in for you,'

Tommy reminded him.

Over the course of the next few hours Robbie recounted the details of Kim's father. He described how life with him had hardened her mother's attitude. In response Tommy filled him in on the events that led to the premature ending of his playing career. As they got stuck into their seventh pint of the night Robbie's phone rang. The bright look of hope in his eyes turned dark and cold when he saw the caller ID. He answered on the fourth ring. 'How's it going Hawk?' he said trying to sound more sober than he felt.

'It's not Hawk, it's Butch.' A confused look crossed Robbie's face as his garbled brain tried to make sense. He took his pint and stepped over to the front door to talk. 'What's the story?' he asked, mid belch.

'You're going to be the bleedin story pal, all over the fucking newspapers.'

'Stop talking in riddles will ya?' Robbie took a long slurp of his Guinness.

'Hawk got a call earlier to say that you made a bollix of the pick up.'

As Butch spoke Robbie got distracted by the TV that was flashing up the words BREAKING NEWS across the screen. He couldn't hear the anchorman speak but he could read the ticker tape headline that ran across the base of the screen. *Major cocaine find in a Dublin port. Sources estimate the haul to be in excess of €5 million* 'Oh fuck,' Robbie said aloud, realising it was too late for him to sort things now. 'Look bud,' said Hawk's henchman, 'I'm only giving you the heads up because of what you did for Macker.'

What I did for Macker? Robbie was confused. I tied him to a chair, he thought, loosely in fairness, but

Hawk had already secured his legs with masking tape. He'd want to have been in the full of his health to break free, which he wasn't. Either way, he hadn't been seen since so Robbie assumed he was swimming with the fishes. 'Did you hear what I just said?' Butch's voice brought him out of his drunken daydream. 'No, what did you say?' Robbie nodded to Tommy who was gesturing if he wanted another pint. 'Hawk is gunning for you man. I've never seen him so angry.'

'So how come you've got his phone?' asked Robbie. His drunken state was clearly reducing his adrenal function, otherwise he'd have fucked off as far away as he could get. 'Just after the call he got telling him about the drugs raid, he got another one,' said Butch. 'Who from?' replied Robbie, struggling with hiccups. 'A hospital. His ma collapsed. They told him she was on the way out. Some sort of brain clot or some yoke. Anyway, he dropped the phone and ran like fuck out of here. He took the van and I haven't seen him since.'

'So he knows about the mix-up at the depot then?' asked Robbie.

'I'm surprised you didn't hear him scream from there. Seriously man, he's lost it. Do you have anywhere you can go?' Robbie looked at Tommy who was smiling at his pint like a lovesick teenager. 'I don't know,' replied Robbie. 'Maybe.

'Everything all right?' asked Tommy as Robbie sat back down. 'No.' His eyes darted left and right around the room. 'What did she say?'

'She?' replied Robbie, momentarily confused. 'No, that wasn't Kim. I wish it fucking had been.'

'What's going on Robbie?' Tommy pulled his seat

closer. Robbie sighed, took a deep breath and braced himself, having made a decision. 'Remember the bloke who I told you about, Hawk?'

'Yeah.'

'Well I was supposed to do a job for him and I fucked up.' He glanced at the repeating headline flashing across the bottom of the news broadcast.

'Don't tell me you're mixed up in that shite,' said Tommy swallowing a belch.

'Not exactly no.' Robbie couldn't look him in the eye.

'Well you either are or you aren't. It's not bloody rocket science.'

'Look I need a place to kip for a night or so,' Robbie said suddenly. 'Kim as well.'

'Only if you tell me what the fuck you've got yourself mixed up in.' Robbie called the barman over. 'We're going to need another couple of pints.'

Over the next hour Robbie gave Tommy the highlights of his career to date. Colourful as it was and pissed as he was, Tommy could recognise an air of reluctance in Robbie's involvement. It was as if he'd been sucked into a vortex of violence from which he could see no escape. At least not while this Hawk character was still around. 'Is this the life you want?' asked Tommy simply. Robbie looked at him, his eyes pleading with him not to go there. 'Come on, tell me Robbie. Is this the future for you? For Kim? Marching to whatever drumbeat this Hawk fella decides.' Robbie slammed his pint down.

'It's not fucking easy okay?'

'Sure it is,' replied Tommy, refusing to be deterred. 'Walk the hell away.'

'It's a bit hard to walk away without your kneecaps.'

'Well, what are you going to do then?' Robbie took a gulp of his pint and looked pensive for a few moments. 'Apparently his ma is after being rushed to the hospital. She's supposed to be on death's door. He's very close to her. If I know Hawk he won't surface till she's sorted or dead. Then I'm in deep shit.'

'I take it this nut job knows where you live?' said Tommy. Robbie nodded. His head was heavy from the drink. 'I don't care about myself, just Kim.'

'Do you think he'd go after her?' asked Tommy in disbelief.

'There's nowhere that sick fuck wouldn't go to get revenge. He's not a fella who likes to be crossed.'

'Can you ring Kim and tell her not to go home?'

'What if she doesn't take my call?'

'She needs to be warned, just in case.'

'Ok, I'll try.' Robbie tapped her name on his phone's contact list and waited. Nothing. 'She's not answering.'

'Send her a text, just to be sure.' Robbie tapped in a message and hit send, the reply was immediate. 'What did you say?' asked Tommy.

'I told her I wouldn't be home because I was doing a job for Hawk. I knew that would get a response. She just text me back and told me to sleep with him tonight because she wasn't coming home any time soon.' Tommy lifted his glass towards Robbie who did the same and they clinked. 'Result,' said Tommy. 'Right then,' he added, slapping the counter. 'After all this stress I say we head back to mine with a few cans.'

'Jaysus I'm plastered already,' said Robbie, his words beginning to slur. Tommy stood up. 'Look at us. A right pair of piss heads and we're supposed to be giving those women on the team a good example.' Robbie looked at him in disbelief. 'Don't try to let on those lot don't do a swan dive into a bottle of wine a few nights a week. Who are you trying to kid? You know in the sixties they used to call Valium "Mommie's little helper"?' 'Yeah,' slurred Tommy. 'Well now the little helper has a new name. It's called Jacob's Creek.'

'Is that what Kim drinks?' asked Tommy. He held up one hand to his eye as he spoke to help his focus. 'She's a demon for the stuff. Only at the weekends mind. I'm always slagging her that she loves the glug glug sound of wine being poured from a newly opened bottle. One time I recorded it on my phone and played it back on a Saturday morning when she was fast asleep. She shot up in the bed and started licking her lips.'

'I better get some in to my place for when she comes to stay so,' replied Tommy standing up and throwing his arm around Robbie's shoulder. 'I'll just go siphon the Guinness and I'll meet you outside.'

Tommy went to the toilets and Robbie walked towards the door. 'Sir, your bag.' A waitress shouted after him. He went back and leaned down to pick up the plastic bag. 'Jaysus the weight of it.' He carried it outside and waited a few minutes before Tommy turned up. 'What's in the bag, a dead body?' he asked.

'Jaysus I forgot it.' Tommy turned to go back inside, not noticing the bag at Robbie's feet. 'It's cool man. One of the lounge lizards reminded me it was there. So spill, what's in it that's so heavy and has to go into the freezer? Is it that tool fella from the club?'

Tommy laughed as they stumbled across the road. 'It's my Christmas dinner.' He reached into the bag and pulled out the long neck and head of a very large, very dead looking bird.

'You're very bleedin eager aren't you? Christmas is a good bit away yet.'

'I know but I did a favour for a bloke and he gave it to me. He hasn't a cent the poor lad and he was too proud to accept charity so I ended up with Goosey Goosey Gander here.' Robbie started laughing. 'What the fuck are you going to do with it? It still has its feathers on for Jaysus sake.'

'I'll stick it in the freezer till I think of something. Maybe one of the team would know what to do with it. A few of them are muck savages from the country. They're bound to have plucked a few birds in their day.' Tommy stopped suddenly, realising what he'd said. 'That's not easy to say when you're pissed,' he laughed. He swapped the bag over to his other hand.

'Here,' said Robbie while lighting a smoke. 'I'll give you a hand.' He grabbed one of the handles of the light plastic bag that was straining under the weight of its contents. The rain came in horizontal waves as they stumbled down the road. The canal was full from weeks of wet weather. 'Does it ever bloody stop?' asked Tommy. 'If it doesn't stop soon some bloke called Noah will sail down Grafton Street and start kidnapping two of everything,' replied Robbie. 'He'd better not go over the north side or the fuckers will rob his Sat Nav.'

The pair ambled down the road swinging the bag back and forth as they walked and made small talk about the upcoming blitz. The booze had dimmed the sense of fear Robbie should have been feeling. As the bag swung forward the bottom gave way and the goose came shooting out and skidded into the middle of the road. 'Fuck,' shouted Robbie. A taxi swerved to avoid the feathered mass but clipped its beak and sprayed them with a large puddle of water in the process. Both men ran to the middle of the road to grab the goose. As they neared it Robbie stuck his foot in a pothole and fell face first on top of the bird and proceeded to break his shite laughing. Tommy was useless. He stumbled around the avian love scene clutching his stomach which hurt from his own laughter. The lights at the junction on the bridge changed from red to green and cars started to approach. Car horns blasted as one after another they swerved violently to avoid them. Tommy, in a useless attempt at traffic direction stood behind Robbie waving his arms about. Robbie, for his part, remained mounted on the bird holding its head in his hand. He seemed to be having a one-sided conversation with it while he tried to get the cigarette into its beak. The sound of a police siren got Tommy's attention. He waved at them while grinning stupidly and continued directing the traffic which he didn't realise had actually stopped. Two very unimpressed guards got out of the car, leaving the blue lights flashing. They approached the prostrate man and bird on the tarmac.

'Do you want to tell us what is going on?' one of them asked. Tommy walked left and right and occasionally straight in an attempt to join them. 'How are yis ossifers?' he slurred.

'It's Garda.' The younger of the two said.

'Sorry ...' belch 'Guard,' replied Tommy swaying like a sapling in a gale.

'There's been an accident,' said Robbie from the ground.

'Have you been hit?' asked the older man in uniform.

'Not today,' replied Robbie, chuckling.

'Sir, have you been the victim of a road accident?' The younger Guard was getting impatient.

'I think his goose is cooked,' Tommy snorted while he gripped onto the Guard to balance.

'Hey c'mere,' said Robbie lifting up the head of the goose and holding its tyre-marked beak up to the man. 'I know this is role reversal 'n' all like Guard, but would you mind blowing into this?'

Both Tommy and Robbie buckled up in laughter as the Guards grabbed each of them by the arm and guided them and the goose off the road. The traffic began to flow once again as the two of them received a strict telling off on the footpath.

Pissed and all, Robbie realised he was lucky this pair were obviously new to the area and they hadn't a clue who he was.

Chapter Twenty Eight

The sound of a drum beating woke Robbie early the next morning. He peeled his tongue down from the roof of his mouth and tried to create some saliva. It was useless. Any moisture in his body had been replaced by pure alcohol. It took a few moments to realise that the sound he thought was a drumbeat was actually his head pounding. Jaysus he felt as rough as a hedgehog's hole. It even hurt to blink. He looked around the room. The walls were covered in floral printed wallpaper. The curtains were blue and cream stripes that clashed beautifully with the walls. The furniture was ancient. As for the bed—Robbie had never actually slept in a bed with *blankets* before. At least not that he could remember. The only modern thing about the room was the floor. It had been heavily varnished and there was a bright red rug thrown on it just next to the bed. He didn't remember coming here in a time machine, but he must have. Pushing back the covers he pulled himself up to a sitting position. It made the pain even worse.

'My fucking head.' He cradled his face in his hands as he spoke. The mobile phone was on the locker beside him. Checking the screen he wasn't surprised to see it was blank. The time on the phone read 8.45 a.m. Kim would be in work by now. He dialled the number. 'Hello, Marketing Department. Kim speaking.' Relief flooded through him. She was safe. That's all that mattered. 'Hello?'

'Kim, it's me. Don't hang up, please.'

'I'm not interested Robbie.'

'Look I promise you. Once this is all sorted I won't

have any more to do with Hawk.'

'I heard it all before,' she hissed in a whisper. 'Keep it for someone who believes your shite. I've had enough. My mam was right all along. I should've listened to her years ago.'

'No you're wrong Kim. This time is different.'

'How?'

'I can't explain it. Just trust me.' Robbie pleaded.

'I'd trust a pit bull quicker.'

'Did you go back to the flat?' asked Robbie.

'No, why?' Her voice was suspicious now. Living with him this long had taught her a thing or two.

'Don't go back there tonight. Come and stay with me. I want you to be safe.'

'Robbie, what's going on?'

'Nothing. I just need to stay away from the flat for a couple of days.'

'You're frightening me now. Tell me what's going on or I'll end this right now, I swear.'

There was no point trying to pretend any longer. This relationship with Hawk was coming to a head and considering how it might turn out, she deserved to know the truth. Sort of. 'You were right about Hawk, Kim,' he said trying to sound contrite.

'No shit Sherlock,' she replied sarcastically.

'He wanted me to move some drugs for him. I didn't and they got lifted by the cops. It cost him five million so he's a bit pissed off.'

'DRUGS! Jesus Robbie.'

'Kim, listen to me. I didn't do it.' That bit was true at least. She didn't need the finer details, especially when this version made him out to be as innocent as a choir boy.

'The thing is, Hawk isn't used to people saying no to

him. He's out for revenge and that means he could go after you to get to me.'

'Oh Christ Robbie. What have you got yourself into?'

'It's nothing. I swear to you Kim I didn't do it. He's just a headcase. I should've listened to you. You always said he wasn't right.'

Kim sighed. 'What will he do if he catches up with you?'

'He won't.'

'How can you be so sure?'

'He doesn't know where I am staying,' replied Robbie.

'Where are you staying by the way?' she asked.

'With Tommy.'

'Tommy?'

'Yeah, remember the bloke you met at the flat? From the Gaelic football team?' he reminded her.

'Oh that's the guy who brought you your wallet after you got kicked in the face by that woman ... '. Her voice trailed off on the last word as she put two and two together. Robbie knew what was coming. 'It wasn't a woman who did that was it?' Even though he knew it was a rhetorical question, he answered it anyway. 'No it wasn't.' 'So what did you do to annoy Hawk that time?' she asked. 'I didn't answer the phone when he rang.' Robbie said quietly. 'He nearly blinded you for not answering his call? What do you think he'll do for costing him five million? Jesus Christ.'

He could almost hear the tears fall as she sniffed. He didn't need to answer the question. They had both grown up around enough violence to know how something like this was dealt with. 'You'll have to go to Sheila in New York, you have to get away.'

'No Kim, I have to sort this once and for all. Whatever that means.'

'I'm coming home. I can't work in this state.' She whispered through her tears.

'Did you not hear me? You can't go to the flat.' Robbie insisted. 'No way.'

'Fine. Well give me Tommy's address. I'll come straight there.' Robbie blew out a sigh of relief and told her where to go. The pain in his head reminded him of his hangover and he remembered how he usually dealt with them.

'Do us a favour will you luv? Stop in the Spar and get us the makings of a full Irish breakfast. I've a fierce goo on me for rashers and sausages.' Death threats from a bat wielding, gun toting homicidal maniac were all very well, but a goo was a goo.

Pulling on his jeans he wandered out onto the landing to see where Tommy was. A sound unlike anything Robbie had ever heard came from a bedroom just across from him. He walked over, fully expecting to see a walrus being buggered up the arse by Moby Dick. Tommy lay diagonally across the bed. His arms and legs fully outstretched like Leonardo Da Vinci's Vitruvian Man. His mouth was wide open and the telltale white mark of dried drool snaked down from the left corner of his mouth to his neck. It looked like a snail had wandered across his face. Had there not been a roof on the house he would've been forgiven for thinking Tommy had fallen from a passing airliner. Robbie coughed and the noise came to an abrupt halt as he woke with a snort and looked around. 'Kim's going to bring stuff to make breakfast,' Robbie said, opening the curtains. 'What?' Tommy sat up in the bed and rubbed his eyes.

'I spoke to her just now, explained what was going on so I did. I couldn't take a chance that she might go back to the flat.'

'Oh grand so,' replied Tommy, slowly remembering the conversation of the night before. 'Go on down to the kitchen and help yourself. I'll be down in a few minutes.'

Robbie closed the door. The rest of the house was as dated as the bedroom had been. There was even a dado rail running down the wall diagonally from the top to the bottom of the stairs. The wallpaper on the top was some sort of white embossed flowery pattern and the one beneath the divider was another striped blue and white creation. Must have been a job lot, thought Robbie. There was a statue of the Virgin Mary on the hall table and a dried out receptacle for holy water hanging from the wall above it. Tommy had thrown his keys into it the night before. Robbie looked around the kitchen and found the kettle which he filled and switched on. There were a couple of pictures of some sort of sea birds on the wall and a team photo from the nineties. He rummaged around and found teabags and a couple of mugs. He made them both tea and went to take a closer look at the pictures. 'Grebes, they're small diving birds,' Tommy said from behind him.

'That's the best type of bird alright. One that likes to go down.' Robbie replied with a wink. Tommy shook his head and pulled a packet of porridge oats from the press. 'Want some?' he asked as he started to measure them out.

'No way man. That stuff will kill you. I'll wait for Kim to bring the proper grub. I'm going for a smoke outside, be back in a minute.'

Tommy cleared away the evidence of their late night drinking. He laughed as he looked at the freezer door and the half wing that was protruding out the bottom on it. He opened the door and stuck the broken wing back with the rest of the goose. Opening the fridge he took out all the ingredients he needed to prepare his food. A short time later he had just finished his bowl of porridge and fruit when the doorbell went. Robbie was at the end of the garden on what Tommy figured was his third cigarette. Any other time he'd have lectured him about how he was shortening his life. Given the circumstances he didn't feel it was appropriate. Even though he knew there was no way Hawk would know Robbie was at the house, he went into the living room and looked out the window to see who was at the front door. Satisfied everything was OK he walked out to open it. 'Kim, good to see you again. Come on in. Robbie's just out having a cigarette or three.'

'I wish he'd give them up before they kill hi ...' She stopped mid-sentence.

'It will be alright, you'll see.' Tommy spoke gently and caught her hand to reassure her. 'I wish I had your confidence,' she replied sadly while following him into the kitchen. 'Take a seat Kim,' said Tommy gently. 'You look wiped out. I'll make you a cuppa.' Kim sat down and noting the dishes, asked, 'Has he already had breakfast? Only he told me to bring stuff for a full Irish.'

'What? Oh sorry about that. I should have tidied it away. No, he's hanging on for that.' He pointed at the bag full of sausages, rashers and eggs that Kim had placed on the table. 'I'll turn on the cooker for you and give him a shout once you've had your tea.'

A few minutes later Kim sipped the warm sweet drink. 'Do you think Hawk will come after us Tommy?' she asked fearfully.

'Robbie will sort it out Kim. He knows it's got out of hand now you're involved. I just don't understand why he's mixed up with that type in the first place,' said Tommy.

'That fella Hawk took advantage of Robbie when his ma died. Everyone on the estate knew it was Robbie rearing his younger sister Sheila. Did he ever tell you about her?' Tommy shook his head. 'He rarely talks about her. He ran all sorts of errands for that tosser Hawk so he could earn enough money to send her away. He wanted her to start afresh, to leave the estate and their shitty father behind. Nobody ever knew why his da hated his own flesh and blood so much. It was like he was jealous of them or something. Thank God Robbie doesn't take after him. He's more like his ma. He has a good heart, he just gets easily distracted. If he could just get away from Hawk and his kind I know he could make something of himself.'

'He will,' replied Tommy with more confidence than he actually felt. Kim finished her tea and started to cook the fry up. Robbie spotted her through the glass and came in from outside. He saw her stiffen immediately. Tommy excused himself saying he was going for a shower. Even as he walked towards her Robbie didn't know what he was going to say. All he wanted was to hold her, to know that she was safe. As soon as he laid his hand on her she crumbled. He turned her around to face him. Her tears broke his heart. He had done this to her. She didn't deserve any of this. Kim worked hard and was well respected in her industry. She always said he could have had a very good job now too if only he had stayed in school and got a degree. But no, Robbie King knew it all. He thought he could do a few nixers for Hawk and fellas like him. Just to earn a few quid like, as he put it. It didn't work out quite as he had planned. Now here he was in a gaff that wasn't his, hiding himself and his mot from a psycho who wouldn't think twice about offing either one of them.

'Kim, when this is over I'm going to go back and do my leaving cert and go to college.'

'Don't Robbie. You know that's not going to happen.'

'I'm telling you, it is. This has all gone too far. I can't have you at risk. It's killing me.' Kim thought of something suddenly. 'Will my mam be safe? Could he go after her?' she asked while horrible scenarios flew through her mind. Robbie didn't think of that. Jaysus, maybe there was an upside to fucking up a multimillion euro drugs haul of an unhinged maniac. He decided not to share his thoughts with her. 'It's me he's after. Your ma won't be in any danger,' he reassured her.

'So what happens next?' Kim wiped away tears and busied herself with the cooking.

'Well if I'm lucky the drug squad will lean on the fella in the customs depot and maybe Hawk's man will crack and drop him in it.'

'Is that likely?' she asked, knowing only too well how good these criminals were at keeping secrets. 'It's the best I can hope for,' he replied. 'Anyway, I have to train the team tonight for Tommy.'

'No you don't.' Tommy spoke from the kitchen door.

Robbie turned to look at him, confused. 'But you have that funeral in Cork.'

'I got someone else to go in my place,' he replied. 'So I'll take the training session tonight. You two have a lot of talking to do and things to sort out.' He handed two plates to Kim as he spoke. 'Are you not having some yourself?' she asked.

'No thanks. My arteries are hardening just looking at that. Enjoy your breakfast. I've to go out to do a few things so make yourselves at home. I'm meeting up with Naomi at lunch time to bring her little one to the playground so I probably won't be back till after training tonight.'

'Oh,' said Kim, grabbing her car keys. 'I have those jerseys in the car Robbie. They came in the other day but I forgot about them, what with the Barbie landslide and everything.'

She ran out to the car and returned with two bundles wrapped in brown paper. She placed them on the kitchen table. 'It was so good of your company to sponsor us Kim,' said Tommy as he began to open the packaging. 'The miserable git in charge of football at the club would expect them to play in their kacks.'

'Jaysus Tommy, go easy. I'm eating here,' said Robbie with his mouth full.

'Robbie King, did your mother not tell you never to masticate in full view of everyone?' Kim scolded, firmly back in her matriarchal role.

'Sure she did,' he replied with a wink to Tommy. 'She used to send me to my room with a jumbo box of Kleenex.' He ducked too late just as the expected slap on the back of the head hit home. Tommy burst out laughing but it wasn't at the smutty comment. He held up one of the jerseys for Robbie to see.   'I thought you'd like them,' Kim said smiling. 'The brand manager thought it was the best fit he'd seen in years.' She looked towards the jersey which Tommy held aloft. It read,

Sponsored by DUREX – Gaelic for Mothers who don't want others!

'They're going to kill you,' whimpered Robbie when he was finally able to catch his breath long enough to speak.
'Relax. They'll see the funny side of it,' Tommy said with a smirk.
'Advertising rubber johnnies? Oh yeah, they'll love that,' laughed Robbie going back to his breakfast.

Chapter Twenty Nine

The ever decreasing beep on the heart machine turned to a flat line as a shattering wail pierced the quiet hospital room. 'I'm sorry.' The nurse said simply as she removed the adhesive pads from the woman's chest. This man had literally not left his mother's side since she had been admitted. He barely ate and had to be coaxed to let go of her hand whenever the medical staff had to check her vitals. He had spent the last two days whispering to her comatose body in the bed. The nursing staff had all been talking about him during their breaks. He was attractive enough, depending on your taste. It was his eyes though. Piercing. They had all heard him speak to his mother about how he would make her a grandmother if she would only open her eyes. He had pleaded with the consultant to make her come around. The frustration of the situation was unbearable for him as he appeared to be a man that was used to getting his own way.

On the first night she had been admitted, the nursing staff in the A&E thought they would need security when he had started to shout at them to fix her. It was an American junior doctor that finally managed to calm him down long enough to explain the situation. His mother had suffered a severe bleed on the brain. There was no hope of recovery and it was now time to tell her anything he felt he needed to say. Maybe it was the shock of the American's bluntness or just a delayed understanding, but after that he just sat with her while he stroked her hand and whispered in her ear.

'Sir?' A middle aged woman entered the

room.   Hawk looked up with wet eyes. He didn't know how much time had passed, still he didn't say a word.   'I'm so sorry for your loss.' The woman said pulling up a seat beside him. He just nodded.

'I'm sorry to have to bother you at such a difficult time but there are some details to be discussed. Did your mother express any particular wishes for when this time came?' she asked in the practised gentle manner of those used to dealing with families after a death.   'We will need to move your mother to the mortuary,' she continued when she got no response. 'If you had any particular funeral directors in mind I would be happy to look after the initial arrangements for you.'

'She always liked that cemetery up the mountains. Didn't you Ma?' He directed the words at the figure in the bed. 'Said it would have a nice view. Isn't that right?' His shoulders shook as he bent his head forward and leaned it on his mother's chest.

'You don't have any siblings or other relatives that you could call?' asked the woman.

'Not a soul.' Hawk replied. Then, as if controlled by an outside force, he stood up suddenly and walked towards the door. 'Contact Murray's Funeral Home in Perryville. Tell them Hawk wants this sorted. They'll take it from there.'

The family liaison woman was shocked by the sudden change in the man. She scribbled his instructions down. Hawk? What kind of name was that? She wrote MR in front of it. Still strange she thought as she followed him out the door. She watched as he strode purposefully away. His mother was dead. His cocaine had been seized and one person was going to bear the brunt of it all. He had nothing else to think about for the last few days as he sat with his mother. He knew she was fucked from what the doctor told him but he still told her all about how he was going to get Robbie and make him pay for making a fool out of him. From the time he was a toddler his mother had always taught him to show people not to mess with him. She had been so proud of him when he punched the neighbour's first two adult teeth out shortly after they had grown. That taught the seven year old a lesson that everyone got to learn over time. You don't fuck with the Hawk. Robbie King should have learned his lesson the last time he got the hiding for ignoring the phone call. Obviously he had gone too easy on him. Hawk didn't normally give people a second chance. He had with Robbie and look how that turned out. There was only one way to make sure he wouldn't get a third.

Chapter Thirty

'She's a grand little kid, your Shona.' Tommy looked at the six year old running around the playground after a girl of similar size. 'Isn't she great the way she makes friends so easily? She must get that from you,' he continued, giving Naomi a nudge.

'I can't argue with you on that,' she replied. 'Her creation was one of those moments of madness we all have in our past.' She looked at him and grinned. 'Well those of us who didn't grow up addicted to a sport anyway.'

'I think we can both agree I had a fairly big moment of my own,' he reminded her, thinking back to his attack on the referee.

'I'll give you that I suppose,' she conceded. 'So you never had any further contact with her Dad then? Was he not interested at all?' asked Tommy cautiously. He felt sure Naomi would put him straight if she didn't want to discuss Shona's parentage.

'Not interested? The prick wasn't even there when I came back from the toilet after the shag.'

'Classy bloke,' Tommy said nodding his head. 'Look. I'm not ashamed. I had a ride with a bloke I met at a party. It was a one night stand and I got pregnant. I'm not the first or the last that has happened to. I have a beautiful daughter and I wouldn't change it for the world.'

'I know. But I just think it's unfair, that's all,' ventured Tommy.

'What? That she doesn't know her dad? She's managed fine without one and anyway, I'm not too sure I'd recognise him myself. I never even got his real name.'

'No I didn't mean her having a relationship with him. I meant him financially supporting you. Kid's aren't cheap to rear as far as I can see.'

'Oh we manage, just. Actually that reminds me. I'm not going to make the blitz tomorrow.' Naomi scrunched up her face as she told him the bad news. She was well aware she was a key member of the team, being as fast as she was.

'Ah Jesus, don't tell me that. Why can't you come?' he asked.

'My mam is sick and she was going to mind Shona for me. I can't afford a babysitter, not for the whole day like that.' 'I'll give you the money,' said Tommy, taking out his wallet. 'How much do you need?'

Naomi held her hand up to stop him. 'I'm not taking your money Tommy but I do appreciate the offer.' He put his wallet away. He had gotten to know her well enough to know that when she said no she meant it. 'Can't you bring her to the blitz and stuff her full of crisps and coke like all the other parents?' He was only half serious. She laughed. 'Seriously Tommy, I do *want* to play. I just don't have anyone who could take her.'

Naomi stood up and jogged over to Shona who had just bumped her head on the slide. Tommy had a brainwave and quickly took out his mobile phone and sent a text to Robbie. The reply came back just as Naomi sat back down. Tommy smiled. 'Cinderella will go to the ball after all,' he said. 'Have you been sniffing glue?' she asked in bewilderment. 'No. But I got you a sitter for tomorrow,' he beamed. She just looked at him. 'Do you want to tell me who?' Tommy explained about Kim and Robbie staying for a few days. He neglected to mention the real reason, suggesting instead that there was a problem with their flat. 'Anyway, Kim thought it would be a good idea to get to know Shona today so she suggested we all meet back at mine and order pizza for tea. Then you can go to training and stay over and go to the match first thing in the morning.' 'Did someone say pizza?' asked Shona excitedly as she bounded over. 'My favourite. Yay!!!' 'Are you sure about this Tommy? Do you have enough room for everyone?' asked Naomi. 'It sounds like you've opened a guest house overnight.'

'It's not a problem. That old house used to be full of people. It will do it good,' he replied.

'OK so,' Naomi answered, giving her daughter a tight squeeze. 'We better go and pack an overnight bag.' Tommy held up his hand to Shona for a high five which she walloped with gusto.

Chapter Thirty One

There was no answer from the phone. It was hardly surprising. The little bollix would know by now that he was on to him. It had been all over the news for the last two days. The Garda Commissioner nearly pissed himself with the excitement. It wasn't every day they got to claim victory over the criminal underworld. Hawk stood outside Robbie's apartment block looking up at the second floor. It was in darkness. He wasn't exactly sure which number Robbie's flat was and the name King didn't appear on any of the bells. He wasn't sure what the mot's last name was. He checked his watch, 8.30 p.m. He could be out with his bird, thought Hawk. But that wasn't likely, not when he knew there would be a price on his head. Robbie was a lot of things but you could never accuse him of being stupid. Not like most of the fellas he'd used over the years. People like Macker, who you could be forgiven for thinking had been lobotomised. Thinking about that double-crossing prick made him even angrier. He had paid the ultimate price.

The door to the complex opened and Hawk saw his chance. He ran over just as the young woman came out. He beamed at her. She looked up initially and then did a double take. It was hard not to be hypnotised by those strange eyes. 'Sorry there gorgeous. Did I give you a fright? Only I forgot the main door key.' He dangled a small key ring as he spoke. The woman blushed and fumbled over her words. 'Oh, it's fine. Did you just move in?' she asked, fluffing up her hair self-consciously. 'Yeah, recently enough. I'm just after splitting up with the girlfriend so I moved in with my mates Robbie and Kim. Do you know them?'

'Oh yeah. They're in 2B. My mam and me live just above them. I don't see Robbie too much but Kim's a dote. Awful good to my mam she is. She's stuck in the house most of the time you see. She has Parkinson's disease so it's hard to get her in and out now it's got bad.'

'Sorry to hear that,' said Hawk. He was anxious to get on with things and wasn't remotely interested in the babbling woman. 'Listen, I've got to go now to get ready for work but maybe I'll see you around?' He gave her a sexy smile and walked into the lobby. The young woman walked away chuffed to bits. She was only going down to the Chinese to order a take away for tea and she'd ended up on a promise with a fine thing. Not bad for a quiet Friday evening.

Once he'd dispatched the ditzy blonde he took the stairs two at a time. The smell of the girl's poxy fake tan hung in the air. Why the fuck did Irish young ones have to make themselves look like bleedin Oompa-Loompas? It was rotten stuff and then when you got your end away with them they got up and left the sheets looking like the fucking shroud of Turin. Dirty skanks. He checked the doors as he entered the second floor. It was his lucky night. 2B was at the end of the hall in a little alcove. He slipped a miniature crowbar from his jacket and broke the lock open within seconds. The flat was quiet. Where was that bastard Robbie? Turning on the lights he rummaged through paperwork that was lying on the hall table. He entered the living room and flicked on the light switch. A sheet of paper jutting out from beneath the couch caught his eye. He yanked it out. SMYTHS

TOYS – DELIVERY NOTE – 10,000 Barbie Dolls. The rush of adrenalin that surged through him would have caused a heart attack in any other man. 'HE FUCKING KNEW?' Hawk roared out to the empty room. 'That fucking cunt knew he'd taken the wrong stuff and he said NOTHING!'

The realisation that Robbie could have warned him and given them enough time to move the cocaine haul drove the rage deeper within him until Hawk decided what to do. He would take everything, one piece at a time, starting with Kim, Robbie's precious fiancée. Good looking sort she was too. Hawk felt a familiar stirring in his boxers. He could kill two birds with one stone. He would enjoy breaking Robbie's arms and legs with a sledgehammer. Imagine how he was going to feel, sitting a few feet away tied to a chair, watching Hawk rape his woman. Maybe she'd even enjoy it, which really would be a bonus. She was a feisty bitch though so she'd probably try to fight him off. Nothing a few thumps to the head wouldn't sort out. Hawk sauntered into the bedroom and pulled out a few drawers letting the contents fall to the floor. She liked her fancy lingerie did Robbie's bird. Maybe he'd bring some along and make her dress up for him before he banged her. He took out a smoke and sat on the bed. Pulling out his lighter he flicked it open and held the flame to the cigarette. Then he had an idea. He smiled to himself as he thumbed through some bits of paper on the bed side locker. When he came across the sheet from the parole officer he started to laugh. Could this get any easier?

Community service: Duration 3 months. Report to Iona Gaels Gaelic Football Club. Contact: Tommy Boylan. Fridays 9.00 p.m.

'Lovely,' said Hawk. He finished his smoke and stubbed it out on the white cotton pillow. He held up his wrist and checked the time. 8.58 p.m. If he left now he would arrive right in the middle of training. There was just one thing left to do. He flicked open his lighter again and held it to the sheet of paper and watched it ignite. He dropped the paper into the centre of the bed and threw all the pages and paper he could find on top of his makeshift fire. He rubbed his hands together as it quickly took hold. Then he turned and walked out of the flat as an inferno grew behind him.

Chapter Thirty Two

'You have GOT to be kidding.' Ruth stood panting with her hands on her hips and stared at Tommy. He was holding up one of the jerseys to show the team, having already listened to roars of laughter from Naomi when he showed them to her earlier. 'If you run quick enough after the ball no one will have time to read it.' He said with a grin.

'Nice try Tommy,' said Ruth looking unconvinced. 'We'll be the laughing stock of the blitz.'

'No you won't. I promise you. Anyway, it will be all over before you know it.'

'Easy knowing that little shite Robbie had a hand in organising these,' said Alison as she searched for an XXL. Not finding one she picked up an XL out of the packet and tried it on. 'Just as well he's not here tonight or I'd break his neck. Where is he anyway? Not as brave as he lets on is he?'

'I gave him the night off,' Tommy called over. 'By the way, I told him not to get the XXL because I reckoned we no longer have anyone who needs it.' He winked at Alison who although still a big lass, had noticeably lost weight. 'I better start feeding myself up,' she replied, trying to look more blasé than chuffed. 'Have to make sure Robbie has something to grab hold of!' Alison wiggled her body suggestively which made Tommy laugh. 'Don't you start frightening that poor bloke again. He'll never come back if you crowd of wagons keep ganging up on him.'

'Don't mind him,' shouted Naomi as she ran to the side of the pitch to retrieve a stray ball. 'Robbie and his girlfriend are minding my six year old in Tommy's house. He's coming to the blitz tomorrow while Kim minds my Shona. If it wasn't for that I wouldn't have been able to go.'

The man in the black jeans and black leather bomber jacket stood in the shadows near the pitch. He had heard one of the fat women call the coach 'Tommy' earlier. So Robbie was in hiding was he? Hawk positioned himself behind a large pole and stared at the youngest looking player on the pitch. He never forgot a face and especially one like that. She was a lippy one when he met her at that party he'd gate-crashed. He remembered exactly when it was because it was the night he got stabbed in the thigh by a junkie near the warehouse. It was only a surface wound really. The bloke had been too out of it to hold the knife properly. Still, that hadn't stopped Hawk nearly killing him before he went and got stitches. He nearly burst them when he got his hole off yer one later that night. He remembered she had some barny with her fella and told the bloke to fuck off home. Then she had flirted her arse off with anyone who looked in her direction. She was a good little ride too from what he remembered. That was nearly seven years ago. She told the women that Robbie was minding her six year old? That meant she would have either been up the pole when he was with her or shortly afterwards. Jaysus, maybe he was the bleedin father. It was a long shot but certainly possible. The thought made him think of his ma. That had always been her biggest wish, to be made a granny. Wouldn't it be fucking typical if he turned out to have a kid after all now she was dead?

The group moved up to one end of the pitch to

practise goal kicks. Hawk slipped away unnoticed and quietly got into the van. He lit up a smoke and waited for the training to finish. This Tommy bloke was going to lead him straight to Robbie. He had to figure out a way to get Robbie on his own. It would be too risky to go in after him if there were a load of others in the house. Any one of them could call for help. He needed to draw him out. An evil sneer crossed his face as he thought of just the way to do it.

The training finished and one by one the women all left. He had overheard the chatter of excitement about some tournament the following day. He hadn't been able to catch where it was on though. It wasn't important. All that mattered was that Kim was going to be on her own with this Naomi one's kid. She and the coach seemed to have something going on between them. He hung back as they put away the last of the equipment and climbed into a car together. They pulled out into the avenue and Hawk followed at a discreet distance. The couple seemed engrossed in an animated conversation. He doubted either one of them would even remotely notice him. After fifteen minutes driving, Tommy's indicator flashed on and off as he slowed down and turned left into the driveway of a modest house. Hawk drove straight past, not even looking in their direction. He pulled over further down the road and turned the van around to study the lay of the land. The house next to Tommy's seemed empty with a large battered looking FOR SALE sign outside. On the opposite side of the road another house had a TO LET sign. It too appeared unoccupied judging by the grass growing out of random cracks in the driveway. Hawk lit another smoke and decided to get out for a closer look at Robbie's refuge. He pulled the lever to open the van's driver door. Nothing happened. Fucking thing, he thought. Butch was supposed to get it sorted. He rattled the lever in its casing for a few seconds and tried again. No change. He clambered over the centre console and cursed Butch when he nearly got buggered up the hole by the handbrake. He tried the passenger door and the same thing happened. 'FOR FUCK'S SAKE,' he growled, almost ripping the lever off in temper. As though fearing his wrath, the door clicked and finally he was free. He closed it quietly behind him and slipped down the street, keeping to the shadows.

The garden of the coach's house was pretty overgrown. Leylandii and holly bushes fought for space down the right hand side. Ignoring the thorns, Hawk pressed through until he was satisfied he was completely unseen from either the road or the house. He stood in his hide and observed the activities in the lit up house. He saw the girl called Naomi. She was definitely the one he remembered. She was chatting to someone and seemed to be laughing but her body was blocking his view. Then she stepped away and Hawk saw who it was. Robbie. Every muscle fibre twitched as he struggled to hold himself back. He could have walked through a brick wall, his anger was so intense right at that moment. Looking on he saw the object of this hatred gesticulating wildly and laughing. It looked like he was recounting a story and when he finished they all laughed. 'Very fucking funny,' Hawk snarled. 'Now tell them the one about the bloke who's going to get to watch as I use this on his pretty fiancée's face as I bang her brains out.' In his hand he held a hunting knife, its six inch blade extended. He touched the point with his tongue and ran it along the shaft. Then he looked towards Kim who was laughing at Robbie's story. He vaguely remembered her as a snooty young one on the Salmon Leap Estate. She threw her head back exposing her throat. Hawk stared at it. He would slice it open just enough to let her bleed to death slowly as Robbie looked into her fading eyes, powerless to help her.

Tommy sat on the couch and looked around him. It felt like the house was back to its old self again with the sound of chatting and people laughing. It reminded him, and not for the first time, how much he missed the old days. He would be off playing a match somewhere and depending on how important a game it was, he would often return home to find the house full of revellers. A few of the team would inevitably end up back in the clubhouse bar, Ray O'Toole for instance, but that was the reason those guys were always warming up the substitutes bench and not top of the selectors lists like Tommy. He prided himself on the fact that he had never once been off the first team and the only way his arse ever saw the bench was if the manager was pulling some sort of stroke to psych the other team out. Everyone knew Tommy Boylan was the key member of the team. Most of the other lads looked up to him back then, not like now. It was also well known about the club that his folks put on a good shindig back in their house after any of the big games. Of course there was a bit of beer available but mostly it was the supporters who took it. Tommy wouldn't go near it nor would any of the lads who yearned for his respect. Instead of drunken banter there was intimate dissection of every moment of the match, irrespective of the result. Back in those days there was no YouTube or play on demand TV so they didn't have the luxury of watching the match back, at least not until the highlights were shown later in the evening. Once the analysis was completed to everyone's satisfaction and Tommy and the lads had been clapped on the back enough to cause mild bruising, someone would start singing. There was always someone with a tin whistle or a guitar and it never took long to turn into a right good session. The house would be heaving and the music and laughter would spill out across the road like ripples on a lake. Having Robbie, Naomi and Kim and little Shona here wasn't exactly the same but it was more than he'd had for years and that suited him just fine. Naomi and Kim were chatting on the sofa.

'Your Shona is only gorgeous,' gushed Kim. 'She's got the most amazing eyes. She reminds me of someone, maybe it's an actress. Like a young Elizabeth Taylor or something. It's driving me mad that I can't think who it is.' Naomi laughed. 'Well just don't let her bat those baby blues at you too much tomorrow when she's trying to persuade you to give her more ice cream.' Tommy smiled at the exchange before he was abruptly interrupted by Robbie flopping down next to him on the couch.

'You must have got the leg over, you're looking that pleased with yourself.' Robbie turned towards him with one eyebrow raised. Tommy's face was giving nothing away as he looked at his new friend. 'Come on, spill the beans.' Robbie nudged him in the ribs as he spoke. Kim and Naomi were totally immersed in a game of snap with Shona and couldn't overhear a thing. 'A gentleman never tells.' Robbie turned to

Tommy as he spoke and took a long slurp of beer before replying. 'Well we're sorted so, cos we've already established you're no fucking gentleman.'

'I beg to differ,' said Tommy, looking slightly put out.

'Look pal, there's a referee out there whose nose is taking up more space on his face than it did before he awarded a penalty against you. Do you want me to give him a quick bell to see what he thinks?'

'That's below the belt Robbie.'

'As was the knee you gave the lad into the bollix. So don't be all holier than thou with me pal. I'm no bleedin angel but I'll tell you something, everyone has a past, some are just better at hiding it than others.'

'Fair point I suppose.'

Robbie leaned into Tommy's ear. 'So are you going to spill?' Tommy looked straight at Robbie. 'No!' 'You're no bleeding crack.'

Robbie pushed himself up off the couch and headed off towards the kitchen to grab another beer. Both Naomi and Kim looked up at the exchange. 'What's that all about?' asked Naomi.

'Just Robbie getting too nosey for his own good,' answered Tommy with a wink just as Robbie returned. Kim narrowed her eyes as she looked at her fiancé. 'Still sticking your big beak in where it's not wanted are you?' Robbie stood with his hands turned out and his shoulders raised. 'Wha? I only asked the lad if he had gotten the l …'

'List ready for the game tomorrow,' Tommy called out suddenly. 'Yeah, I should get cracking on it actually.' Naomi gathered up the cards. 'It's getting late. I'm going to get Shona to bed. Tommy, is it alright if I have a shower after that? I feel minging after the training.' Tommy jumped up and Robbie stepped in front of him. 'I'm sure I could write out the positions for tomorrow's game if you felt the need to help Naomi build up a lather.'

The smack on the back of the head surprised Robbie. He turned to see Kim standing there with her other hand on her hip. 'Honestly Robbie King, you are the biggest dirtbird I have ever met. Leave this pair alone.'

'Spoilsport,' muttered Robbie as he stood to one side. Tommy laughed as he went to step past. Robbie caught him by the arm and whispered in his ear. 'Them floorboards are very creaky in the landing. I'll be listening out for you later on.' Tommy shook his head and looked back at the younger man. 'You're obsessed.' Robbie pulled Tommy close and whispered in his ear. 'Not obsessed, just horny. Kim has me on rations till I sort this shite out with the Hawk. I think I'd prefer if he put one in my head.'

'You don't get your end away much when you're dead though.'

Robbie considered his point for a moment, 'Fair point.'

Chapter Thirty Three

Robbie woke early on Saturday morning and spooned Kim. He'd been surprised at how relaxed he felt. Maybe it was the innocence of being with a six year old but he felt he could put Hawk out of his mind, albeit temporarily. No playing the hard man but instead enjoying the moment and most of all, the giggles between her and Kim. The two of them had talked for ages when they went to bed. They came to an agreement. Once he sorted things out with Hawk, they would settle down and try for kids of their own. They both realised they might have to leave the country because the only way to get Hawk off his back was to turn supergrass on his enterprises. They would go to his sister Sheila in New York for a while. He knew a bloke who could get him a passport and swap around his first and second name. He'd become Patrick Robert and that, hopefully, would ensure him sidestepping any problems his previous convictions would present. Kim was willing to give up her job to go with him. Knowing his life could be in danger made her realise how much time they had been wasting. She wanted to get on with their life and the sooner the better. She was willing to go against her mother's wishes, finally. Well, Robbie thought, there was another way they could rid themselves of Hawk but there would be no coming back if he went down that road and got caught.

Getting up quietly he pulled on his new tracksuit. Tommy had surprised him with it the night before. It was one with the Iona Gaels crest on the breast. When he was handed it he couldn't speak. He had welled up but it was all on the inside, a man had his image to think of. It was the first time in his life that he felt like he really belonged. He scrawled a note for Kim and Tommy saying he was gone to get the team bus and he would meet the women at the clubhouse car park. He set off on the Honda towards the garage lock up that held the spare Viking Splash boat. He'd made a copy of the key before he was kicked out of the place. He had a few things up his sleeve to make the blitz a bit more fun. He had to collect some essentials off a mate along the way. As he busied himself thinking of the quickest way to get there, he didn't notice Butch and another bloke on a motorbike one hundred yards behind.

'So this is where they kept all the sporty looking ones hidden.' Robbie had parked up the yellow boat, much to the amusement of the other Gaelic for Mothers teams. Scores of women wandered about wearing shorts and their team jerseys. Some local newspaper reporter had shown up and was organising a photo of the Iona Gaels women. He commented that their Durex sponsorship logo would probably make the front pages of the broadsheets. Kim's boss would be delighted. The team, on the other hand, wanted to thread the eye of his mickey with a hot poker. Robbie pointed to another team who were beginning to gather. 'Looks like I spoke too soon. There's a few muffin tops out there.' Tommy glanced at the group of well-fed ladies.
'Scratch that,' said Robbie staring, as several more women with bulging midriffs walked out. 'They're not muffin tops, they're the whole shagging bakery.' The two men looked toward a woman who was

struggling to pull on an under armour body top. 'Jesus, would you look at the big tattoo on her side. What is it?' asked Tommy squinting his eyes to try to make it out. 'I think it's the Goodyear logo,' laughed Robbie with a wink.

'Iona Gaels?' A woman's voice called out to them from the side.

'Yes, Tommy Boylan,' he said offering his hand to one of the organisers. 'Where do you want us?'

'If you need to use any changing facilities they are in there,' she said pointing the way. 'When you are ready head out to the pitches for your warm up. Here's a list of your matches, best of luck. Oh, and there's tea and refreshments in the clubhouse for you if you fancy it.' The women milled around Tommy and Robbie. 'Where's the toilets then? Did she say?' asked Tracey.

'Oh Jesus, don't tell me you had another dodgy curry last night?' said Robbie feigning disgust. Then he turned and spoke loudly to the open car park. 'Everyone? Keep your kit bags zipped up tight or this one is likely to puke into them.'

'ROBBIE!' shouted Tracey. 'I'm scarlet. Will you stop?'

'Well you have form is all I'm saying.' He shrugged his shoulders and picked up the bag of balls Tommy had taken off the boat. 'Let's take five minutes for a loo break,' said Tommy, 'and then meet me out at that pitch over there.' He pointed towards the area marked 1. The girls scarpered. 'It's the adrenalin,' said Tommy with resignation. 'The bowels can't handle it. When I used to play the inside of my colon must have looked like aluminium piping. There used not be a thing left in me by the time I hit the pitch.'

Robbie grimaced and nodded to the entrance to the club house. 'I'm just going to run into the jacks myself. I'll see you in a minute.' He jogged over with his rucksack on his back and slipped inside. Women were sitting around drinking tea and coffee while horsing into sandwiches and buns. He slipped over beside the catering area and quickly took the large bowl of sugar and put it underneath the table. Then he poured hot water into two Styrofoam cups and popped a tea bag into each.

'Sorry there luv, would you have any sugar?' he asked the girl in charge. She looked around the table, perplexed. 'It was there a minute ago.' 'Maybe someone took it into the kitchen to refill it. You wouldn't check would you? Only I'm gasping for a mug of scald.' His big brown eyes were hard to refuse. 'Give me one minute,' she said as she scurried off. Robbie pulled two large bags of Movicol powdered laxative from his rucksack and poured one into the sugar bowl and the other into the large tin of instant coffee granules. Quickly mixing each of them with a spoon he set them back on the table and walked away chuckling to himself. Alison turned into the hall just as he left. 'I'll be right out Robbie. I'm just getting a quick coffee for energy.' Slipping his arm around her shoulder he guided her outside.

'Not today blobby. Coffee is off. So is the sugar.' She stopped and looked at him with suspicion. 'You're a dirty little bastard Robbie King. What are you up to?'

'It's the lack of trust that hurts me most you know,' he replied in a girly whimper as he pretended to wipe a tear from beneath his eye.

'Now I know you've done something dodgy!'
'Bet you're glad I'm on your team though eh?'
'Bloody right,' she laughed.

The two of them walked out together and joined the others on the pitch for a warm up session. Tommy was taking the women through their paces. It was the first day in ages that it wasn't raining. A look to the ominous black clouds gathering hinted that might be about to change. The women had almost perfected the drill where they passed to the second person to their left and followed the ball. Next Tommy made them go through some sprints and stretches before calling them all together.

'Ok ladies, our first game is against Moorville. Stick to what you've all learned and just do your best. The important thing is that you enjoy it, right?' He looked around the team for agreement. 'Bollix,' said Robbie much to Tommy's surprise. 'The important thing,' he continued, 'is that you lot get stuck in and remember everything you learned.' He didn't need to spell it out. He had told them previously that he wanted one dirty tackle each. Ruth fiddled with a silver and diamond crucifix around her neck as she listened. Noticing this Tommy held up his finger.

'That reminds me. No jewellery allowed on the pitch. It's for your own good. It will either get damaged or worse. A ring could get caught in something and rip your finger off.' The ones wearing jewellery took various pieces off.

'Does a vajazzle count? I'm not taking that off.' Naomi was deadly serious.

'That's the second time I've heard that word,' said Robbie. 'What in the name of Jaysus is a vajazzle?'

Naomi locked eyes with him and with an impish grin

replied simply, 'Fanny art.' Hardly missing a beat he replied, 'Well don't get kicked in the hole so.'

A shadow fell across the group. Robbie turned to see an exceptionally tall woman in a Moorville team jersey carrying a large cup of coffee. He nudged Tommy and whispered 'Shit, it's an eclipse.' 'Don't let her hear you,' he replied. 'She could take out the both of us.'

'We're playing you guys first I think,' she said. 'We got here a bit late so we're just having a quick caffeine fix, then we'll be right out.' Robbie smiled and patted the wall of muscle on the shoulder.

'Sure have a second cup. It's supposed to be a fun day out.' He winked at Alison and walked away. Tommy's team continued with their drills while they waited in an effort to take their minds off the tough looking Moorville team, some of whom had started to walk out. 'Jesus would you look at that one,' said Ruth in disbelief. 'She's like a character off LA INK. I've never seen so many tattoos. She'll be like a kids copy book left out in the rain in a few years when it all starts seeping through the wrinkles.'

'I dunno,' said Naomi joining in. I sometimes fancy getting a cute little tattoo.'

'I'd get one too' said Tracey to everyone's astonishment. 'But only if they could tattoo Angelina Jolie's face onto mine.'

'Are you OK there, you look a little lost?' Tommy had noticed a man looking quite out of place. He walked away from the group to speak to him.

'I'm here to have a look at the tournament. When does it kick off?' asked the man in an American accent.

'First match on this pitch is Moorville v Iona Gaels.

That's us by the way, I'm Tommy Boylan.' He extended his hand in greeting.

'Jerry McGrath,' replied the man shaking hands. 'Very pleased to meet you.'

'You're not local by the sound of things,' said Tommy.

'I'm over from the United States on a bit of a road trip. I heard some people talking about this so I thought I'd take a look. Kill some time, you know how it is.'

'Are you familiar with Gaelic football?' asked Tommy.

'A little.'

'This is a new initiative that Croke Park, that's the headquarters of the game, is trying to promote. It's called Gaelic for Mothers.'

'Who don't want others, according to their shirts.'

'Yeah, they weren't too happy to wear them at first but they came around. We had to find a sponsor ourselves. The club don't really take us seriously. I suppose it's because we are not in the running for any of the big competitions.'

'I think they are making a mistake,' said Jerry sincerely. 'I can imagine the posters. A mom running down the pitch with a football under one arm and a baby under the other.'

'I can't see us getting funding for anything like that. Their focus is on the men's seniors' team and to a lesser extent the women's seniors. Most of this shower,' said Tommy indicating his team, 'never even picked up a football till six weeks ago.'

'And yet they signed up for a tournament?' replied Jerry, stunned. 'I'd say that's pretty impressive.'

'Yeah,' agreed Tommy, a smile of satisfaction

crossing his lips. 'They certainly can't be accused of not trying.' Robbie joined them as he spoke and Tommy introduced him. 'Mind if I hang out to watch you guys a while?' asked Jerry. 'You can be our team mascot,' Tommy said with a smile. 'You might even bring us some luck.'

Alison jogged slowly over looking decidedly uncomfortable. 'Tommy, please tell me you're putting me into goals.'

'Actually I was going to put Tracey in for the first half. Why? What's the problem?'

'I wasn't thinking when I got dressed and I put on an underwire bra,' she answered. Tommy was none the wiser and looked at her with a blank stare. 'I'll be filletted if I run in it Tommy.'

The American's eyes sparkled with amusement. Noticing this Robbie nudged him with his elbow. 'Stick around. You wouldn't believe the stuff they come out with. See yer one over there?' He pointed to Ruth. The American nodded. 'She just told me her thong had gone so far up the crack of her arse she'd need a proctologist with a miner's lamp to get it out.'

'ROBBIE!' shouted Tommy, knowing full well Ruth was too ladylike to say such a thing.

'Wha?'

Tommy shook his head.

'So how long have you been involved in the game then?' Jerry asked him.

'Me? Since I was a kid. It's true what they say. It gets into your blood.'

'Were you any good?' asked the Yank, smiling.

'I scored the odd goal alright.' He was nothing if not modest. The conversation was interrupted by the approach of the referee. 'Howya lads. Look eh, your opposition have only nine players available.' He seemed a little sheepish.

'Are you messing?' said Robbie. 'I saw them getting off their bus. I'd say the only mammies left in Moorville are the ones still pushing the babies out.'

'It seems some of them have a bit of a bug. I'm told by their coach that the jacks looks like it's been crashed into by a flock of starlings. Half of them didn't even make it to the toilet bowl.'

'Jaysus, that's shocking. Must have been all that coffee they had. Sure we'll manage with nine so. Are they ready to start?'

'Yeah, let's go,' said the ref. The girls made their way into their respective positions as Tommy called out to them. 'Do your best now girls.'

'And don't forget yis promised me one each. Right?' Robbie roared after them. Tommy turned to him with his eyebrows raised.

'What's that's all about?' Robbie seemed to consider the question for a moment then grinned. 'Nothing.'

The teams got into position. Ruth and Stretch went centre field for the throw-in. Their opposite players looked at each other and exchanged a confident smile as they towered over Mary. Noting this she was more determined than ever to show them how she got her nickname. The ref blew his whistle and the ball was thrown high up in-between the opposing players. Stretch sprung up into the air like something shot from a rifle, much to the horror of the Moorville centre field. She wasn't able to grab the ball with both hands though so she whacked it straight into the arms of Naomi. 'Yes,' shouted Ruth and darted off down the middle towards Moorville's goal. Naomi was fast. She managed to solo and bounce the ball once before she was taken out by a shoulder to the right tit. 'Ref!' she roared as the girl tore off with the football. The ref wasn't interested. 'Fuck that,' she said as she chased after the game.

Moorville tried to hand pass the ball from one player to another. Brid pounced on it like a leopard, then panicked and kicked it down field. Naomi sprinted against her opposite number and got to it first. She bent down to get it and the woman leaned over her. Naomi couldn't even stand up with the weight of the player on her back. She tried turning left and right to get away. All the while her arse was cocked up in the air and her head was down between her knees. Still the woman leaned over her. 'Are you wearing a strap-on?' Naomi shouted to her. 'Are you trying to ride me or what?' The whistle blew and the ref came over. 'Moorville ball,' he said pointing to the opposition.

Naomi was fuming. 'She gets the ball for trying to take me up the arse?' Trying not to laugh the ref replied, 'You were travelling with the ball.' 'Travelling? I couldn't take a step.' She looked toward Tommy on the sideline as she spoke. He held his forefinger up to his lips. She knew exactly what he meant. You don't argue with the ref in Gaelic football. Jesus, he was one to talk! She felt her blood start to simmer as the Moorville forward took the ball and booted it down the pitch towards Iona's goal. It was picked up by another forward who let it fly. It came at Alison with such force it hit her square in the chest and sent her onto her arse. But she still held it in her hands. 'No goal,' shouted the ref. The Moorville players surrounded him to argue but he blew the whistle to resume play. Alison caught her breath and kicked the ball up to centre field. Naomi launched herself into the air and grabbed it with two hands before pulling it into her chest. She took off at a sprint. Seeing she was about to be blocked she was preparing to hand pass to Ruth when she got an elbow straight into the right tit. It was the same girl as before. She had come out of nowhere. Naomi shoved her away. She kicked the ball on to Ruth who had gone ahead. Then it was passed to Tracey who found herself unmarked by any of the opposition. She ran her four steps and bounced the ball because the solo still eluded her. The other team were bearing down as Naomi roared 'TAKE YOUR SHOT.' Tracey looked toward the goal, sent the ball downwards to her left foot, made contact and stuck it in the back of the net. 'Oh my God. Oh my God,' she screamed, waving her hands in front of her face like a teenager trying to stem the flow of fake tears. The Moorville goalie looked like she'd just eaten a jellyfish. Her lips were pursed with determination as she kicked the ball up to mid field. The rain that had been threatening started to fall as a misty drizzle. 'That goal will have pissed them off. This is going to get interesting,' said Tommy.

'It already is,' replied the American. He was glad he'd thought to wear a waterproof coat because he planned to watch a lot more of this.

Two Iona players converged on the player with the ball as she thundered her way up the pitch. She shouldered one of them out of the way and gave the other an elbow to the face. She ran on and Stretch came straight for her. With one shoulder to the chest she sent Stretch flying. Two steps later she took aim at goal and BOOM! Alison couldn't react fast enough and the ball shot past her. 'Hey ref,' shouted Robbie from the sideline. 'Easy knowing you're not sponsored by Specsavers anyway.' Stretch was still winded on the ground as Moorville celebrated. 'Right girls, it's time to play for pints,' shouted their captain.

'Did she say pints?' Stretch asked Naomi who was helping her up to her feet. 'Yeah,' she replied. 'Brid said she overheard them saying whoever scores a point gets a pint bought for them in the bar afterwards.'

'Well they can shag off. What do you say we use Robbie's tactics and send them home thirsty?'

'Game on.' The two girls hit their palms together mid-air. 'Pass it on,' called Stretch as she ran back to mark her player on the wing. She caught Robbie's eye as she passed and winked at him. He nodded his head in return. 'Is there something going on with you two? I thought she was married,' remarked Tommy, having noticed the exchange. Jerry looked on for the response also out of curiosity. 'Don't mind yer man,' Robbie said to him, flicking his head toward Tommy. 'Sure what kind of a pervert would ride one of his own team? D'ya know what I mean like?' Tommy's face reddened.

'I'm intrigued,' said Jerry. 'Which one is it?'

'See yer one out there with the spiky black hair and the good figure?' said Robbie.

'She's hard to miss alright. But you know some of those others are good-looking women even if a few of them are carrying a few extra pounds.'

'Ah yeah, but you fellas in America like everything super-sized. Me?' said Robbie holding his hand upturned as if trying to grip something. 'I think any more than a handful is just being greedy.'

'Jesus,' said Tommy turning back to them. 'Would yis stop lads?'

'Go on Ruth,' shouted Robbie, ignoring Tommy. She was making her way up the pitch while Naomi and Stretch were running alongside, blocking the Moorville player's attempts to tackle her. 'Ow! Watch it you bitch,' roared one of them at Stretch who had accidentally on purpose stamped her studded boot into her foot as they ran along. 'Sorry, didn't see you there,' Stretch called out as she carried on.

Meanwhile Ruth had lost possession and a girl took aim to kick the ball back towards Iona's goal. The kick sent it up high. As the ball started to come back down Naomi and a Moorville girl stood side by side. With it just a few feet away Naomi nipped behind the girl and jumped up kneeing her as hard as possible into the kidneys. The ref who was to the front saw nothing except Naomi grabbing the ball while the other woman was rubbing her back and cursing like a sailor with knob blisters. The ball was passed to Brid and back to Naomi before Ruth received it and sent it over the bar for yet another point. The goalie kicked the ball out as the referee blew three short whistles to indicate the end of the match. The final score was 1-5 to 1-1. The rain was heavy now but it didn't stop Tommy beaming with pride. Robbie's smirk turned into a devilish grin as the team gathered around whooping and patting each other on the back. 'Ladies that was only brilliant. You did me proud. One thing though,' Tommy paused. 'Where did you learn all those sneaky tactics?' Robbie whistled as he pretended to count the water bottles. The women all looked at each other and grinned. Some of them stifled laughter. Tommy turned to him. 'You wouldn't know anything about it would you Robbie?'

'Me?' he responded, his face the picture of innocence. 'Don't know what you're on about.'

An official from the club approached the group. 'Which of you is the coach?' he asked. Tommy stepped forward. 'That's me. You're not calling it off on account of the weather are you?'

'No, we'll play on. We're almost finished anyhow.'

'Finished?' said Tommy, confused.

'Yeah, see you were due to play a team from Kilbradden and then Rosehill. Thing is, they've only four players fit between them.'

'Are you serious?' replied Tommy. 'Jesus, that was hardly worth their while travelling over here.'

'They had sixteen each when they arrived,' said the official, 'but it seems they've all had an attack of the trots.' 'Them as well? That's some coincidence,' said Tommy, narrowing his eyes while looking at a blank-faced Robbie. 'Yeah,' the steward answered. 'We've closed the refreshments area just in case something in there gave them food poisoning.'

'That's probably a good idea.' Tommy held Robbie's eye as he spoke. 'So anyway, both teams have had to concede the game to your lot. That means that with the win you just had, you're straight into the final. Looks like it's your lucky day.' 'Who are we playing in the final then?' asked Tommy.

'The hosts. Rathburn. Pitch 2 in twenty minutes.' The steward walked away. Ruth stuck her head in between Robbie and Tommy. 'Did he just say we are in the final?' 'Yeah,' replied Robbie. 'Seems a few of the other teams had to pull out. They've all got a dose of the hurry-go-fasts.'

'The what?' asked Ruth, puzzled.

'The squirts.' Still she looked baffled.

'The scutters. You know, the type of shites that mean you can't trust a fart.'

'STOP, I get it.'

'It's just amazing none of us have it. I wonder why that is?' Tommy asked, eyeing Robbie. 'We were all drinking water,' replied Brid. 'Robbie said the coffee would be bad for us.'

'Clearly.' Tommy picked up his gear. 'Come on, we better have a bit of a warm up for the final. This should be interesting. They seem to have a full squad. Obviously they only drank water too.'

The women followed him over with Robbie and the American bringing up the rear. 'So what do you think of this Irish style football then? Bit different to the stuff you Yanks play isn't it?'

'I never had much time for American football myself. This is great stuff. Plus I get to see the game played in its natural home.' Jerry pointed to the surrounding houses. 'The heart of the community.'

'I suppose it's nice if you're a tourist to see things in their natural habitat,' said Robbie. 'Flowers, animals, north-siders.' Turning around he walked off towards the dressing rooms leaving Jerry staring after him.

Chapter Thirty Four

Kim was talking to her mother. It wasn't going well. 'Mam, just listen to me now. Robbie is going to change.' She walked up and down the hall as she listened to the voice ranting at the other end of the phone. 'No, he's not just like my father. He is different. We might go abroad for a while but if we stay here he's planning to go back to school. I believe him this time. Something has changed.' A child's hand caught hold of her blouse from behind and gave it a little tug. 'Do you know where my dolly is?' Shona spoke before Kim had even turned around. 'Hang on a sec Mam.' Kim put the phone to her chest and bent down on her hunkers to talk to the girl. Her brilliant blue eyes sparkled as they teetered on the edge of tears. 'I can't find her anywhere,' she sniffed. 'Well where did you have her last?' asked Kim, rubbing Shona's shoulder gently. 'I don't know. I think I showed her the old swing in the garden.' The little girl said sadly. 'Ok, well I'll tell you what. You go check in the garden to see if your dolly is out having fun. I'll just finish off on the phone and I'll be right out to help you search. Ok?' Shona nodded and ran down the hall and into the kitchen.

'Sorry about that Mam, I've a little one here that I'm minding for a friend of Robbie's. It's made me a little broody to be honest.' Kim had to hold the phone away from her head as her mother screeched a response. 'Jesus,' she whispered, shocked at the ferocity of the outburst. She walked into the living room and stared sadly out the window at a van parked on the kerb a few houses down. Her shoulders sagged under the weight of her mother's disapproval. She heard the back door close. There wasn't any sound of crying she noticed, which meant Shona must have found the dolly. In a way it would have been better if she'd come in bawling. At least then she would have had an excuse to get away from the earbashing she was getting. 'Mam, look,' she finally managed to get a word in. 'Robbie is going straight right? He told me he's going to give the cops whatever they need on that Hawk character and I believe him. That's why we might have to leave the country for a while till things blow over but Mam listen. I've known Robbie all my life. I've seen what a good person he is, the way he took over the family when his ma died. He never once lashed out at his da even though most other men would have. He earned my respect years ago Mam and I will go anywhere to be with him. Now, I'm really sorry but I have to go. I've to take care of Naomi's kid.'

Kim hit the button to disconnect the call and threw the phone onto the sofa. It was very stressful being torn between two people you loved. 'Shona?' No reply. 'Shona honey? Did you find your dolly?' She walked toward the back door. The kitchen was empty. The back door was shut but where was the little girl? 'Shona?' Kim's voice was a little louder now. She hurried over to the back door and hurried down the steps to the garden. It was empty. The old iron swing swayed ever so slightly as though only recently abandoned. Retracing her steps she returned to the kitchen. 'Shona?' There was the faintest hint of panic in her voice as she climbed the stairs. A chill descended on her as the silence enveloped her.

Something didn't feel right. Then she saw something lying on the landing—blonde hair cascading over a little pink dress thrown carelessly on the ground. Shona's doll was lying at the top of the stairs. Still there was no sound. Kim couldn't understand it but she felt scared. She reached for her phone in the back pocket of her jeans. Shit. She remembered that she'd chucked it on the sofa. She opened the door to the bedroom that Naomi and her daughter had slept in the night before. Relief battled with concern as Kim rushed to the perfectly still body lying on top of the duvet. Shona's little tummy rose up and down as she breathed.

'Don't worry. She's not dead.' The man's voice made her scream with fright. She swung around and looked straight down the barrel of a gun. 'You,' she managed to whisper as she stumbled backwards and fell to a sitting position on the bed. 'The others are going to be back any minute,' she lied in desperation. Hawk sat back in the armchair in the corner of the room and laughed. 'We both know that's not true now, don't we?'

'No. I swear. I was just talking to him,' she replied. Her voice rose in panic. 'He said they were on their way.'

'Stop talking bollix,' he roared. 'The only person you were on the phone to was your oul one. Or have you some kinky reason for calling Robbie "Mam"?' Kim turned back to the little girl who was out cold.

'What have you done to her?' she asked.

'Just a bit of chloroform. She'll be passed out for a bit. Enough time for you and I to get better acquainted.' He licked his lips as his eyes settled on her pert breasts. Her nipples, still erect from the cold winter air in the garden, pushed against the thin cotton blouse. Hawk stood and walked over toward her. Using the tip of the gun's barrel he traced the outline of each one. His cold eyes stared into hers, challenging her to try to stop him.

'Go fuck yourself,' she hissed, too terrified to move. 'The only thing getting fucked around here is you sweetheart. And you're going to love every minute of it.' Kim spat right into his face. The stub end of the gun crashed against the side of her head. The room began to spin as she felt herself losing consciousness. The last thing she was vaguely aware of was someone pulling off her jeans. Then everything went dark.

Chapter Thirty Five

'Let's go over a couple of things before the final.' Tommy stood in front of the semicircle of women. Robbie was beside him and Jerry stood a little further back. The rain was driving across the pitch from the west. The women looked like they had been used as target practise for the local fire brigade. Even so, they all stood to attention to see what the boss man had to say. 'That last match was great but it's over now. The Rathburn team is at full strength. There's no scutters in their dressing room. So don't go thinking this is going to be easy because it's not. Alison, no more standing still with the ball and your arse cocked up in the air okay?'

'What's wrong with my arse?' she said feigning insult.

'Nothing, but if you keep it up like that for too long the council will use it to park bicycles in.'

'Don't be talking dirty Tommy,' Alison laughed, 'You'll ruin my concentration.'

'I'm serious ladies. Remember to keep moving. In this rain if you don't, you're liable to rust. If you get the ball and panic they will be all over you like a rash. You've got to take your four steps. Then you either bounce, solo, pass the ball or take a shot. Got it?' They all nodded their acknowledgement. The Rathburn team came out to warm up and Tommy nodded to their coach. 'Good to go in about ten minutes?' he asked. He got a thumbs up. 'Did you see that?' Ruth asked Naomi.

'See what?' she replied.

'Two of them were wearing headbands that said Docklands Triathlon.'

'Shite,' said Naomi. 'They must be super fit.'

'Bollix,' said Robbie, sticking his head in between them. 'They probably nicked them off some buggers as they ran by. The only triathlons people from Rathburn know are smoking, drinking and shooting up.'

'Come on you lot,' Tommy interrupted. 'Do some stretches. By the way, do any of you need your boot studs tightened? It's going to be slippery out there now with all this rain. I don't want any of you getting injured.'

'It's not football boots we need Tommy, it's flippers,' Ruth laughed.

The girls all began to follow him through the now familiar routine. Robbie watched as Jerry fiddled with his iPhone. Noticing this he looked over and smiled. 'I was just posting a comment about the match on Twitter. I'm not sure what hashtag to give it though.'

'Hashtag? Is that something you smoke or what?' asked Robbie. 'No,' replied Jerry laughing. 'But I can see how you'd think that. The hashtag is the name that marks a topic out. So for instance, if I mentioned football in the topic it would attract people who are looking for similar content.'

'Do you know what I just heard?' asked Robbie, a serious look on his face as he lit up a smoke. 'No, what?'

'Blah, blah, fucking blah!' Jerry laughed. 'I'm guessing you don't tweet then?' Robbie looked back at him, bemused. 'Why do people keep asking me that?'

'It's a very popular pastime' replied Jerry.

'So is tossing off. No, I don't tweet or lay eggs or any other poxy thing that birds do. In my opinion mobile phones are for ringing and texting. Nothing else.' He wandered over to where Tommy was going through some stretches. '... and bend and hold. One, two, three and release.' FART! 'That wasn't the release I meant,' laughed Tommy.

'Here, I was thinking,' said Robbie as he waved his hand in front of his nose. 'Maybe we should put the girls here in for some kind of eco award.'

'A what?' asked Tommy.

'They could be the first wind powered Gaelic football team.'

'Very funny. Now come on,' Tommy clapped his hands together and called out to the women. 'Assume the position.' He ignored the titters of laughter, as he normally did. Ten minutes later the referee blew the whistle and threw the ball up between the two opposing players. Wise to Stretch's tactics having watched their previous game, the Rathburn centre field player used her elbow to block her. She grabbed the ball and landed back on her feet before tearing off like a hare. Naomi raced after her and counted three steps in her head. After the fourth step the player was going to have to do something with the ball. She took a step and then dropped the ball toward her foot to solo kick it back up. Naomi shot her fist out and punched the ball away before the other player could make contact. The ball went out on the wing while Naomi was taken out by the girl colliding against her. She landed hard on her shoulder and was winded for a few seconds. The game continued with Rathburn owning the ball for the next few minutes. Alison stood in goal waving her arms in an attempt to distract the oncoming player who was eyeing up the goalposts greedily. She took her kick. It went high and looked to be going straight over the bar. Apart from growing an extra six feet in two seconds, there was nothing Alison could have done to stop it. At the very last second the ball dropped from its curved arc and snuck in under the bar for a goal. 'Fuck,' said Tommy and half the team in unison. The game continued with Rathburn dominating play. The same player sent two more goals in using the same style from the half way line. 'Has yer one got a shagging remote control on that bloody ball or what?' Tommy said to Robbie as they looked on. 'There's fellas playing senior county football for Dublin couldn't do what she's just done, three times! And these are supposed to be mammies just playing for a laugh.'

'You wouldn't see that in Croke Park,' said Jerry, watching in fascination.

Tommy was beginning to wonder if the Yank knew more about the game than he was letting on. He watched as Jerry made an excuse and went to talk to the coach of the other team. Alison kicked the ball well into centre field. Brid bent to pick it up and instead of taking her four steps she passed it off right away. 'It's not bleedin ticking luv,' roared Robbie. 'You don't have to get rid of it straight away you know.' Ruth caught the ball and managed to do a dummy pass that fooled the oncoming player who tried to tackle her. Realising it had worked she ran as fast as she could and pulled off a solo like she was playing since she was in nappies. She passed the ball out to Naomi who had come to shadow her. Naomi saw she was about to be tackled and passed it back to

Ruth who took a shot at goal. The goalie, caught by surprise only managed to punch it out. Ruth had fire in her belly and she launched herself into the air, caught the ball with two hands, landed and belted it straight into the back of the net.

Robbie and Tommy cheered at the sideline but were drowned out by a man standing under a brolly who was screaming his head off in excitement. Tommy did a double take when he saw who it was. 'Lorcan?'

'How's it going Tommy? Did you see my Ruthie, wasn't she great?'

'She certainly was. Does she know you were coming to see her?' asked Tommy.

'No, I thought I would give her a surprise.' Lorcan was grinning like a teenager on a first date.

'That's nice. She'll be dead chuffed.' Tommy was thrilled for her. When he was playing competitively he knew some girlfriends of players who said the game caused their relationships to drift apart. In Ruth's case, the opposite was true.   The Rathburn women were surprisingly rattled by the goal. Tommy had sussed out their strategy very quickly. Their forward players did everything possible to get the ball to the girl who had scored the three goals. None of the others had been anywhere near target when they took a shot. 'You've got to intercept the ball before it gets to number 8.' Tommy called to Stretch on the wing. 'Pass it on.'

Robbie had noticed the same thing but took a slightly different approach. He ran up the sideline and caught Naomi's eye. He held up eight fingers and lifted up his boot and hit it with his hand. She winked at him. Message received and understood. Stick the boot in to their number 8. The word spread around the Iona Gael's team like chickenpox in a crèche. Every time the number 8 got the ball she was surrounded. She was fast though and it meant Stretch, Ruth, Brid and Naomi had to do more running than normal. Ruth managed to intercept a ball after she and Brid raced down the pitch after the player. 'Stay with me Brid and I'll pass off to you.'

'I can't Ruth, I'm wrecked.' Brid wheezed. Tracey looked on as she jostled with another girl. They had exchanged a few pleasantries at the start of the match and Tracey had owned up that it was her first ever blitz. The ball was kicked into their area and Tracey got to it first. The other girl tried to block her path and Tracey barged through her and kicked the ball away.

'You've awful pointy elbows for someone who's never played before.' Tracey shrugged her shoulders and said nothing. She was afraid to in case she got a smack in the mouth. Meanwhile Stretch and Ruth were still all over number 8. No matter which way she turned, one of them would block her. It didn't matter that the ball wasn't even near her.

'Do me a favour luv will ya?' The girl asked Stretch.

'What?' asked Stretch, a little confused.

'Would you ever fuck off?'

'Did you see that Ruth?' The little red-haired dynamo called to her team mate. 'She's getting pissed off. We have her rattled.' 'We certainly do,' replied Ruth beaming brightly as Naomi scored another goal. Stretch pushed against the number 8 and said, 'We're going to stick to you like shit to a bunny's bum. You better get used to it. Luv.'

The referee blew his whistle. The teams went

to opposite sides of the pitch. Tommy got the girls in a huddle and passed the water bottles around. 'You're doing great. There's only three points in it. Remember, if the goal is covered take your point. They all add up.' Jerry wandered over as Tommy was going through some pointers. 'Their number 8 played inter-county football for Waterford for ten years,' he said to Robbie.

'She could probably kick the ball through the eye of a needle if you held one up,' replied Robbie. 'All the more reason to take her out so,' he added within earshot of Naomi who hadn't managed to do it as yet. 'Now now, I thought you were supposed to play nice,' said Jerry. 'They'll say sorry when they do it.' Robbie looked up at the American. 'What's nicer than that?'

'Girls, get out and play now like your lives depend on it.' Tommy was well fired up. 'Imagine walking into the clubhouse at home having won the bloody blitz. Those feckers had us written off before we even started.'

A light cough from behind made a few of them turn. 'Don't tar everyone with the same brush there Tommy.'

'Lorcan!' Ruth ran over to him and gave him a sweaty hug. 'You came.'

'You didn't really think I would miss this.' He smiled at her warmly. 'Did you see the goal?' she asked, full of excitement.

'See it? Not only that. I think the vibration of it hitting the back of the net knocked out a few fillings.'

'Do you think you could do it again Ruth?' Tommy asked. 'Bring it on!' She shouted and the whole team cheered. Robbie grinned. He couldn't wait to tell

Kim all about the day.

The second half started with Stretch winning the ball from the throw-in, only to be elbowed right in the eye very deliberately by her opposite number. 'Oi!' she roared. The ref awarded the ball to Iona Gaels and Naomi, having the strongest kick, took the shot. She managed to get it deep into the Rathburn back line where Ruth was waiting. Brid, Stretch and Naomi all ran to her aid. 'For fucks sake, spread,' roared Robbie. The girls remembered his instruction from the night he trained them and they took off to various areas around the field of play. Ruth reached both arms in the air, thumbs touching at the tips. The spread of her hands looked like a W, just as Tommy had taught her to catch. The ball slammed into her hands, she drew it towards her chest to protect it when bam! A hand came from the right hand side and smacked up hard beneath the ball. It shot out of her grip as a gloveless hand followed through and walloped her in the face. Ruth felt a stinging sensation and took off her glove to feel what was causing it. Pulling her fingers back she saw red. There was blood on her hand. The girl's nail had sliced through the skin on her face. There was no way to know if it was intentional or not. Still, thought Ruth, it fecking hurt. Rathburn had managed to score a point and the ball was now back in play. Naomi collided with another player while chasing a long kick out by Alison. 'Fuck,' she roared as her boot flew off her foot mid stride. 'Keep going,' shouted Tommy from the sideline. He tried not to laugh at the sight of her muddy wet sock flopping about as she ran down the centre of the pitch after the girl who'd managed to get to the ball. Seizing the opportunity the player ran straight for Naomi clutching the ball. At the very last second she smashed her studded boot hard into Naomi's unprotected foot. 'That's for my cousin on the Moorville team. One of your lot did just the same to her.' The girl spoke menacingly into her ear before legging it down the pitch. Naomi hit the deck and grabbed her injured foot. The referee blew his whistle and ran over.

'Did you see what she did?' she asked from the ground. 'Unintentional foul.' The ref raised his hand to indicate a free kick to Iona. 'Unintentional my arse,' she argued. 'It couldn't have been more planned if she'd painted a bloody target on my foot.' 'I could change my mind if you like,' said the referee, a sarcastic smile crossing his face. 'Are you going to take the free yourself?'
'Yes. I'll just collect my boot first if that's alright with you.' She stomped and sloshed her way back to where her sodden boot lay forlorn in the mucky grass. 'Jaysus, this is wicked rain,' said Robbie to Tommy looking on. 'Kim will be raging. She was planning to take Naomi's young one to feed the ducks in the park. I'll give her a ring to say we're on the last game. Will we go out later for something to eat? All of us like. We might have something to celebrate by the looks of things.' 'Yeah,' said Tommy rubbing his hands together. 'That sounds like a plan.'

Naomi took the ball and kicked. Robbie tapped the screen on his phone a couple of times and held it to his ear. It rang and rang. Ruth caught the ball and ran, evading two defenders and kicked for a point. The goalie jumped up expecting to be able to punch it out but instead hit off the ball, sending it into her own goal. 'Yahoo!' shouted Ruth while doing a little shimmy to celebrate. Lorcan laughed and blew her a kiss. Robbie took the phone from his ear and checked the screen even though he knew he had dialled Kim's phone. 'Problem?' asked Tommy.

'No. It's weird is all,' replied Robbie. 'The phone rang for ages and then when she answered she said nothing.' 'She probably dropped it,' said Tommy without looking over. 'I'm always doing that. They're too bloody small these days, that's the problem.

The game was in its final stages and Iona Gaels were one point ahead. The ball was sent high into the air by a Rathburn player. Naomi and her nemesis, the girl who stamped her foot, were shoulder to shoulder jostling for position as the leather ball came down through the air toward them. Just as it came within reach they both fell forward as each of them felt a studded boot on their arses. 'What the hell ...' Naomi started to shout before she saw the cause of the foul. Stretch had jumped and then used the two of them as a climbing frame to get to the ball before they did. 'Casualties of war,' she shouted and winked at Naomi who was so full of stud holes at that point she feared she might actually drown in the rain. Stretch was thundering down the pitch ducking and weaving as she went. Seeing Tracey left unmarked she passed the ball over. She took it and sent it over the bar. The goalie cursed and ran to retrieve it before booting it out. But it was too late. The ref blew the final whistle. The girls shook hands with the other team before jumping all over each other in the middle of the pitch. Tommy stood at the sideline beaming with pride. 'I knew they could do it,' he said.

'You must feel very proud,' Jerry shook his hand. 'I still can't believe you only started training them less than two months ago. That's pretty amazing, I don't mind telling you.'

'They did all the hard work,' Tommy replied.

'Bullshit. They would be nowhere without you. I've never seen such dedication and self-belief. You have a big heart Tommy Boylan and I bet it's shaped like a Gaelic football.' The American stuck out his hand again which Tommy shook vigorously. 'It was a real pleasure. Thanks for letting me be part of your team today. I haven't enjoyed a match as much in years.'

'Next time you're touring around Ireland be sure to look us up,' Tommy said warmly.

'Maybe you'll get to New York before I get back here again. Who knows?'

All Tommy could do was wave his goodbyes as he got grabbed and pulled into the middle of the pitch. The entire team tackled him to the ground.

'You can't be the only one all clean and tidy,' said Naomi as she dived on him smearing his face with muddy wet grass. 'Jaysus, get a room will you?' shouted Robbie. He saw her coming too late. Alison threw her arms around him in a big bear hug. She held his head to her chest just like she'd done in the Croke Park dressing rooms. 'Come to Mama,' she roared. Her arms were wrapped so tightly around his head he couldn't hear his mobile ringing in the back pocket of his jeans.

Chapter Thirty Six

'Robbie?' Kim mumbled. ·'What happened?'
Her head felt cloudy and she wanted to be sick. Her
eyes flickered. She tried to rub them but her hand was
caught in something. She was always wrapping
herself up in the duvet when she slept. Robbie used to
say it was like tearing open a birthday present every
day, trying to unravel her in the mornings. 'Robbie?'
This felt wrong. She really was stuck and something
pinched her wrist each time she tried to move her
hands. She was freezing too. Opening her eyes fully,
she saw that her blouse was lying open and the
buttons were ripped off. The cups of her bra dangled
from either shoulder. It had been cut at the front. Her
jeans were pulled down over her hips. Then it all
came surging back to her. Hawk. He had hit her with
a gun.

'Oh Jesus,' she cried, fearing what he must
have done to her. Oh dear God, she suddenly
remembered. Not Shona too! Please no. Not to a six
year old girl. What kind of animal was he? But she
feared the answer to that question. The ties that
bound her were much too tight to manoeuvre even
slightly. Lifting her head she looked around the room
as best she could. Nothing. Shona had been passed
out on the bed, she remembered that much. Hawk had
given her chloroform. Please don't let her have
woken up and started screaming, thought Kim.
Lifting her bum and then her shoulders alternatively
she inched herself to the edge of the bed. No matter
how hard she tried she couldn't pull herself into a
sitting position. Her arms pinned behind her back

made the balance all wrong. There was no other choice. With one great effort she leaned onto the shoulder nearest the edge of the bed and toppled nosily to the floor. Turning on one side she managed to pull one knee up slightly more than the other. Her jeans were just below her bum now impeding her movements. Progress was difficult. Thinking of what that monster might be doing to the little girl drove her on. She had been supposed to keep an eye on her. Kim raised her head and neck as far as possible and hooked her chin onto the mattress. Twisting her body and pulling with all the strength she could muster, she managed to get herself onto both knees. The effort was immense and still she was only halfway there. Tucking her head once more into the mattress, she pushed from her knees until her body appeared like a plank leaning against the side of the bed. Bit by bit she shuffled her bare feet forward. Finally she was standing. She was perspiring heavily from the effort. She strained her ears to hear any sound of movement outside the closed bedroom door. Nothing stirred.

Then she heard it. The Super Mario Bros music. Robbie had downloaded it from iTunes and set it up as her ringtone. He did it as a joke because she had been so shite at playing the game on the Wii and he always beat her. She almost cried as she remembered how chuffed he was when he managed to set the ringtone for his incoming calls only. He'd set her mother's number to play Nellie the elephant. 'Robbie,' she whimpered, cursing herself yet again for leaving the bloody phone downstairs. Moving awkwardly across the bedroom floor she progressed slowly towards the door. With every shuffle of her feet the jeans inched down further on her thighs. If she went too quick they would end up around her ankles and topple her over. Eventually she made it and turned her back to the door. Her hands gripped the lever and pushed down quickly. Shouldering it wider she took baby steps out to the landing. The faint hum of talking came from the kitchen. A child's voice. Shona! If she was talking it meant she was alright, that she wasn't hurt. Didn't it? Kim's breasts were exposed and she desperately wanted to cover herself up. But that wasn't possible. Trying to walk down the stairs wasn't a safe option. Breaking her neck wasn't going to help Shona. Instead she fell heavily onto her backside. She took one step at a time on her bum like a toddler. She tried not to think of Hawk seeing her as good as naked again.

Kim had no memory of what happened after he hit her. That was nearly worse because images of what he might have done flashed through her mind. Tears fell and she wanted to be sick. With two steps to go she leaned into the banisters to push herself upright.   She heard her phone ring again. She whipped her head toward the sitting room where she had left the mobile. The tune wasn't coming from there. Her blood ran cold as the realisation dawned. Hawk had found her phone. It was hopeless. The kitchen door opened and there he was. His sapphire eyes that she remembered once telling Robbie were stunning now bored into hers. What was it about them that nagged at the back of her mind? He approached her slowly, like a snake. 'Looking for more are you?' He licked his index finger and slowly ran it down her neck and over her left breast. Her heart thundered in terror beneath it. His eyes stared coldly into her own as he pushed his face up close to hers. 'Your fella

fucked me over sweetcheeks. Five million he cost
me.'

'That's nothing to do with me, or the kid,' she
pleaded. 'Leave her out if it.' He spat the words out.
'See the thing is luv. You're a grand tight little ride
but you're no five million worth.' The bile rose in
her throat as he confirmed her worst fear. 'So you've
got a lot of work to do before I'm finished with you.'

'Robbie,' she cried out.

'Him? He'll be no use to you. He sent my gear up in
smoke, so I'm going to do the same to him. And you
can't fuck dust, can you luv?' Kim looked at him,
confused.

Hawk gripped her breast tightly in his hand
and squeezed. He pushed her up against the wall and
pressed his groin into hers. His buttoned jeans felt
rough against her nakedness and tore at her skin.
'I'm going to break his arms and then his legs,' he
hissed into her ear. The tears fell steadily down her
cheek as she shut her eyes trying but failing to shut
him out also. His rough fingers grabbed hold between
her legs. He twisted his hand causing her to cry out in
pain. 'Then I'm going to screw you in every hole I
can find or maybe make some new ones.' He pulled
out a knife from the back pocket of his jeans and held
it next to her face. 'You want to know what happens
next?' he asked. Kim didn't move. 'I'm going to half
slit his throat and cover him in petrol. Then I'm going
to throw a match on him and turn him to dust. His
dying sight will be his precious Kim getting pounded
by the Hawk. Nobody messes with me luv. You
remember that.' He pulled her jeans up and fastened
them before tying the open ends of her blouse
together in a knot. The sound of the back door

opening and closing startled Kim. Hawk shot his hand up to cover her mouth. Her eyes bulged and stared at the kitchen door, willing Robbie to come through it.

'Shona pet, is that you?' Hawk called out in a gentle voice.

'Yes. I put all my things in the van like you said but I can't shut the door properly.' Her voice got louder as she approached the kitchen door.

'Get yourself a treat from the fridge sweetie, I'll be right in and then we can go.' Kim felt his hand press harder against her mouth. 'One fucking word to her and you're dead.' He released his grip.

'Please don't hurt her, she's only a kid. She's nothing to do with Robbie.' Kim pleaded in a whisper.

'I only just found her. I would never hurt her,' he replied. Kim didn't understand what he meant until the door opened and Shona walked out and stood next to them. 'Are you better?' she asked. 'The man said you drank too much wine and bumped your head.'

If the little girl had gouged his eyes out and popped them into her own sockets they couldn't have been more similar. That's who Shona reminded her of when she had spoken to Naomi about the colour of her eyes. She had seen that unusual blue before. On Hawk. She looked from the kid to Hawk and back again. Could it be? Naomi had opened up to Kim the night before over a bottle of wine. She'd told her how Shona's father was a rough sort she had shagged at a friend's party. She hadn't been able to remember his name, just that it was something to do with an animal. She knew it was a nickname but that was all. What were the chances? Kim wouldn't have given it a second thought if it weren't for the eyes. They said it all. 'I'm OK Shona sweetheart. Are you OK? You're not hurt are you?' she asked.

'Why would I be hurt? I'm a big girl you know. I'm nearly six and a half. I was just bringing my stuff into the man's van. He's helping mammy bring it all home because Tommy's car is broken he said.'

'That's nice,' Kim said, feeling it was anything but.

'It's really exciting. He even has a mattress in the back so we can be comfy. See, there's no booster seat in the front so he would get into trouble with a policeman if I sat up there.' Her innocent face was serious as she relayed the details. She was relishing the fact that she knew so much.

'We couldn't have that now, could we?' Hawk ruffled her hair. 'Why don't you run out and get the most comfy spot. Kim and I will lock up here.' 'OK,' she chirped and skipped off.

'So much for not talking to strangers,' muttered Kim, feeling momentarily brave.

'I shagged her ma about seven years ago. By my reckoning she could be my kid. There's no denying she's got my good looks.' He pulled her toward him by the hair and licked his tongue all the way up the side of her face.

Grabbing her by the elbow he shoved her into the kitchen and forced her down on to one of the chairs. With his back to her he took out a bottle and a dry J-cloth. Suddenly the sound of Super Mario Bros filled the room. Robbie! She had to warn him. She scanned the room frantically looking for her phone. Hawk turned to face her and pulled the mobile from his jacket. He looked at the screen. 'Looks like it's time for loverboy to join the party.' He ran his finger across the screen to connect the call and held it to his ear without saying a word. 'Kim? Are you there?

Kim?' She could hear Robbie's voice and it broke her heart. 'Kim? What's wrong with this poxy phone?'

Hawk smiled and used his shoulder to hold the handset to his ear. With his hands free he unscrewed the top of the bottle and poured some of the liquid onto the J-cloth. The smell sickened Kim and all of a sudden she realised what it was. Chloroform.

'ROBBIE HEL ...' The shout was smothered by Hawk's hand pressing the cloth to her mouth. She struggled and tried not to inhale but it was no use. She was overpowered and slumped forward onto the table.

'KIM!' Robbie's frantic voice screamed out of the phone. 'I'm sorry.' Hawk put on a high pitched voice like a girl. 'I can't come to the phone right now.'

'Hawk. What have you done to her?'

'Listen to yourself. Straight in with the accusations. You're well suited the two of you. She was a gobby sort too till I shut her up.'

'Oh Jesus no. You didn't hurt her, please say you didn't.' Robbie could hardly breathe.

'Well, listen to you now eh? Full of manners aren't we? You weren't so fucking polite when you bollixed up my shipment of cocaine.'

'It wasn't my fault,' Robbie pleaded.

'Whose fault was it so? Mine?' Hawk laughed down the phone.

'Look, I'll sort something,' said Robbie quickly.

'So you just happen to have five million stashed in a piggy bank somewhere do you?'

'No but ...'

'But nothing. Shut your fucking mouth and do exactly what I say.' Robbie listened as Hawk told him to meet the three of them at the warehouse. The three of them? Shit, he had forgotten about Naomi's kid. 'Oh yeah and Robbie?' Hawk said, his voice ominous. 'What?' 'You never told me your Kim was such a screamer in bed.'

The line went dead. Robbie threw his head to the black clouds lashing rain upon him and let out a roar to rival the thunder.

Chapter Thirty Seven

Tommy ran over to where Robbie had fallen on his knees, sobbing. 'What is it?' he asked. 'What's happened to Kim?' Naomi ran over too, her voice trembling. 'Is Shona alright?' Robbie ignored her and looked straight into Tommy's eyes. 'He has them. He must have followed me when I went to your house.' He wiped his face furiously. Tommy helped him up from the ground as the rest of the team gathered around in a small group. 'What's going on?' asked Alison 'Who has taken them Robbie?' Naomi asked in fear. 'I've got to go.' He started walking towards the car park where the Viking Splash vehicle was waiting. 'Hang on,' called Alison. 'You can't just leave us here.'

'He's got Kim. You don't understand.' Robbie shouted over his shoulder as he started to run. 'He's an animal.'

'What? Who is?' Naomi shrieked.

'Hawk.' Tommy replied on his behalf in a calm voice as the lot of them followed Robbie. 'Oh my God.' Naomi put her hand up to her mouth in shock. Tommy noticed and looked at her, confused.

'What does he look like?' She caught up to Robbie and pulled on his arm to make him wait.

'Like a fucking maniac. Jesus Naomi, I don't have time for this. What the hell does it matter what he looks like?' Clutching his arm tightly she continued.

'Does he have strange blue eyes, like a husky dog?' she asked, ashen faced. Robbie nodded, 'Yeah, why?' 'And a scar on one cheek?' she added, still holding him tightly. Tommy stood behind her shoulder and rubbed her back. If Robbie hadn't been so wired about Kim he probably would have copped on by now himself. It didn't take a geneticist to figure it out.

'You think it's the same guy? Are you sure?' Tommy asked. 'If he had called himself John or Alan maybe I could have my doubts. But Hawk? It's not exactly common is it?'

'Excuse me,' Robbie asked, his patience almost gone. 'But what the fuck are you on about?' Tommy stepped forward. 'Naomi thinks Hawk might be Shona's father.' Robbie stared at her, stunned. 'You've GOT to be shitting me. Does he know?'

'No he doesn't bloody know. I never laid eyes on him since the main event. That was nearly seven years ago. He wouldn't hurt a child would he?' She asked, searching Robbie's face for any hint. He was silent. 'You've got to know,' she screamed. 'I thought you were his mate.'

'He was never a mate of mine,' he shouted back. 'All I know is that he is one sick bastard and he is using Kim to get to me. None of this fucking talking is going to help her alright? I'm going to do as he said.'

'What does he want?' asked Tommy pulling Robbie back by his arm. 'Jaysus man, will you stop? He's got Kim. I have to go. He will hurt her, bad.'

'He's got Naomi's little girl too Robbie, she's only six years old. You're going nowhere without me.' The grip of his hand coupled with the look in his eye showed he meant business. 'Or us.'

Robbie looked around to see the entire Gaelic for Mothers team bunched up behind him. 'This isn't a fucking joke alright? This man has battered the shite out of people for fun. He has killed people. He's not going to be frightened off by a gang of mammies.'

'We're not a gang of mammies,' said Ruth. 'We're a team of mammies and we stick together. If nothing else we can create a diversion.' Robbie grabbed a handful of his hair in frustration. 'Will yis listen to me for fuck's sake? Am I speaking bleedin Russian here? The man is a nut job. You think he won't hurt yis because yis are women? Bollix. The only woman he ever respected was his ma and she just died. He probably hasn't even buried her yet. This guy is fucking psychotic. Macker, the last lad who pissed him off? He ended up tied to an anchor and fucked into Dublin Bay.'

Naomi had been silent while all this arguing ensued. She caught hold of Tommy's hand and squeezed. 'I don't care about any of this,' she cried. 'All I know is he has my daughter and your fiancée. Every minute we stand here arguing is another he has with them to do God knows what.'

'She's right Robbie,' Tommy used the voice of reason. 'This isn't just about you anymore.'

'Well don't say I didn't warn you,' said Robbie climbing up the three steps to the Viking Splash vehicle. The others quickly followed. He turned the key and the engine roared to life. He stuck his foot down on the accelerator and swung the yellow boat out of the car park and down the road leaving a trail of broken wing mirrors behind him.

'So,' Tommy said as he climbed into the front seat beside Robbie, 'having seen what he did to your face when you didn't answer the phone, I'm guessing he'll have something more in mind this time. It might sound like a dumb question but do we have a plan?'

Robbie took no notice of red lights as he shot through

junctions at top speed. The women all held on with white knuckles.

'Jeepers,' said Ruth. 'This is a bit mental, isn't it?' 'I know,' said Alison nervously, 'I just hope Robbie knows what he's doing.'

'Robbie,' Tommy spoke in a voice devoid of alarm. 'How much use do you think you'll be to Kim if you collide with a double decker bus? Besides, you'll get the cops after us and if they stop us you'll never get there. Slow down. The more hurry, the less speed.' Robbie glanced quickly at him as they hurtled towards a bridge crossing the Liffey. He slammed on the brakes and waited when the lights turned red. His fingers tapped impatiently on the wheel as Tommy continued. 'You've got to think this through Robbie. You can't just go in there balls out and expect it all to go your way.' Robbie didn't look around as he answered.

'You know Kim is my entire world right?'

'Yes I do.'

'Well, because of me her life is in danger. Not only that, but Naomi's young one is caught up in my shit as well. As if that wasn't bad enough to wreck my head,' he used his thumb to point behind him, 'now I'm about to chuck that lot into the line of fire too.'

'They wanted to help Robbie, just like I do,' replied Tommy.

'What if he kills one of you?' Robbie challenged.

'It won't come to that,' Tommy said, tossing a football from hand to hand.

'It fucking might Tommy, really.'

'Do you know something Robbie? When I played for Dublin in the early years they used to never give us a chance. Always the underdogs we were, written off before we even stepped on the pitch against the stronger teams.'

Robbie was growing more impatient, unable in his hassled state to see where the story was going.

'The point is, being considered the weaker opponent is a huge advantage. Hawk is a tough bastard. I get that. But I also get that he's an arrogant prick. Arrogance causes mistakes Robbie. You and he know what to expect from each other but he hasn't a baldy what to expect from the rest of us.'

'OK OK.' Robbie replied. 'Just do me one favour. Once I get Kim and Shona out of harm's way, promise me you won't let any of this lot risk themselves. I'm the one he wants. If I can get him to follow me you can get Kim, the kid and the team to safety. I can take care of myself once I know Kim is safe. Promise me you'll do that.'

Tommy nodded but didn't utter a word.

Chapter Thirty Eight

The street leading to the warehouse was almost empty. Robbie didn't know whether it was the expectation of what lay ahead or the fear of what Hawk may have already done, but the hairs on the back of his neck stood up as they approached. The white van was facing them as they neared the warehouse entrance. Tommy put his hand on Robbie's shoulder. 'What about getting the cops involved?' he whispered, already sure of the response. 'No cops, this has to be just him and me.' Unusually the heavy metal security shutters were raised. Robbie drove the large yellow vehicle through but stopped it halfway.

'Don't sit under the metal bit in case the fucker drops it. I can't drive the whole way in or we'll be like fish in a barrel.' The noise of the big diesel engine blocked out the sound of a large green motorbike that had pulled into the street behind them.

Robbie got up slowly and peered around the dimly lit space. 'He could be anywhere,' he said, turning to the women as he jumped out onto the ground. They were nervous but at least they were together. 'He always hits first and doesn't bother asking questions later, so stay put.' The women gathered around Alison and Ruth as Robbie left them. Climbing down out of the Viking boat, Tommy began to bounce the football on the floor. Thud! Thud! Thud!

'So I guess sneaking up isn't the way it's going to be then Tommy eh?' Robbie hissed as he swung his head left and right looking for danger.

'He'd be expecting that Robbie,' he whispered in response. 'What he won't expect is a gobshite footballer walking around like he's in the museum at Croke Park.' As if to add to the incongruous picture he was painting, he started to whistle.

'Tell your pal to shut his hole.' The thick Dublin accent came from the shadows to their left. Tommy looked to the source and watched as the little light that was there illuminated the bright blue eyes of a madman. In his hand he held a chrome handgun which he pointed menacingly at Robbie's head as he began to talk. 'I could pop one in your head right now but that would ruin all the fun. Kim is going to help me put on a little show for you.'

'Where is she?' Robbie shouted, lunging in Hawk's direction.

'Ah—Ah—Ah. Don't be getting all shirty now.'

'Tell me where she is Hawk.' Robbie pleaded.

'Ask me bollix,' he replied with a sneer, 'because her and my bollix have become quite close. If you know what I mean like.'

Robbie made a dive towards him but Tommy caught hold of him just in time. 'You've got to find out where they are first,' he whispered. Hawk moved further toward the two men. His face was now fully visible from the light of a street lamp just outside the entrance.

'Tell me what you've done with my daughter.' Tommy whipped his head around as a female voice surprised the trio. 'Naomi, get back on board,' he urged. 'I'll sort this out.' Ignoring his words, she turned to face the man she had last seen briefly almost seven years ago.

'Naomi is it?' I never was one for names me.

But then I didn't recognise you with all that clobber on. Why don't you get your kit off and we'll see if we can pick up where we left off. Robbie's missus needs a rest after all.' Tommy struggled to hold him back as Hawk spoke.

'Are you joking?' Naomi laughed as she continued to walk towards him, ignoring the gun until Tommy held her back too. 'If I'd known what kind of animal you were I would have gotten a tetanus shot after the last time.' Hawk clutched his chest with his free hand in an exaggerated fashion.

'You're breaking my heart.' He pretended to cry.

'I'll break your face if you've done anything to my little girl.' She spat the words at him.

'You will yeah.' Hawk dismissed her with one wave of the gun. 'So she's mine then is she? You can't deny she's the spit of me.'

'What does it matter? You'll be having nothing to do with her anyway,' Naomi was insistent. 'You're hardly a good role model are you?'

'Why would I give a fuck about your opinion?' he laughed.

'Because I'm her mother and your name isn't on the birth cert so you don't get a say.'

'You've got it all arse about face sweetheart,' said Hawk lighting up a smoke. 'She's with me now luv and in case you didn't notice, I've got a gun.'

A noise from near the entrance made Hawk turn and look. 'What the fuck?' He laughed as Alison, Ruth, Tracey, Brid and the rest of the team came towards them cautiously. 'I see you brought the heavy squad with you Rob.' Ignoring Hawk, Alison called out. 'There's noises coming from the van outside Robbie. Someone is ...'

Hawk took aim.

'SPREAD!' Robbie roared as he saw it. Instantly, the women ran in every direction. Hawk was taken by surprise for just a moment but it was long enough for Robbie and Naomi to turn and make for the entrance. Hawk raised his gun again and pointed after them. The football hit his hand with such force it knocked the gun flying and sent it scuttling into the darkness. Tommy stood from where he had kicked the ball and smiled. He'd always been able to hit the target. Hawk sprinted after Robbie and Naomi. Catching her by the hair he threw her against the wall. Her bottom lip split open and blood gushed down her face as she slumped down to the ground, stunned. Robbie was nearing the van. They had to be in the back otherwise he would have seen them sitting in the front when he'd pulled up. He slipped on the cobbles as he raced forward bashing his shoulder off the van's side panel. 'KIM,' he shouted as he heard the muffled screams coming from within. 'I'm coming.'

'No you're not,' whispered Hawk in his ear as he sunk the six inch blade deep into him.

Every nerve ending screamed agony to his brain. He fell to his knees and his back arched in a vain attempt to escape his attacker. It was too late. The blade was buried up to the hilt in Robbie's shoulder. Hawk put his left hand on the other shoulder and with his right hand pulled the knife out to use it again. For the second time a football smacked into him. This time it was his face that took the brunt of it. Robbie's right arm was useless, with his left he tried to push his way up using the side of the van. Hawk grabbed him up by the collar and pushed him into Tommy who was fast approaching.

He jumped into his van shouting, 'I'm going to kill her Robbie.' He slammed the door and started the engine.

'Get the boat,' Robbie roared as the van pulled off. Tommy ran to the Viking Splash and leapt aboard. He gunned the engine and reversed quickly, then jumped down to help the girls lift Robbie on. 'We don't have time to get everyone on,' he shouted. Naomi hopped aboard before he'd finished the sentence. 'I'm coming.' Her tone didn't invite discussion. 'Go, Go,' shouted the others. 'We'll phone the Guards.'

Tommy dove behind the wheel and smashed his foot down onto the accelerator. The yellow boat's wheels spun and lurched forward sending Robbie flying back smashing his shoulder against the hard plastic seat. 'AHHHH FUCK,' he screamed in pain.

'Jesus sorry,' said Tommy, easing off the speed.

'What the fuck are you doing?' shouted Robbie.

'Your shoulder,' Tommy called back. 'I don't want to make it worse.'

'Fuck my shoulder, he's got Kim. I don't care if I bleed to death once we get her back. Now floor it.'

'That's not going to happen.' Naomi struggled to pull one of the kit bags out of the storage area between the seats. Pulling out the first aid kit she tore some cotton wool wadding, ripped his jacket and tracksuit further apart where the knife had gone through and placed the wadding on the widening gash. 'It's not perfect but it's better than nothing,' she shrugged squeezing his knee. 'You can get the stitches in once Kim's with you to hold your hand.'

Robbie caught her hand and held it tight, looking her straight in the eye. 'I'm sorry I got you mixed up in all of this,' he said quietly.

'I know,' she replied. 'I know.'

'There he is!' shouted Tommy. They were driving down through Ringsend now, heading towards the coast road. 'We have to get ahead of him somehow, slow him down.'

'You might be in luck if he heads towards the level crossing. It might be down for a train passing,' shouted Naomi from the back. 'Where are the cops? They should be here by now.'

'He'll lose it if he sees cops,' said Robbie quickly. 'We've got to try to sort this. Listen Naomi just so you know, his mother really wanted him to be a father. I can't see him hurting her intentionally.'

'I hope you're right,' she cried. The white van approached a small roundabout. Robbie pulled himself up and moved into the front next to Tommy. 'Go round the other side, try to block him off.'

'And drive head on into someone?' Tommy shouted. 'Are you out of your shagging mind?'

'In a game of chicken, the bloke with the biggest car wins. We're driving a boat with horns for Jaysus sake. They'll get out of the poxy way.'

There really was no other choice. The level crossing was looming. Tommy put his foot to the floor and pulled the wheel over to the right. The Viking ship swung around the mini roundabout. Less than three hundred yards away from the crossing, a green Kawasaki 900 came shooting out on the other side of Hawk's van. The biker opened up the throttle and raced forward in line with the Viking ship. Two burly men sat on the bike, their faces obscured by helmets. 'I assume these are some of his henchmen?' shouted Tommy. Robbie tried to see but the bike had dropped back behind the van. Hawk must have called for backup. It was probably Butch and some other bloke. Oncoming cars mounted the footpath to get out of the way of the large yellow vehicle hurtling towards them down the wrong side of the road. Tommy inched ahead of Hawk. 'The fellas on the bike will have brought him a new gun,' said Robbie. 'We've got to draw him out before they get it to him. Get over the railway track and wait till he's on it then turn sideways. If our luck is in we'll block the whole road and the cars behind him will box him in.' He put his hand to the blood soaked shoulder of his shirt and turned to Tommy. 'I'm going to need your help Bud.'

'I know,' said Tommy quietly.

The Viking ship got ahead of Hawk as they approached the tracks. Tommy gunned the engine further to draw him on them. A few seconds after he felt the rear wheels bump over the track line he slammed on the brakes. Hawk's van jolted to a stop. Robbie and Tommy jumped out followed by Naomi. 'You get them out,' shouted Robbie as they ran to the van. 'I won't be strong enough with my shoulder fucked. I'll keep Hawk distracted.'

'Don't let him kill you Robbie,' said Tommy quickly. 'You're the best mate I've got.' The two men held each other's gaze briefly. 'Let's do this,' said Robbie.

Hawk's wild eyes glared out the windshield as they approached. 'What the fuck is he at?' whispered Robbie to himself. 'Why isn't he getting out?' Then he remembered. The internal handles of the van were fucked. Butch had been supposed to fix them. He mustn't have bothered his hole. Robbie edged closer to the door as Tommy ran around the back. The thundering roar of a motorbike could be heard over the sound of car horns beeping at the hold up. Shit, thought Robbie. His back up has arrived. Through the closed window he could hear Johnny Cash belting out one of his best known tracks. Robbie looked as Hawk pushed and bashed at the inside of the door. Clearly the windows were banjaxed too. The sudden clanging of the level crossing warning bell rang out.

'FUCK,' shouted Robbie to Tommy. 'Train! Hurry up!' He looked towards the back of the van and his heart almost stopped. Naomi was standing with her hands up in the air. Tommy was in the same position but was talking to someone. The barriers continued to drop as far as they could and go back up, their sensors picking up the obstruction. 'THERE'S A TRA ...' roared Robbie. His last word was drowned out by the sound of a gunshot. 'KIM! TOMMY!'

The high pitched scream of the Dublin-Wexford express train shattered the air. Everything happened at once. Robbie looked to the rear of the van, no sign of anyone. He went to take a step towards the other side of the tracks when something made him look toward Hawk. But he wasn't looking back. Instead his head was turned the other way. Suddenly he whipped around and started frantically kicking at the windscreen and banging on the door. The noise was intense. The thunderous bellow of the huge diesel engines. The blaring horn. The screeching of brakes. The screaming of onlookers. Even with all that, Robbie could still hear Johnny Cash coming from the van. Maybe he was imagining it. Then he saw what Hawk already had. The express train was coming right for them. Hawk looked at him and he saw something in his eyes he had never seen before.

Sheer terror. Robbie knew he'd never make it to Kim on time. He dived out of the way screaming her name as he flew through the air. He landed badly on his wounded shoulder and cried out in agony.

The impact was immense. The white van flew up into the air in two pieces. Hawk's body shot through the windscreen and landed with a lifeless thud on the roof of a nearby car. The van's front bonnet hung off the roof of the Dart commuter train station. People started to get back slowly to their feet, their faces frozen with shock. An elderly man from one of the cars nearby hurried to Robbie to help him. 'You're hurt son,' he said noticing the blood-stained clothes. 'Sit here till the ambulance arrives.' Ignoring the man's advice Robbie leaned on his outstretched arm and struggled painfully to his feet. 'I've got to get to the other side. My fiancée was in the back of that van.' 'I'm sorry lad. Nobody could have survived that impact.' 'KIM.' Robbie screamed her name. The wailing sirens could be heard in the distance over the continuing rumble of the train's engines. Everything seemed to be happening in slow motion. One by one the train doors started to open and white faced passengers jumped off onto the ground. Robbie saw his chance. 'Can you help me up there?' he asked the old man, pointing to the train carriage. 'I have to get over there to check for my fiancée.'

'I'll help you but son maybe you should wait for the emergency services to get to her. It won't be a pretty sight.'

'I don't care. I have to be with her. This was all my fault.'

The old man nodded and held his two hands

with fingers intertwined as a makeshift step. Robbie put his foot into it and used the leverage to climb up onto the empty train carriage. Two steps later he jumped down from the opposite open door and ignoring the pain in his shoulder, started looking for Kim. Naomi was kneeling on the ground clutching something wrapped in her coat. Shona. The little girl was bawling and her mother looked up at Robbie as she stroked her hair in an effort to soothe her. With the slightest movement of her head, she indicated towards two men to her left. Butch stood beside a large man who was holding Kim in his arms. Robbie didn't know who the other man was because he was still wearing his motorcycle helmet. She wasn't moving. 'Kim!' Robbie sprinted towards them and grabbed her into his arms. 'She's here,' shouted Tommy as he ran towards them with a paramedic motorcyclist. Robbie looked up suddenly. The paramedic took Kim and laid her on the ground. 'She's unconscious,' he said after a brief examination.

'Unconscious? You mean she's not dead? But I heard a gunshot.' The big man took his helmet off just behind Tommy. When he spoke Robbie felt a shiver up his spine.

'Hawk had padlocked a chain though the door handles. Butch shot it off. She wasn't in the van when the train hit.'

Robbie's mouth fell open in shock. It couldn't be. The man continued talking, obviously pleased with the reaction his presence was getting. 'Butch pulled the kid out just in time, that's why his hand is splattered all over the gaff. I pulled your bird out just before that. She was out cold whatever Hawk did to her.'

'But you're dead,' was all Robbie could say.

'I never had you down as a stupid bollix,' replied Macker. 'I guess I was wrong.'

'But Hawk told Butch to dump you into the harbour. I helped tie you to the chair. You were wearing an anchor for fuck's sake. They're not known for their buoyancy.'

'I got sick of that fucker telling me what to do.' Butch's voice called out from behind the other man. He was sitting on the ground now as another paramedic was desperately trying to stem the flow of blood gushing from the place where his hand should have been. 'Anyway, you didn't exactly tie the ropes too well on old Macker and he was always a strong cunt. That's when I realised you weren't as keen on Hawk as I thought.'

'Butch? I thought you were here to help Hawk.'

'You *were* wrong Macker,' said the burly man in a weak voice from the ground to his friend. 'He *is* a stupid bollix.'

Robbie shook his head trying to fathom what was going on. He was dazed. As the paramedic searched his bag for something he caught hold of Kim's hand. 'Why won't she wake up?' 'Chloroform,' replied the paramedic. 'I can smell it from her mouth. All her other vitals are normal, although she's taken a nasty gash to the head. That will need stitches. They will check her out fully in the hospital but she's not in any immediate danger.' Robbie bent to her ear as she lay unconscious. 'Kim, it's me. Robbie. You're going to be fine. Hawk's dead.' He clutched her hand and held it to his lips. A low moan came from her mouth. Her body shivered.

Robbie pulled off his damaged coat and placed it on top of her. Two ambulances pulled up with sirens wailing and four men in paramedic uniform approached pulling stretchers and equipment. 'What happened to you?' asked one of them, noticing the makeshift bloodied bandage stuck to Robbie's shoulder.

'Has that been looked at?'

'No,' Robbie replied. 'I'm not going anywhere till she's sorted. She's going to be my wife.' His eyes were full of tears.

'Well you can travel together then,' said the man as one of the ambulances reversed towards them.

The police had arrived and were busy directing traffic away from the junction. The fire brigade began the task of extracting the van from the various places it had ended up. The train was reversed back off the level crossing and Hawk's body was covered by a sheet. The young ambulance driver walking beside Robbie nodded towards the scene.

'What was he doing going onto the tracks if the exit wasn't clear?' he asked.

'Dunno,' replied Robbie stifling a laugh as he thought of the Johnny Cash tune that had been playing. He winked at Butch and Macker. 'I guess he didn't hear the train a coming!'

Chapter Thirty Nine

'That bang to the head didn't knock any sense into you I see.' Tommy got up from his seat in the bar and hugged Kim warmly. 'You're still hanging around with this tosser?' As he spoke he nudged Robbie on his good arm. The knife Hawk had plunged into his back had run along the shoulder blade so didn't do any catastrophic damage. Still, he had loads of stitches and his arm was in a sling so the birds on the team gave him plenty of TLC. It was a full week after the events at the level crossing. Kim's initial fears that she may have been raped by Hawk were unfounded. To her huge relief it seemed Hawk had just been messing with her head. In the days that followed, Shona had calmed down and spoken about the ordeal to Naomi and a counsellor. It seemed that she had interrupted Hawk's intentions. She said that she woke up on the bed and 'the man' was pulling down Kim's pants. He stopped when he saw her and took her downstairs. Then he started talking 'gobbledegook' as she put it, about daddies and their little girls before he locked her and Kim in the van. The Guards almost did somersaults when they identified Hawk's body at the mortuary. It always made their job easier when the criminal toe-rags bumped each other off. It meant less work for them. Of course they had come to interview Robbie at the hospital. As always he told them fuck all of any use but swore he was now going to go straight...ish.

Tommy had organised a table in a posh restaurant called The Quail's Egg to celebrate their victory at the blitz. They had arranged to meet first at the clubhouse. The place was jammed. Tommy hadn't paid too much attention but apparently there was some big shot American in town. He was the guy selecting teams for the tournament in New York.

'Sorry I'm late,' Ruth said as she arrived. 'My son Garry rang from Sydney so I didn't want to rush him off the phone.'

'You haven't missed anything anyway luv,' said Robbie. 'Apart from Tommy here blowing kisses over to yer man. If you hold him I can still give him a box, I always punched better with this fist,' Robbie held up his uninjured arm while he spoke to Tommy. They were both looked across at Ray O'Toole.

'I thought you said you were going to smarten up your act?' said Tommy with a grin.

'I can throw on a suit before I deck him so. Would that be alright?'

'Behave.'

'Ah seriously man,' said Robbie. 'Look at him. He's practically asking for a smack in the mouth.'

Ray was being patted on the back by a host of different men, each of them congratulating him on running a club that would be sending their senior men's team to America. 'Big headed git,' Robbie muttered into his pint. The Gaelic for Mothers team all sat around Tommy, Naomi, Robbie and Kim. 'We'll just wait for the official announcement. Then we can shag off to the restaurant. The seniors are a cracking team. They deserve this,' said Tommy. Ruth touched Tommy gently on the arm. 'I was telling my son all about your heroics today. He still feels really bad about what he did to you.' Tommy was baffled. He'd never had any real dealings with the young lad when he was at the club. Then he'd been banished to the UK and hadn't laid eyes on the bloke since.

'What are you on about? Sure I haven't seen Garry since he played for the senior team that time.'

'That's what he's talking about. He always meant to apologise in person but time passed and then between one thing and another it never got done.'

'Now I'm totally lost Ruth.' Tommy's face told her that she'd obviously put her big size nines in it.

'Oh my God, you didn't know. Garry assumed it would have come out over the years. He just never thought to mention it until he heard you were coaching us. Forget I said anything.' Tommy looked at her intently.

'I have no idea what you're talking about but whatever it is, spit it out.'

Ruth quietly relayed the story of how Ray O'Toole had bribed her son and other players all those years ago to say that their violent behaviour was because they wanted to be like him. When she finished speaking she held her breath, praying that he wasn't going to self-combust. Tommy just sat and stared across at the man you had destroyed his life. Ray joined a group of Iona Gaels committee members who were stood huddled in the corner of the room. One by one they all reached out to shake hands with the President of the GAA who had brought along the American whose face Tommy couldn't see.

'That must be the American bloke over there with them,' said Robbie. 'I reckon yer man O'Toole has a horn with the excitement.'

'ROBBIE!' Kim went bright pink.

'Wha? I was only saying.' He looked indignant.

'These nice ladies wouldn't be used to that kind of

talk,' she insisted.

'You'll have to join the team pet,' he laughed. 'You wouldn't believe the shite this lot have said and done to me.'

'You probably deserved it.'

Mick, the Senior's coach cast an eye in their direction and spoke to Ray. 'What are Tommy's lot doing here? We're not having a cake sale are we?'

'No,' sniggered Ray. 'They are going out for dinner. They're just meeting for a drink first. Once they shag off we can get down to some serious celebrations with our lads. Now I better get the show on the road.' He took the microphone and stood on a small raised platform at the top of the hall. He could feel Tommy Boylan's eyes boring into him. After a few minutes talking about the accomplishments of the senior's team he made an introduction. 'Can you all please give a big Iona Gaels welcome to a man who has spent the last few weeks standing on countless sidelines? He is here tonight to make an announcement about the team who will represent Leinster in New York. Put your hands together for Jerry McGrath.'

Tommy and Robbie looked at each other, eyebrows raised. 'Isn't that yer man who watched us at the blitz?' asked Robbie. Staring at the man who took the microphone from Ray, Tommy nodded slowly, his mind suddenly distracted from Ruth's shocking revelations.

'Well fuck me pink,' he whispered.

'You're not my type,' answered Robbie. The American took to the podium.

'I've been involved in this wonderful association since I was a boy. Gaelic Park in New

York is, as you know, the home of GAA in America. It's a sport that is growing globally. We decided to engage with expat clubs in other parts of Europe and the rest of the world. This has been eighteen months of planning but finally we are there. This is a massive event aimed at further promoting the game in all these new markets. When choosing teams to take part we looked at more than just skill.' Ray O'Toole nodded and smiled as the speech continued. 'It was a very close call in the end. When I witnessed the commitment this team displayed, their courage in the face of overwhelming odds was admirable yet unsurprising given who their coach is.' Ray patted the senior's coach on the back. Jerry continued. 'I was quite frankly bowled over by their uniqueness and total self-belief but most of all, their ability to build something out of absolutely nothing in just two short months.'

'What's he on about?' Ray turned to the senior's coach who shrugged his shoulders and replied.
'Maybe he's pissed.'
'Gentlemen and most importantly Ladies, the team who won the honour of an all-expenses paid trip to compete in New York ...' He gestured towards Tommy.
'Oh please God no,' Ray whispered. Tommy, realising what was about to happen, looked over at his nemesis and started to laugh. Jerry's voice boomed over the microphone,
'... is the Gaelic for Mothers team from Iona Gaels.'
The screams and shrieks of shock and delight almost shattered the glass behind the bar. 'Are you having us on?' Ray jumped up to ask the American. 'No

Sir,' he replied. 'I certainly am not. Now if you will excuse me, I want to congratulate Mr Tommy Boylan, if they ever release him.' Neither Robbie nor Tommy could get up from their seats. The entire team of women had dived on top of them and were still cheering and whooping. Jerry laughed. 'I might have a pint while I'm waiting.' When Tommy managed to scramble free he took out his phone. He keyed in a message quickly and pressed send. As the women grabbed Tommy once more Ray O' Toole picked up his mobile to read the incoming text. *Payback's a bitch, isn't it?*

Tommy was far too excited to eat his meal at the restaurant when they finally got there. Jerry joined them and bought several bottles of champagne to celebrate their news. Every time Tommy thought of the smug look on Ray's face changing to one of utter horror, he burst out laughing. Robbie was eyeing up the cutlery as Jerry, Tommy and the team chattered. Noticing this, Kim leaned in to whisper in his ear. 'Don't even think about it. Your thieving days are over, remember? I'm going to the loo then we'd better head home. We still have to unpack the stuff in the new flat.' He watched as the love of his life walked towards the door. He had promised her he would change, and he would. Soon. Everyone began hugging to say their drunken goodbyes. Tommy shook Robbie's hand and helped him put his coat over his shoulders. 'I couldn't have done it without you,' he smiled. 'Guess that makes two of us,' replied Robbie.

He left with Kim on his good arm. Snow was

threatening and the air was freezing outside. Kim shivered. 'Here, take this.' He shrugged off his coat and she happily slipped into it. They stood at the corner waiting for a taxi. Kim zipped up the coat and put her hands in the pockets to keep warm. There wasn't any room.

'What the hell? She pulled out a handful of silver cutlery.

'Robbie! You promised.'

THE END

About the Author

Sinead Hamill lives in Dublin with her husband and two children. She is also the creator of "Get your ditties out", a blog which offers her unique observations of everyday Irish life and other humourous situations.

Acknowledgements

This story would never have happened were it not for the famous Askeaton rooster who denied me so much sleep. In addition, many thanks to Denyse Woods and Yasmin O'Grady for helping me find my true voice. To Maria McGuinness for editing so patiently. To Graham Holbrook for his illustration. To Catherine Ryan Howard's book *Self-Printed* for guiding me through publication. To Designforwriters.com for the book cover. To Tricia Holbrook, Elaine Banfield and Sara Power for their never-ending encouragement. To John Joe Young and the football team, forgive me for even suggesting that any ladies fart in Gaelic football, I'm sure they don't. To Tony, Susan Cormican and Aileen Murphy for battling through first drafts. To Tony, Hazel and Dawn, love as always and finally to all the fabulous women that play on Gaelic for Mothers teams throughout Ireland – what wonderful characters you all are!

www.sineadhamill.com

Twitter: @sinead_hamill

CPSIA information can be obtained at www.ICGtesting.com
Printed in the USA
LVOW08s1519130314

377295LV00003B/87/P